ANGEL IN JEOPARDY

ANGEL IN JEOPARDY

Christopher Nicole

This first world edition published in Great Britain 2007 by
SEVERN HOUSE PUBLISHERS LTD of
9–15 High Street, Sutton, Surrey SM1 1DF.
This first world edition published in the USA 2007 by
SEVERN HOUSE PUBLISHERS INC of
595 Madison Avenue, New York, N.Y. 10022.

British Library Cataloguing in Publication Data

Nicole, Christopher
    Angel in jeopardy
    1.   Fehrbach, Anna (Fictitious character) - Fiction
    1.   World War, 1939-1945 - Secret Service - Germany - Fiction
    2.   Suspense fiction
    I.   Title
    823.9'14 [F]

ISBN-13: 978-0-7278-6542-7   (cased)

All Severn House titles are printed on acid-free paper.

Typeset by Palimpsest Book Production Ltd.,
Grangemouth, Stirlingshire, Scotland.
Printed and bound in Great Britain by
MPG Books Ltd., Bodmin, Cornwall.

Prologue

'*What a magnificent tree,*' I remarked.
   Some forty feet tall, with a thick trunk and many branches, its green foliage studded with deep-blue flowers, it was situated about a hundred yards behind and above the villa, which was built into the upper slopes of Montgo, the high, lion-like hill that dominated the Costa Blanca resort of Javea.

'It is a lovely tree,' Anna Fehrbach agreed, her voice soft and, when she spoke English, still retaining a trace of the brogue she had inherited from her Irish mother. 'But it requires careful watching. It is a jacaranda and has an insatiable thirst. As you can see, we keep a hose on it several hours in every day. But as you also see, we planted it a good distance from the house and, more importantly, the swimming pool. I know some people here in Spain who planted a jacaranda about thirty feet from their pool; they thought it would give shade when they were lounging on the coronation. Well, it certainly did that, but its roots also went in search of moisture, and before they realized what was happening, those roots had eaten their way right through the concrete walls of the pool to suck out the water.' She sighed, and looked around herself at the flower beds and weeping willows that she also culti-vated. 'I hope I am not boring you. I love this garden. I never had the opportunity to have a garden when I was a girl, or a young woman.'

'You could never bore me, Anna,' I assured her.

I was not attempting to flatter her; it was the simple truth. This was the fourth time I had been privileged to spend a few hours with Anna Ferhbach, the Honourable Mrs Ballantyne Bordman, best known as the Countess von Widerstand; the title, which loosely translates as the Countess of Resistance, would have been ridiculous in any average woman, but anyone who supposed that Anna Fehrbach was an average woman, or an average human being, would have been making a grave mistake. Several who had made that mistake had come to a sudden end.

She was now in her late eighties, and for walking on the uneven surface of the hillside used a stick. But she stood perfectly straight, her height still only an inch under six feet. I had never been privileged to see her legs, as nowadays she always wore trousers, but I could see from her waist and hips that they were very long, and from the exposed ankles and bare feet in her sandals had no doubt that they were still the legs for which, it was said, men had been prepared to die . . . and quite a few had. She remained very slim, a result of her many years of arduous physical training, but there was still sufficient shape to her shirt to remind one that men had not died to get their hands only on her legs.

Yet the erstwhile physical beauty that remained evident was as nothing compared to her face. Her skin had become a little tight, and there were crows' feet seeping away from her eyes, but the perfection of her slightly aquiline bone structure remained, perhaps more obvious now than in the past, because the magnificent long, straight, pale-yellow hair that had once been her crowning glory was now white, and cut short. But the deep-blue eyes had not, I surmised, changed at all. Those eyes had never been other than soft when they had looked at me, but I knew enough about her to understand that they could become as cold as sapphires when necessary, just as I also knew that they had looked upon sights as terrifying as anything ever dreamed up by a Hollywood monster-movie magnate. But more important, they also masked one of the most remarkable brains in history, not merely because she had an IQ of 173, but because of the almost unearthly speed of thought, reaction and decision that had made her the most deadly assassin of her time – and enabled her to survive a hundred close brushes with her own death. They were eyes which, far more than her body or her hair or her face, had lured many a man, and woman, to disaster.

Sadly, I sometimes reflected, I had never known those eyes save in this twilight of her life, when she was utterly relaxed, willing, and even anxious to talk about her past before it was too late. The only visible evidence of what had once been was her exquisite jewellery, the tiny gold bars of her earrings, the gold crucifix round her neck, the huge ruby solitaire on the forefinger of her left hand, all so feminine, and so contrasting with the man's gold Rolex on her wrist. She wore this jewellery, as I knew, less because she wished for decoration, than as a symbol of what she considered her greatest triumph. Save for the watch, it had been given to her by her Nazi masters, to enhance the image they wished her to project – that of the wealthy socialite. Obviously they had intended to reclaim it at some time. But they were all gone, and she was still here – with the jewellery. She found that immensely satisfying.

I had tracked this woman for some forty years, when I could spare the time, ever since I had first come across the occasional mention of her in the various memoirs I had studied while writing about the Second World War. I had been fascinated both by the legend of her beauty, by her ruthlessness, and by her sudden disappearance when still at the height of her powers, as much as by the many famous and infamous characters she had known intimately, both during World War II and during the chaotic years that had followed. Most historians of the period assumed that she had died; some refused to believe that she had ever lived. But I had been unable to accept that so vibrant a personality could either be a myth or have wound up in an unnamed grave. And as I had searched I had come across tantalizing snippets of information that had led me ever onwards – until I had been told of a lonely old woman who apparently lived with her memories and a single servant, a woman who moved with incredible grace, was clearly enormously wealthy, who had been born, I was able to discover, on 21 May 1920 – and who spoke several languages but, when she used English, had an Irish accent. All of those straws in the wind fitted with what I had already gleaned.

So I had taken my life in my hands, quite literally if her record was at all accurate, called at this villa on the hillside and embarked on the mental voyage of a lifetime. The woman herself! If it is possible for a man to fall in love with his own grandmother, I had done so. More importantly, I came upon her at a definitive moment, when she had understood that she was coming

*to the end of her life, and after so many years of the utmost
secrecy, with the memory of who she was and what she had
done no more than a whispered legend, she wanted to leave her
memorial to the world. And here was a journalist arriving on
her doorstep, obviously, as she quickly established, totally innocent of any connection with her past, but eager to learn. Thus
she had welcomed me, and by the time of this fourth meeting,
we were the closest of friends. So I ventured, 'Do you regret
your childhood? – I mean, the things you did not have, like a
garden.'*

'That would have happened anyway,' Anna pointed out,
beginning to walk back towards the house. 'My parents lived
in a town house in the centre of Vienna, and they were both
working journalists, like you. They had no time for gardens.
But I had a very pleasant girlhood, until March 1938. I was
the nuns' favourite, because I was bright, hard-working, well
behaved . . . Do you know, at the age of seventeen I was the
youngest head girl the convent had ever had.'

'And then you just disappeared. Do you think the nuns ever
knew what happened to you?'

'Oh, certainly. Up to a point. Everyone in Vienna knew that
my father had been arrested for editing an anti-Nazi newspaper, and he and all his family carted off to, as they supposed,
a concentration camp. They would have assumed that was the
end, for us.'

'And it would have been, but for you.'

'Don't make me sound like a heroine, Christopher. I was a
seventeen-year-old girl, who was told, obey us, work for us,
and your family will live and may even prosper. Disobey us,
in any way, and your family will die. So I obeyed.'

'But within two years you were fighting them, actively if
secretly. That makes you a heroine, in my book.'

'You say the sweetest things.' She opened the back door
and led me into the cool interior of the house, where Encarna,
her maid, waited with an open bottle of champagne. I had
always found Encarna hardly less fascinating than her
mistress, because I had no idea how much she knew about
that mistress, how close they were. Certainly Anna never
attempted to be secretive in her presence. She handed me a
glass, raised her own, and sipped. 'Things turned out more
fortunately than I had ever dreamed they could.'

'*But far more dangerously.*'

She led me on to the naya and sat down, crossing her knees. '*Being a spy, much more an assassin, is a dangerous business,*' she commented, with her usual ingenuousness. '*And you were the best. By the time you were twenty-two you had . . . eliminated twenty-two people. Have you any thoughts about that?*'

'*Nightmares, you mean? Some of them. The first – that poor, helpless concentration-camp inmate I was ordered to kill, simply to prove to the SD that I could . . . that was awful. Gottfried Friedemann . . . he was such an innocent, who had stumbled upon something too big for him to handle. The two British agents in Prague . . . I did not know they were British agents.*' She sipped champagne, reflectively.

'*That's only four,*' I ventured.

'*The others . . . the NKVD people who raped and tortured me . . . I told you, I had never fired a tommy-gun before. I remember only a feeling of exultation as they came at me and I squeezed the trigger and watched them falling about. The Gestapo agents who tried to arrest me, that was pure self-defence.*'

'*And the women? Elsa Mayers and Hannah Gehrig, and Hannah's daughter, Marlene?*'

'*They were all about to betray me, which would have meant an unpleasant end, for me and for my family. Hannah actually shot me, as you know.*'

'*And you still bear the scar. On your ribcage.*'

'*Yes.*' She glanced at me. '*Would you like to see it?*'

'*Ah . . .*'

She smiled. '*I will show it to you. When I know you a little better.*'

'*And Heydrich? The secret one?*'

Anna made one of her enchanting moues. '*I hated him more than any man on earth. But I was his mistress for very nearly two years – his sexual slave, you could say. One cannot have that kind of relationship with a man, and not have . . . well, a relationship. I was actually relieved that my instructions from London were to set up the assassination for the agents they were sending from England, but under no circumstances to become involved myself. As far as I was concerned, it was execution by remote control.*'

'*But you still had to take over yourself.*'

'*I had no choice. In the first place, London's instructions had been explicit: Heydrich had to die before he was returned to Germany. They felt, correctly, that he was going to be made Hitler's heir, and immediately begin to share power, and they also felt, again correctly, that, evil as Hitler was, he was a child compared with Heydrich. And then, the assassination attempt went disastrously wrong. The tommy-gun to be used by the lead operative jammed, can you believe it? And his back-up, who was armed with a grenade, didn't throw it accurately enough. Oh, Reinhard was very badly injured, but the doctors had no doubt that he would recover, and the assassins had all been killed or captured . . .*'

'*So you finished the job yourself.*'

'*It wasn't difficult. As everyone knew how close I was to him, I had no difficulty in gaining access.*'

'*And no one was suspicious?*'

'*A great many people were suspicious. But by then I was under the protection of Himmler, who, as I told you, was more than happy to see the back of Heydrich; at that time he aspired to be Hitler's heir himself.*'

'*So you landed on your feet, as usual.*'

Another moue. '*That is one way of putting it.*'

'*And to this day, no one knows the truth of it.*'

'*You do, now.*'

'*You never even told Clive Bartley?*'

'*No. I was tempted, but I never did tell him the whole truth. To the world, to history, Heydrich died as a result of wounds suffered in the grenade explosion.*'

'*And was his assassination your greatest coup?*'

'*Heydrich? Good God, no. Even then, there were much bigger fish to be fried. The biggest fish of all.*'

'*You don't mean . . . But . . .*'

'*Yes,*' Anna Fehrbach said. '*I had my failures, too.*'

Voices from the Past

S tefan Edert's greatest pleasure was overseeing the Countess von Widerstand train. In this summer of 1943 he had been her personal coach for two years, and whenever she had been in Berlin she attended the gymnasium for a workout several days a week – which, ever since her return from Prague the previous May, had been just about every week. Yet he never tired of watching her.

He could do no more than that, as she had established at their very first meeting, in the summer of 1941. He could watch her run, sweatshirt straining across her nipples. He could watch her on the indoor range, when she used her pistol with such relentless speed and accuracy. He could watch her doing fifty press-ups, the smooth muscles in her shoulders rippling, her buttocks thrusting against her shorts. He could even wrestle with her on the mat, occasionally pinning her, while always aware that to her it was a game, and that, had it been the real thing, she would have disposed of him before it had even begun.

Above all, he could watch her shower, as now, face turned up to the flooding water, hair soaking, flesh glistening as the liquid flowed over hills and into valleys he dreamed of exploring. But they would remain dreams, unless a miracle happened. She allowed him these intimacies because to her he was not a man: he was her trainer. Sometimes he was so frustrated he felt like strangling her. But that too was impossible: he knew she could kill him before his fingers could close on her throat. And then he wondered if she ever had any sexual impulses at all. Of course she must have. She had been Reinhard Heydrich's mistress for more than a year. But it was now more than a year since 'the Hangman', as he had been known, had been murdered by Czech patriots. And in that time her name had not been linked with anyone else – not even with her boss,

Heinrich Himmler. If only he could break through that cocoon of self-possessed reserve.

Anna stepped from the bath, towelled vigorously. 'Are you satisfied?' she asked, her voice low, caressing.

'You are in perfect physical shape, Countess.'

'I meant, have you looked at me long enough for one morning.'

'Oh . . . ah . . .' He knew he was flushing. 'It is my business to look at you. To be sure of your condition.'

'And you are pleased. That makes me very happy. Do you still have that photograph you took of me, a couple of years ago?'

'It is on my mantelpiece.'

Anna wrapped her wet hair in a towel, put on her camiknickers. 'What does your girlfriend think of that?'

'I do not have a girlfriend, Countess. I have your photograph.'

Anna paused in pulling on her slacks. 'And you can get off on that?'

Stefan licked his lips. 'I did not mean to insult you.'

'You did not insult me, Stefan. I am complimented. But I am sorry you have such a sterile existence.' She fastened her slacks, picked up her shirt.

'May I take another?'

'Have I changed that much, in two years?'

'No, but the photo is . . . well . . .'

'Perhaps a little tattered? Yes, Stefan, you may take another photograph of me.'

'I have my camera here.'

'I do not wish to be photographed like this.'

'But you would . . .'

'Take off my clothes? Of course. But even so, I have no make-up, my hair is a mess . . . Listen, come to my apartment . . . tomorrow evening when I am home from work. I will pose for you there.'

Stefan could not believe his ears. 'I can come to your apartment?'

'I have just invited you, Stefan. Six o'clock tomorrow evening.' She replaced the towel round her head with a cloche. 'Ciao.'

*   *   *

It was not far from the SD gymnasium to the apartment building, also owned by the SD, where Anna lived, and she enjoyed the early-morning stroll, even if she was surrounded both by the evidence of last night's air raid and by anxious people, on their way to work, reading their newspapers and muttering to each other. The contrast between the immaculate, ebullient city to which she had returned from England in 1940, one step ahead of the British SIS, as her SD masters supposed, and these increasingly decrepit and depressing surroundings, was so great as to be unbelievable.

In 1940, the only word had been victory. People smiled, and cheered at every bit of good news from the west. In the summer of 1940 there had been no eastern front to think about. But even in 1941 there had been nothing but victories. Now . . . the government, for which she officially worked, insisted that victory in Russia was still just around the corner, and would certainly be achieved this summer. The thousands of German families who had had a husband, a father, or a son serving at Stalingrad found that very hard to swallow, even if no one dared say so in public.

While she . . . Back in 1939, when she had willingly been 'turned' by Clive Bartley, it had been in a mood of outrage at what had been done to her, and her family, by the SD, the Sicherheitsdienst, the most secret force in all secrecy-bound Nazi Germany. Then she had had to accept the British claim, which had seemed entirely without foundation, that they would win in the end. Now she no longer had any doubts. Last year's victories of Midway and Alamein, not to mention the Russian triumph at Stalingrad, and now the surrender of the entire German army in North Africa, were disasters from which there could be no recovery.

Now she also worked for the Office of Strategic Services, the most secret of *American* counter-espionage departments, even if, after more than a year, they had not yet called on her services. Clive Bartley, MI6, had agreed to share her even before America had entered the war in December 1941. So she had not yet discovered exactly what they had had in mind. Her visit to America almost seemed like another existence. Had she really lain naked in Joe Andrews's arms, feeling utter peace and contentment? Could she admit to herself that she had found Joe even more satisfying than Clive Bartley? Or

had that all been part of the American ambience, that feeling
of total security which everyone over there seemed to assume
was theirs by right, but which she had never known, at least
after the age of seventeen.

But Clive was the man who had rescued her from the hell
into which she had been sucked by the SD. He was the man
who had promised her eventual salvation. He was the man to
whom she had given her all, including her very life much less
her body. Life without Clive was not conceivable. And she
had seen neither him nor Joe for nearly two years.

Thus she did not know if either of them was aware how
much her entire existence had changed since Heydrich's death.
Heydrich had supervised her education and training as an SD
agent, and although he also had enjoyed the use of her body,
he had never allowed that to divert him from his reason for
employing her in the first place. If she had proved her worth
as a spy, she had proved even more valuable as an assassin,
and he had never hesitated to use her in that role, certain that
by holding her family in secure but not harsh confinement he
held her obedience just as firmly. She suspected he had always
known she hated both him and the regime he represented –
although once, in a moment of weakness, he had actually
proposed marriage – but he had never doubted that he held
all the high cards.

Himmler, who had actually taken her over before his sidekick's death, when Heydrich had been sent to Prague as
Reich-Protector, was an entirely different man, and because
she had always been a sexual object to every man she had
met, she could not figure him out at all. He appeared to
enjoy her company. He certainly liked to look at her, sometimes when she was naked. But his touch always
perfunctory.

Of course, he suspected, on some fairly substantial evidence,
that she was a lesbian, quite *un*suspecting that the woman
with whom she had been reported to be intimate had been
another British agent to whom she had been conveying information in the only safe way, lips to ear while they had shared
a bed. But in addition, for all the omnipotent and apparently
ruthless power he wielded as head of both the Gestapo and
the SS, and therefore the SD, the apparent careless disregard
for human life embodied in his orders and directives, he was

essentially both timid and of limited intellectual powers. In *her* powers of decision and lethal determination he saw an alter ego he wished he himself possessed. That she was a beautiful woman and he actually did possess her, as he supposed, was a bonus, but not one he would ever have risked losing, or even tarnishing, by seeking to discover what might lie beneath the cold beauty and the sexuality.

Which suited her well enough. She dreaded the thought that one day his so far sublimated desire for her might get the better of him, and she be exposed to that so white flesh and feelingless fingers. But he had certainly changed her life over the past year; he had refused to let her leave Berlin, after she had spent the previous four years travelling, seducing, and killing, for the Reich. But that had been when she had been Heydrich's to command.

Himmler was keeping her as his own private . . . what? From the point of view of MI6 she was better placed than ever before. As both the Reichsführer's Personal Assistant and his confidante in so many things she had access to so many secrets, of both the Party and its strategy, military and political, and these she faithfully remitted to London via her Berlin contact. She had no idea what London did with the information, whether they shared any of it with the Americans. But being no longer required to travel, she had been unable to make physical contact with either Clive or Joe. Thus her sense of loneliness, of isolation, was growing. She did not even know if either of them was alive or dead, healthy or ill.

She realized that she had been so lost in thought she had covered the five blocks from the gymnasium without realizing it. Her apartment building was in front of her . . . and there was a man walking at her elbow. She stopped, and turned towards him, not the least apprehensive. Whether he was City Police, State Police, Abwehr, Gestapo or even SS, as a member of the SD and of Himmler's personal staff, she was inviolate. 'Are you following me?' she inquired, quietly.

He licked his lips. He was a tall, heavy-set man, with bland features and yellow hair. The perfect Aryan, she thought. 'Forgive me, Countess.'

'I don't know that I should. I dislike being followed. Especially when I am not properly dressed.'

'I only wished to have a word. My card.'

Anna took the cardboard rectangle. 'Lars Johannsson, *Stockholm Gazette*. Are all Swedes named Johannsson?'

'Well, no, of course not. Ah . . .'

'Just my little joke. And does the *Stockholm Gazette* really exist?'

'It does indeed.' Johannsson looked up and down the street. 'Do you think we could have a talk?'

'Isn't that what we are doing?'

'I meant, in private.'

'I don't think that would be a good idea, Herr Johannsson. I never give interviews to the press.'

'Not even if I were to tell you that my middle name is Joe?'

Anna studied him even as she felt her stomach muscles contract. But she had to accept that he had just given her the OSS identification code. Yet to be contacted like this, after so long . . . 'Well,' she said. 'I might be able to make an exception.'

'Thank you. In your apartment?'

'That would definitely not be a good idea. The building is owned by the SD and is bugged. You can buy me a cup of coffee. Over there.' She led him across the street to the coffee shop that was just opening and at which she was a regular customer.

'Good morning, Franz,' she said to the waiter. 'Two coffees, please.'

'Right away, Countess.' He glanced at Johannsson and hurried off.

'You understand that I can have no secrets from my employers, certainly as regards anything I do in public,' Anna said. 'Therefore I must inform them of this meeting.' She smiled at his expression. 'But not necessarily the true contents of our conversation. However, as you are supposed to be interviewing me, and Franz may well be asked about it, I suggest you produce a notebook and make notes.'

'Ah. Yes.' He took out his book and a pencil.

Franz served the coffee and left the chit.

'Now remember,' Anna said. 'Be confident, casual and concise.'

Johannsson sipped his coffee and grimaced.

'I know,' Anna said. 'It is dreadful stuff. It is made from

chicory. But real coffee is unobtainable here in Germany. Do write something.'

Johnnsson doodled. 'There is a man we wish you to see. Friedrich von Steinberg.'

Anna put down her cup.

'I imagine you already know him,' Johannsson said.

'He is a Foreign Office official. You mean, *you* know him?'

'We have met, yes. We regard him as potentially useful.'

'And you have told him about me?'

'Does that bother you?'

'For God's sake!' Anna snapped, keeping her voice down with an effort.

'I have said, we believe that he may be of use to us.'

'You have still placed my life in his hands.'

'He knows nothing of you, save that I have told him you may be sympathetic towards a project he is trying to get going. Believe me, he was even more alarmed than you when I suggested you get together. You have quite a reputation.'

'Thank you for those kind words.'

'Countess, all I am asking you to do is meet with him and listen to what he has to say. If you think it is impractical, walk away.'

'Herr Johannsson, I hate to be rude, but you do not appear to understand anything of this business. If Count von Steinberg is prepared to work for you, then by definition he is working against the Nazi Party. That means he is a traitor to the Reich. That means anyone who knows his secret is a threat, and anyone who knows of his secret and does not go along with him is a terminal threat. Who sent you to me?'

'Colonel Donovan.'

Anna leaned back in her chair. When she had met the so-called 'Wild Bill' in New York, two years previously, and been recruited by him, she had liked him enormously, although even then she had never doubted his ruthlessness, whatever his charm. But this . . . 'Is MI6 involved?'

If they were they had certainly not informed Bartoli. But then, Clive, like her, did not entirely trust Bartoli.

'Not to my knowledge,' Johannsson said.

But they would have to be, and sooner rather than later; MI6 was her principal, no matter what Wild Bill Donovan, or

Joe Andrews, might choose to believe. 'So when is this meeting to take place?'

'Your call. But it should be soon. It must be soon.'

'I know. Everything is urgent. Is it to be accidental?'

'That would be best.'

Anna considered. She needed time to contact London and see if they knew of this highly dangerous turn of events. 'I sometimes go jogging in the park. Before I go to work, as I must now do, as soon as I have changed my clothes.'

'You work in Reichsführer Himmler's office?'

'That is correct. So let us make it a week, Tuesday, 10 August. I shall jog in the park next Tuesday at six. I am always finished by half past.'

'A whole week? Not until then?'

'Not until then, Herr Johannsson. I have other commitments.'

He hesitated, but her tone had not suggested that she was open to either argument or persuasion. 'I will inform Count von Steinberg.'

'Now tell me what this meeting will involve.'

'I am not in a position to do that.'

'Do you mean that you do not know, or that you are refusing to confide in me?'

'I am obeying orders, Countess.'

Anna regarded him for several seconds. If he was setting her up . . . but she had no doubt that she could convince Himmler that she was going along with him, and Steinberg, merely to find out what they were up to; her boss had always accepted everything she had told him in the past. As for being dumped in the middle of some anti-Nazi plot . . . Clive Bartley had warned her that the Americans were difficult people to work for because of their pragmatism: only the end result mattered. 'Will I see you again?'

'Regrettably, I am returning to Stockholm as soon as I have spoken with Count von Steinberg.'

'Well, then . . .' Anna stood up. 'I won't say this has been a pleasure, but thanks for the coffee.'

'And you will be in the park next Tuesday morning at six.'

'That is what I agreed, Herr Johannsson. Good morning, Franz.' She smiled at the waiter, and left the coffee shop.

*   *   *

Anna crossed the street, smiled at the concierge behind the desk in the lobby of her apartment building – as it was owned by the SD and he was in its employ he was required to note all non-resident comings and goings, which was the main reason she had not brought Johannsson inside – and took the lift to the sixth floor.

Over the years she had carefully trained herself to take each day, and each problem, as it arrived and, most importantly, never to overreact; any other approach to her precarious life might have involved a mental breakdown. But this . . . The trouble was, she supposed, that over the past five years, working for Heydrich and now Himmler, while they were both absolutely vile, bloodthirsty monsters, as she had been thinking just before the appearance of Johannsson, she had always felt they cared about her survival. Even when sending her to Moscow to assassinate Stalin, Heydrich had provided her with an out. It hadn't worked, of course. It had never been going to work, even had she not been betrayed before she had reached her target. But she had always felt he had hoped it would. He wanted her back, not because he had the least genuine affection for her – she did not suppose he had ever had the least genuine affection for anyone save perhaps his daughter – but because he knew her value.

MI6 had always provided her with an even greater sense of underlying security, thanks to Clive Bartley. Four years ago she had seduced him in a mood of angry rebellion against her employers and her fate, and discovered that he was the first man she had ever met of whom she could be genuinely fond, because he was the first man she had ever met whom she felt she could trust, absolutely. More than that she was reluctant to consider, at this time. She had been trained to seduce men, to learn their secrets, and then, if required, to destroy them. Never to love them. But Clive was her future, and thus the future of her family as well. Yet even he had been unable to prevent his superiors from giving her the task of overseeing the assassination of Heydrich. Through Bartoli she had learned that they had been very pleased with the outcome of that coup, even if all their agents had been taken or killed. All except her. And London did not know that it was she who had completed the job, despite their instructions not to become personally involved.

She could not feel that the Americans had any personal interest in her survival. Even Joe Andrews. He had once saved her life, but that was because Clive had sought his aid. And when she had repaid him, in her fashion, he had said he loved her. But after the business in Washington, when she had had to shoot her way out of an NKVD trap, leaving six bodies scattered about the place, she had been given the choice between working for the American Secret Service or spending the rest of her life in prison even if she managed to escape the electric chair. Then he had been required to hand her over to his boss in the OSS and the situation had changed. Wild Bill Donovan had clearly been as smitten by her looks and her charm and lethal potentiality as any man, but he had made it clear that he intended to use her, regardless of any personal risk to herself, when the occasion arose. Then this long silence. But now she had a nasty suspicion that the occasion had arisen.

The lift stopped, and she crossed the lobby, opened the door to her apartment, stepped into the inner lobby and closed the door behind her, then leaned against it for a moment. Home! She adored this apartment. She had been brought up in Vienna in comfortable but never luxurious surroundings; her father had been a liberal newspaper editor always at odds with the various right-wing Austrian governments even before the Anschluss. And when she had been commandeered by the SS she had assumed even that comfortable existence was gone for ever. Instead she had wound up here, in the very lap of luxury, from the thick-pile rugs on the parquet floor, the expensive drapes, the hardly less expensive prints on the walls, to the superb ensuite master bedroom . . . None of it was hers, of course, any more than the priceless jewellery waiting on her dressing table or the expensive clothes hanging in her closet. Like the entire building, it and they belonged to the SD, who had given it to her to match the image they wanted her to project – that of a hugely wealthy socialite. She recalled with some amusement how astonished Donovan, with his typically money-oriented American point of view, had been to discover that she received no salary, merely had her bank account topped up by the SD accountants as and when they felt she needed it. *He* was now paying her a large salary, the money being deposited in a bank in the States. She wondered if she would ever be in a position to claim any of it.

The inner door opened, and Birgit, her maid, emerged, looking anxious. A small, dark-haired woman with pert features, only a few years older than Anna herself, Birgit always looked anxious. She had now been with Anna for three years, and if she had never actually shared in any of the several traumatic events of those three years, had been close enough to them to know that her mistress often lived on a knife-edge. But she also knew that Anna worked for the SD, and that where that most secret organization was concerned, the one mistake one could make was to ask questions. And this last year, since their return from Prague, had been quiescent, at least for her. But now she was definitely agitated. 'Countess,' she whispered. 'There is someone here to see you.'

'Who?' Anna asked. After the disturbing sudden appearance of Johannsson she was in no mood for another crisis.

'She says . . .' Birgit drew a deep breath. 'She says she is your sister.'

'What?' Anna demanded, and stepped past the maid to throw open the door to her lounge and regard the young woman who had been sitting on the settee, but had risen to her feet. She might almost have been looking at herself, a few years ago. Almost. Katherine Fehrbach was a couple of inches shorter, and somewhat more solidly built. Her hair, if worn equally long, was a darker share of gold. Her features, although very handsome, just failed to match Anna's poignant beauty, though at this moment they wore an attractive mixture of defiance and apprehension. . But . . . she should have been in the prison camp along with her mother and father. 'What are you doing here?' Anna demanded.

'You could at least say hello,' Katherine suggested.

'What has happened to Mama and Papa?'

'Nothing, so far as I know.'

'But you are out.'

'Well . . .' Colour crept into Katherine's cheeks. 'I volunteered. To be like you.'

Anna went to the sideboard, poured two glasses of schnapps. It was still not yet nine o'clock, but she desperately needed a drink. 'To be like me.' She handed a glass to her sister. 'What did Mama and Papa say?'

'Well . . . they weren't happy.'

'Because they think you have signed up to become an SS whore. They think I am an SS whore.'

'They don't know the truth.'

Anna frowned. 'What truth?'

'What you do.'

'And you do – know what I do.'

'Yes. Now. Dr Cleiner told me.'

Anna sat down. 'You have been to the SD training camp?'

Katherine sat beside her. 'I completed the course two days ago. That is why I am here. They told me I could come to see you before I commenced my final training.'

'You have completed the initial course,' Anna said slowly, remembering her own experiences, five years before. 'You mean you have . . .'

'I have killed a man, yes. He was a condemned criminal, anyway.'

'And that makes you happy.'

'Well . . . you had to do that, didn't you? Dr Cleiner considers you his most successful pupil.'

If he does, Anna thought, it can only be because I defied him. But the implications of what she was hearing were shattering.

Katherine squeezed her hand. 'And now we'll be working together. I am so proud.'

Oh, you silly, silly girl, Anna thought. I have done what I have done for the past five years in order to keep you, and Mama and Papa, alive, even if they are not aware of that. But I am also committed to destroying every vestige of Nazism . . . and that now includes you. Did she dare tell her the truth? But that way lay suicide; she had no faith in her sister's strength of character. She could only hope to rescue her when this whole filthy edifice came crashing down. Which meant an added responsibility, both then and now.

'Hardly together,' she remarked.

'Oh, I understand that you are far senior to me,' Katherine said.

'Yes,' Anna agreed. 'But I am sure we'll see each other from time to time. Now, I must change my clothes and get to the office. When do you start your final training?'

'I start the day after tomorrow. They say it will take another month. I understand that it is to do with deportment and that sort of stuff.' She followed Anna into the bedroom, looked at the jewellery on the dressing table. 'Will I be given things like that to wear?'

'When you have completed your final training, and if they are satisfied with you.'

'Anna . . . will the additional training involve . . . I mean . . .'

Anna threw her shirt and slacks and camiknickers on a chair.

'Anna?' Katherine asked. 'That mark on your side . . . you didn't use to have that.'

'True. I was shot.'

'Shot?' Katherine cried.

'The risk goes with the job,' Anna pointed out. 'And as I am sure you can see, I wasn't killed or even crippled.' She clipped on her suspender belt and sat down to put on her black stockings. 'Your final training will be intended to make you into a lady. Didn't you like what happened at the SS school?'

Katherine licked her lips. 'I didn't know what to make of it, at first. But I kept telling myself that you had done it all. I still found it hard to accept.'

'Well,' Anna said, pulling on a clean pair of camiknickers and then her white shirt, and black calf-length skirt. Then she knotted her black tie, made sure it was the right length. Now she was correctly dressed as an SS secretary. She sat at her dressing table to apply make-up and brush her still damp hair, before securing it with a tortoiseshell clip on the nape of her neck. 'It did happen to me, as it happened to all the girls who trained with me. We all had to strip naked and be "examined" by Cleiner; we all had to learn how to handle men, both physically and mentally . . .'

'You mean you actually . . . used your mouth?'

'Didn't you? You must have, or you wouldn't have passed.'

'I hated it. And that was something I just couldn't imagine you doing.'

'Well, if it's any consolation, I didn't care for it much, either, then. Because I didn't care much for any of the men we were given to practise on. If you ever get someone you can really like, it can be a dream.'

'Anna, did you know that they all regard you with total reverence? They talk about how you shot your way out of England and the hands of the British.'

The only people I shot in England were three Gestapo agents trying to arrest me, Anna thought. I broke Anna Gehrig's neck, after she had shot *me*.

'About how you shot and killed two enemy agents in Prague.'

Two *enemy* agents, Anna thought. The nadir of my career. At least so far.

'About how you shot your way out of the Lubyanka Prison in Moscow.'

With Joe Andrews at my side, Anna remembered. She attached the tiny gold bars to her ears; the clips were also gold. Seven people for the Reich, she thought. And another fourteen they did not know of. And Heydrich. 'You don't want to believe everything you hear. Now, I have to go.'

'Will I see you again?'

'I said that we would get together, from time to time. But when will depend on what job you are given, and whether we are both in Berlin at the same time.'

She strapped on her Junghans watch; she did not wear her ring to the office, but her crucifix had never left her neck, as Katherine had noticed while she was dressing. 'Anna . . . how do you go to church? I mean . . . well, how do you confess?'

Anna went to the door. 'People like you and me do not go to church, Kate.'

Incident in Geneva

A nna walked to Gestapo Headquarters. It was not far, and walking was easier than summoning a taxi; the streets were so cratered and rubbled it was impossible to drive very fast and one never knew when one would encounter a 'No Entry' sign. People hurried to and fro, but most gave at least a glance at the tall, strikingly good-looking young woman, so officially dressed, and exuding such confidence. How little they knew, she thought.

She found it incredible that she actually felt a sense of

homecoming when she entered this building, inferior only to that given her by her apartment. Of course she had now worked out of here for five years, but equally she was aware of the horrors that could go on in the cellars – she had once suffered those horrors herself, for a breach of discipline. But yet, so far as anyone knew, she was now 'one of them', her future no less than her past tied to them and their success. Thus she gave her invariable smile to those men and women who greeted her as she went up the stairs to her office, sat behind her desk and checked her diary. There was no mail. She never received mail.

There was nothing in her diary either. Himmler, not recently having employed her in her original role as the SD's number one executioner, treated her as a super-secretary. What he wanted most was her brain; thus there were several files waiting for her to peruse, select the important items, and commit them to her photographic memory, to be recalled as and when he required the information. She picked up the first one and opened it, but she knew that this morning concentration was going to be difficult, even for her. Both Johannsson and Katherine – and thus, by extension, her parents – were on her mind, the trouble being that in cold terms Johannsson, and the fact that after more than a year she had been contacted by the OSS and given instructions, was by far the more important.

Her intercom buzzed.

'Anna.'

'Good morning, Anna.' Himmler's voice was as coldly impersonal as ever. 'Come in, will you?'

'Yes, Herr Reichsführer.'

She closed the file, left her office, smiled at the real secretaries in the lobby outside the Reichsführer's office, knocked, and entered the huge room, blinking at the sunlight streaming through the great windows, one to each side of the full length portrait of Adolf Hitler, looking suitably noble, on the wall behind the large desk, and then came to attention and threw out her right arm. 'Good morning, Herr Reichsführer. Heil Hitler.'

'Heil!' Himmler regarded her from behind the rimless glasses which largely obscured his eyes. If his black uniform was pristine, the cross-belts highly polished, it was still difficult to consider him as an insatiable god of war. The thinning pale hair, the equally pale and hardly noticeable moustache, the pasty complexion, the rimless glasses and the twitching hands – all combined to present a picture of anxious indecision.

Neither suggestion was the whole truth, Anna knew. Himmler was quite capable of ordering the execution of a thousand men, women and children, as he had done many times already, and he was now engaged in building a huge extermination centre at Auschwitz in Poland, to get rid of many thousands more of those, principally Jews, regarded by Hitler as unfit to belong to the Reich. But on the rare occasion he had been required to witness an execution he had been physically sick. Just as when he had sent her to Prague the previous year, her instructions to obtain the proof that Heydrich was seeking to usurp his powers, and perhaps even those of the Führer, he had shrunk from ordering the assassination of a man he had virtually created, and whom he had come to fear.

'Anna!' he said. 'You exude so much health. You have been training.'

'Of course, Herr Reichsführer. I train every morning, either in the gymnasium or in the park.'

'How I wish that all of my staff were as dedicated as you. Sit down.'

Anna sat before the desk.

'Are you pleased to have your sister in the department?'

'I am surprised, sir. I think I should have been advised.'

'She volunteered, you know.' A subtle reminder that *she* had been conscripted.

'So I believe, sir.'

'You have seen her?'

'This morning, before coming to work.'

'And what do you think? I have not met her yet, but I am told she is very nearly as striking as you.'

'Very nearly, sir.'

'And I am sure she will turn out to be as dedicated. Tell me, Anna, are you a happy girl?'

She was utterly surprised. 'I think so, sir.' Part of her training had been to learn how to lie, convincingly.

'But you are aware of what is going on?'

Alarm bells jangled in her brain. 'I try to be, sir.'

'I am talking about the Kursk offensive.'

'Yes, sir,' she said cautiously.

'We committed almost our entire Panzer army, to shatter the Russian salient, pinch out their forces, and regain everything we lost at Stalingrad last February.' He stared at her.

'And the battle has commenced, sir.'

'The battle is over, Anna. The final communiqué has just arrived. We have been beaten.'

It was Anna's turn to stare. 'Those were the new Tiger tanks.' Though she had advised MI6 of the coming battle plans, and had no doubt that the information had been passed on, she had still expected the Russians to lose.

'The Soviets knew of our plans and anticipated them. How, I do not know. But our forces are falling back everywhere.'

Another triumph, she thought. But one which might bring with it unimaginable catastrophe. If from an Allied point of view any Russian victory had to be tremendous news, the thought of the Russians entering Berlin, with her condemned to death by the Kremlin, before the British and Americans could gain a foothold on the continent, was terrifying.

'Add to that,' Himmler said, 'this landing by the Allies in Sicily, it is a pretty sombre picture. In fact . . .' Another long stare. 'Can I trust you, Anna?'

Anna got her brain into gear. 'I hope so, sir.'

'I hope so, too. I made you what you are, you know. Everything you have is a gift from me.'

'I do understand that, sir.'

'Without me, you are nothing. But as long as I am here to protect you, the world can be at your feet. And that of your sister.'

He certainly believed in laying it on with a trowel. 'I appreciate that, sir.'

'So, we stand or fall together, eh?'

God forbid! she thought. But she said, 'Of course, sir.'

'So everything I say to you, every instruction I give you, is in the most complete confidence.'

'I understand that, sir.'

'So there is something I wish you to do for me, which must be known only to you, me and the person you are going to visit.'

'Sir?'

Himmler opened a drawer and took out a large envelope, the contents of which he emptied on to his blotting pad. 'I have had these prepared for you.' He held them up in turn. 'One passport, in the name of Anna O'Brien. I always think it is better to retain one's Christian name, where possible, to avoid mistakes. You are a citizen of the Republic of Ireland, and therefore neutral. A first-class return train ticket to Geneva. Now . . .' He reached down beside his chair, and lifted an attaché case from the floor, placing it on his desk; it was obviously very heavy. 'In Geneva you will visit a Herr Laurent, to whom you will deliver this case. I have written down his address; memorize it and then burn it. You will open the case for him, and he will check the contents. Then he will give you a receipt, and you will return here. Understood?'

'Ah . . . yes, sir.' She could only wait, as he could not possibly stop there.

As he also understood. He produced a key and unlocked the case. 'Come round here.'

Anna got up and stood at his shoulder, gazing at the piles of bills, pounds sterling, French francs, Swedish kroner, Italian lire, even US dollars. 'Herr Laurent will convert this money to Swiss francs, and give you a receipt in that denomination, as well as in American dollars.'

'Yes, sir. May I ask . . .'

'I actually have no idea what it will amount to, in Swiss francs. I believe that in US dollars, it totals something like half a million.'

'I see, sir.'

She would have moved to return to her seat, but he suddenly put his arm round her thighs and hugged her against him. 'This is merely the first instalment, and it is yours as much as mine. I am taking care of our future, Anna. I am sure you understand as much as I that things are not going well. We are being crushed. Oh, it may take a few years yet, and in those years the many secret weapons our scientists are working on may well come to fruition and turn the tide back in our favour. But a sensible man covers every possible angle.'

'Of course, sir,' Anna agreed, her brain racing. 'Have you then abandoned the intention of succeeding the Führer?' That had, after all, been behind his wish to get rid of Heydrich.

'I would like you to forget that we ever discussed such a

possibility. It is not our place to do so, in such a time of crisis. And frankly, my dear girl, one has to wonder, supposing things do not change for the better, if there will be anything worth succeeding the Führer for. But as I have said, I intend to cover every possible contingency. Both for you and for me. Always remember that.' He closed the case, locked it, and held out the key. This was attached to a fairly long looped cord. 'Wear this around your neck, and do not take it off until you hand over the case.'

Anna dropped the loop over her head, raised her hair over it, and then pulled down her tie and unbuttoned the top of her shirt to lower the key and settle it next to her crucifix.

'The most fortunate of keys,' Himmler remarked, watching her. 'You will of course be adequately armed for this mission, just in case someone tries to rob you.' He held out a sheet of paper. 'Should anyone official attempt to prevent you completing your mission, whether at the border or anywhere else, here is your carte blanche.'

Anna scanned the sheet of SS notepaper, on which he had written: *The bearer of this note is travelling on official business for the Reich, and is to be given any assistance that she may require. Reichsfüher Himmler.*

'Is that satisfactory?' he asked.

'Entirely, sir.'

'However, bearing that in mind, it follows that under no circumstances must you open that case to anyone but Herr Laurent.'

'And if someone insists?'

'Handle it as you think best. Whatever happens, whatever you have to do, you will have my full support . . . providing the contents of the case are not revealed. So. Any questions?'

'When am I to leave?'

'Immediately. You may go home to pack an overnight bag, and then Colonel Essermann will pick you up at a quarter to twelve, in order that you may catch the twelve o'clock train. A seat has been reserved for you. You will be in Geneva by nine o'clock tonight. You are booked into the Hotel Gustav. It is small, quiet and discreet, but I understand it is comfortable.'

'Yes, sir. This room . . . is it ensuite?'

He raised his eyebrows. 'Is that important?'

'It is to me. Privacy is important.'

'I understand. I will have one of my secretaries telephone and make sure that it is ensuite. Now, sleep with the case beside you. Call on Laurent at nine tomorrow morning. He is expecting a messenger, and will respond to the word 'donation'. Once he has checked the amount, and given you the receipt, you will return here. You will report to me the moment you are back, no matter what hour that may be.' He opened the deep drawer of his desk and took out a bottle of schnapps and two glasses, poured, and held one out. 'To the success of your mission. But I know that you will not fail me. Heil Hitler!'

Anna took a taxi from Gestapo Headquarters to within a block of Antoinette's Boutique, paid the driver off, and walked the rest of the way, the precious attaché case in her right hand. It was extremely heavy but, apart from not wishing to be driven to the door, she needed to give her heart time to settle down, and her mind time to evaluate what had just happened.

Her boss was preparing to do a runner! And take her with him! And Katherine? What was he thinking of – setting up a harem in his retirement? But he had placed his life in her hands. Save that she did not know if she dared take it. She could only betray him to Hitler, and she had no idea what the response might be. Although the Führer had expressed an interest in her work, and indeed in her – so much so that she had almost feared he was going to take her over for himself – the events of the past year had been so dramatic, and indeed, from his point of view, traumatic, that she had only seen him once or twice, and then fleetingly. But she did know that he relied on Himmler more than anyone else in his government, save perhaps for Dr Goebbels, and to accuse the Reichsführer of potential treason might rebound catastrophically.

In any event, she could do nothing without instructions from London. She entered the opulent showroom of the boutique, which was quite busy; Himmler might be despairing of Germany's prospects, but the average well-to-do Berliner was still prepared to accept the official word that victory was just around the corner, and thus intended to enjoy life to the maximum allowed by the RAF.

A smartly dressed young woman hurried forward. 'May I be of assistance, Fräulein?'

She had assessed the secretarial uniform and also spotted the absence of a wedding ring, but she was not someone Anna had ever seen before, and clearly had no idea who she was. 'I wish a word with Signor Bartoli,' she said.

'Ah . . . do you have an appointment? He is very busy.'

'I do not have an appointment,' Anna said. 'Just inform him that the Countess von Widerstand wishes to see him. I will wait in his office.'

She walked towards the inner door, and the girl scurried beside her. 'You can't go in there, Fräulein. Oh, Frau Bartoli,' she gasped in relief. 'This lady—'

'Good morning, Edda,' Anna said. 'This young woman appears to be confused. Will you tell Luigi I wish to see him, urgently.'

'Ah . . .' Edda Bartoli hesitated. She was a slim, somewhat hard-faced woman, who wore her dark hair long as she wore her husband's elegant clothes with panache and ruled her husband's staff mercilessly, but who was always uncertain in the presence of Anna. As the couturier's wife, she had had to be included in the network, though Bartoli had promised that she knew nothing about their real purpose; he had told her they were actually working for Mussolini – a man she apparently worshipped – just to keep an eye and a finger on the Nazi pulse. Anna had never trusted her, had in fact more than once begged London to do something about the set-up, but as London had no other contact so well placed in the German capital, and did not wish her to be personally involved in the sending and receiving of messages, they had not yet responded.

'It is urgent,' Anna repeated, opening the office door and then closing it behind her, before sitting down and crossing her knees.

She did not have long to wait before the door opened and Luigi Bartoli bustled in. Short and stout, with a balding head and a little moustache, he had long got over the initial sexual euphoria of three years before, when he had been presented, as he had supposed, by London with an utterly beautiful and delightfully young agent to control. But not only had his advances been firmly rejected, the young lady had proved quite impossible *to* control. 'You come charging in here,' he complained, 'without an appointment . . . I was with an important client.'

'I am sorry, Luigi,' Anna said equably. 'This is urgent.'

'It is always urgent.' He sat behind his desk and shot his cuffs. 'Well?'

'I wish you to get a message off to Basle immediately.'

'Very well. It will go tonight. What is it?'

'Luigi, I said immediately. That means now.'

'You are being absurd. You know I do not use the radio during the day. That is far too risky. You will endanger us all.'

'There is nothing incriminating in the message, even if anyone here manages to decode it. You will just say, Belinda will be at the Hotel Gustav, Geneva, tonight, using the name Anna O'Brien. Personal contact is urgently needed. Tonight only.'

'You are going to Geneva?'

'Your perception never fails to fascinate me.'

He ignored her sarcasm. 'On urgent business. What is this urgent business? And under the name of Anna O'Brien? What sort of a name is that?'

'It is an Irish name, Luigi, as I am half Irish, as I believe you know.'

'And you think you can get out of Germany using a false name?'

'I know I can get out of Germany using a false name, because I am doing so with the blessing of Reichsführer Himmler.'

'You are travelling on his business?'

'Again, your powers of deduction amaze me.'

'So tell me what it is.'

'It is what I am going to tell whoever meets me. If London decides you should know of it, they will inform you.'

He leaned back in his chair. 'This is absolutely impossible. I am your controller. Yet you continually send messages which I do not comprehend. Suppose I refuse to accept this situation any longer?'

'Then you should complain to London. But if I am not met in Geneva tonight, *I* will complain to London, and I would not care to estimate what they will do about it.'

He glared at her, but he had never been able to determine how much clout she had in London – he knew nothing of her

American connection – and equally, he had never been sure just how much clout she had with the SS: he knew she was Himmler's PA.

So she smiled at him. 'I will see you when I come back. Ciao.'

Birgit was dusting and polishing enthusiastically, but paused to point at a window. 'Look at the crack, Countess. One of those bombs must have been closer than we thought.'

'Well, tell Rudolf to get hold of a glazier, if he has not already done so; I'm sure we cannot be the only apartment with a broken window. Now, I am going away for tonight.'

'Oooh, Countess! Am I coming with you?'

'No, you are not. You are staying here to attend to the window. I will be back tomorrow night, but it may be late. So listen. There is a man coming to see me tomorrow after-noon, only as I will not be here, you will have to receive him and tell him that I have been called away, but I will contact him when I return.' She was suddenly overtaken by her wicked sense of humour. 'The gentleman – his name is Stefan – is actually coming here to photograph me. But if you like, you can let him photograph you, instead.'

'Oooh. May I? I have never been photographed.'

'Then I suggest you try it. You might enjoy it. You under-stand that he will wish you to be in the nude?'

'You mean, with nothing on? Oh, Countess, I couldn't do that.'

Anna reflected that although her maid knew all about her various lovers – well, nearly all – the only romantic attach-ment *she* had ever revealed was for Marlene Gehrig, the young woman who had attempted betrayal and had had to be disposed of. But that had been two years ago. 'Who knows?' she suggested, '– you might enjoy that also. Now I must hurry.'

She went into her bedroom, had another shower as it prom-ised to be a long day, and put on clean clothes, a severe black calf-length dress. To this she added a black cloche, tucking her hair out of sight. She knew that she could not prevent herself from attracting admiring glances, but she could make herself as inconspicuous as possible. Then she packed a complete change of dress and underwear, stockings and her make-up in a large shoulder bag, added a Luger nine-millimetre pistol, a spare clip, and her silencer, surveyed herself in the mirror, and returned to the lounge to sit on the settee, remaining absolutely still, staring in front of herself, the black attaché case resting against her leg. Birgit knew better than to interrupt this routine, which she had observed her mistress following on previous occasions, without the least understanding of the reason for it.

Anna was concentrating, so that she could present to the world a picture of a slightly inconsequential young woman, going about her obviously inconsequential business, while actually being totally prepared for what she had to do and, more importantly, for what she might *have* to do, to carry out her task and return safely. The most important distracting thought was how London would respond to her message, and who would contact her in Geneva, because, perhaps . . . But of course it could not possibly be Clive: there simply wasn't time. She was dreaming, and her business had no room for dreams. But it was essential that contact was made, both from the Himmler point of view, and to find out what the Americans were up to, supposing London knew.

The doorbell rang. Anna looked at her watch. Quarter to twelve on the button. But that was how the SS, and even more the SD, worked. She got up. 'I will see you tomorrow night, Birgit,' she called, and went to the door. 'Good morning, Colonel.'

Hellmuth Essermann clicked his heels; as always he was handsomely immaculate in his black uniform, with his yellow hair and perfectly Aryan features. Anna had known him for close on two years, and if she had never been able to like him, or fully trust him – he was a dedicated Nazi – she could never forget that he had saved her from the horrors of 'interrogation' at the hands of the Gestapo, albeit at Himmler's command, following Heydrich's death. But she also knew that he would like to get closer to her, as he had revealed on several previous occasions, and again now. 'You are as beautiful as ever, Countess.'

'Why, Colonel, you say the sweetest things.'

He eyed the attaché case. 'That looks very heavy. May I carry it for you?'

'Thank you, no. I can manage.'

Again he clicked his heels, and escorted her downstairs to

the waiting car. They were at the station a few minutes later, and he accompanied her on to the platform. 'I am told that I must meet the late train from Geneva tomorrow evening. I assume you will be on it?'

'That is my intention.' She looked along the platform at the two trench-coated men, standing together and watching her.

'Gestapo,' Essermann remarked. 'They oversee every foreign departure, or arrival.'

'In your company, I am sure they will not interfere with me.' It was no business of the Gestapo to become involved with the SS, much less the SD.

'But you will not have my company on the train. Would you like me to have a word with them, warn them off.'

'Do you think they know who I am?'

'Every Gestapo agent knows who you are, Countess. And every Gestapo agent dreams of one day being able to pin something on you which will get you into their torture cells.'

'Because of Feutlanger?'

'Feutlanger in Prague, Groener in Moscow . . . They still hold you responsible for the collapse of their London operation three years ago.'

Even if neither they nor you know the truth of any of those events, Anna thought. 'How nice to be hated,' she commented. 'Is Feutlanger still around?'

'Very much so. You will be passing quite close to him when you cross the border. He may have failed to get his hands on you after the Prague disaster, but no disciplinarian action was ever taken against him, although one could say that his upwards career has been arrested. He now commands the Munich office.'

'I shall remember that. But I don't think I will need your protection on this trip, Colonel, although I appreciate the offer. I shall say auf Wiedersehen. Until tomorrow.'

She boarded the train, and was shown to her reserved seat. The attaché case she placed beside her, resting her arm on it; it would have to accompany her to the dining car for lunch in any event. She was joined in the compartment by a man and a woman, whom she assumed were husband and wife, smiled at them, looked out of the window at Essermann, fluttered her fingers, and then leaned back and relaxed.

Feutlanger, she thought. The very name made her skin

crawl. As Essermann had reminded her, they had first met in Prague in 1940, after that disastrous shoot-out in which she had inadvertently shot and killed two British agents. It was that example of supreme skill and Nazi dedication, as was supposed by her superiors, that had earned her reputation as the SD's most accomplished assassin. But Feutlanger, in charge of security at the Hradcany Castle and, in that capacity eagerly taking over the investigation into what had happened, had been outraged to discover that he was outranked by a twenty-year-old girl, as she had then been. When she had returned to the Czech capital, two years later, her brief the destruction of Heydrich, he had still been there, his hackles again raised at the sight of her. And on Heydrich's death, so clearly the result of a conspiracy, he had thought he had his chance . . . even if he had had no proof. But he had had, momentarily, the power. She could still feel his hands sliding over her flesh as he had told her what he was going to do to her, his fury when Essermann had turned up with the order from Himmler that she was to be released into his custody.

But her feelings towards him had not weakened, either.

'Despatch from Basle,' Amy Barstow announced standing before Clive Bartley's desk and leaning across it to place both the original and the decoded version before her boss, and then straightening with a quizzical expression. 'It's very early, but there seems to be a flap on. It's from *her*.'

She sighed as Bartley almost snatched at the paper. She had now worked with him for three years, and had the highest regard for him, both as a man and as a superior. This was partly because of his reputation as one of the most successful MI6 field agents, which he had earned long before she had come into the service, and also as a man. In this he represented her ideal, being over six feet tall, powerfully built, ruggedly good-looking . . . and quite beyond her reach. This, she felt sure, was less because she was the hired help or even because she knew she was overweight and had unremarkable features, than because he was already apparently committed, here at home to a high-powered fashion editor, even if their relationship was somewhat on and off, but more importantly with the agent he regarded as his private property. Amy had never met the Countess von Widerstand, although she had seen press photographs of her published in the glossies when she had been living in England as the Honourable Mrs Ballantyne Bordman. She could not deny that the beastly woman was a knockout. What she resented was the way her hard-boiled boss sprang up like a puppy offered a bone whenever she deigned to communicate with him.

Now he scanned the transcript and stood up. 'I'll be upstairs.'

'Arranging a visit to Geneva?' Amy asked acidly. 'There simply isn't time, sir.'

'There is always time, Amy,' Clive Bartley said.

William J. Baxter studied the transcript in turn. In the strongest contrast to his senior assistant, Billy Baxter was a small and untidy man, who invariably looked harassed. Clive could sympathize with him; his job consisted of trying to control a batch of field agents who were congenitally *un*controllable, otherwise they wouldn't have been field agents in the first place. And of them all, the one who gave him most grey hairs was Anna Fehrbach. He had been reluctant to take her on at all, even when she had been 'turned' by Clive in the course of a furious love affair. He accepted that, positioned as she was in the heart of the Nazi establishment and that by the Nazis themselves, she was the most valuable of his people, but her propensity for sudden, extreme and often lethal violence kept him in a constant state of apprehension as to who was next going to cross her path and live to regret it . . . only living did not often come into it. 'So she's got her knickers in a twist,' he remarked. 'But then, she's always getting her knickers in a twist about something or other.'

Clive sat before the desk. 'If Anna says it is urgent, then it is urgent. You know that, Billy.'

'But she can't tell us what it is.'

'She doesn't feel she can use Bartoli to tell us what it is. She doesn't trust him. And neither do I. When are we going to replace him?'

Baxter started to fill his pipe, a sure sign that he was unhappy with the situation. 'When we can locate an adequate replacement, and when we can get rid of him without blowing the entire system apart. Anna wants him replaced simply because she doesn't like him. She has never supplied us with any concrete evidence that he cannot be trusted. All right, keep your shirt on.' He struck a match, puffed contentedly, and obviously felt better. 'I agree this may be important. If Anna is paying a brief visit to Geneva it is obviously on the instructions of her SD employers. And when Anna goes visiting out of Germany somebody generally drops dead. Get a message off to Basle. I assume they already have someone on the ground in Geneva. They can contact him, or her, and tell him to check out this Hotel Gustav, after nine o'clock tonight.'

'Then you are likely to have another corpse lying about, and it will be one of ours.'

'He'd use the Belinda code.'

'That would depend on how quickly he could get it out, and how lethal a mood Anna is in when he makes his play. She has a hang-up about being betrayed.'

'Tell me about it. God, what a fuck-up. How the hell I ever allowed you to foist this walking reincarnation of Lucretia Borgia on me I shall never understand.'

'Because she is the goods, and she's ours, body and soul.'

'You mean she's yours, body and soul. You hope.'

The opening he had been waiting for: 'She is mine,' Clive said. 'That is the point I am making. She trusts me, and only me.'

Slowly Baxter took the pipe from his mouth. 'Oh, no,' he said. 'Oh, no, no, no, no, no. Anyway, you could not possibly do it.' He looked at his watch, and then at the transcript. 'It is now ten thirty. Anna is spending one night at this place. God knows how many people she is planning to eliminate in that time. But there is no way you can get there for tonight.'

'Billy, it is only nine thirty in Germany. Or Switzerland. And you can get me there. You got me to Moscow in two days two years ago.'

'To rescue Anna. You are both becoming an expensive luxury. Do you seriously expect me to go to the boss and ask him to persuade Fighter Command to let us once again have the use of a Mosquito?'

'Yes, sir, I do.'

'They have their own duties, you know. I happen to know that something very big is in the wind, which is going to require the services of every available RAF aircraft.'

'I believe this occasion warrants it. Anyway, do you seriously believe that the absence of one Mosquito for one night is going to ruin their plans?'

'Two nights. You have to get back.'

'I can take my time about that. I can cross into France and contact Jacques, and you can send a Lysander to pick me up.'

'Are you out of your mind? France is no longer Vichy, you know. It's all German, now.'

'I can get to Jacques. And once I do, he can get me out.'

Baxter sighed, but he studied the transcript again. 'Most urgent,' he muttered. 'It had better be.'

'Cancel any appointments I may have for today and the next week,' Clive told Amy, pausing only to pick up his overnight bag, which he kept permanently packed with the necessary changes of clothing he might need on the continent.

'Ah . . . you are taking Miss Hoskin out to dinner tonight.'

'Bugger it. Well, you will have to telephone her and tell her I can't make it.'

'Don't you think you should do that, sir? The last time you gave me a message like that to deliver, she cursed me out.'

'Remind her there's a war on,' Clive recommended.

The train reached the border at six, but at the end of July it was still broad daylight. Several policemen came on board, and a couple of very obvious Gestapo agents. They moved slowly through the compartments, checking passports and travel documents. Anna had had a good lunch, the case always beside her, and had actually dozed during the afternoon. She felt totally relaxed. Whatever its implications, her assignment was one of the least exacting she had ever had, and while she was curious as to who might be waiting for her, as she was sure it couldn't be Clive, there was no point in thinking about it. Just to be in touch with the world outside Germany was a treat. Now she opened her eyes to blink at the uniformed man standing over her. 'Your passport, Fräulein.'

She opened her shoulder bag – the Luger was well concealed beneath her change of clothing – and handed over the booklet.

'Anna O'Brien? Is your journey business or pleasure?'

'I hope to combine the two,' Anna said, pleasantly.

'You are leaving Germany?'

'I shall be returning to Germany tomorrow.'

'You mean you live in Germany.'

'That would seem to be obvious.'

'But this passport says you are an Irish national.'

'So it does. That is because I am – an Irish national.'

'Travelling on business in and out of the Reich.' He looked at the attaché case. 'I hope there is nothing illegal in that case, Fräulein.'

'Of course there is not. The case contains my clothes and personal effects.'

'But you say you are returning tomorrow. It is surely a very large case to be taking for one night.'

'I am attending a dinner party, and have my ball gown, with accessories.'

'I think I will have to look inside.'

'And I would prefer you not to.'

He gazed at her, uncertainly, while the other two passengers seemed to huddle against each other. But before he could come to a decision, they were joined by one of the Gestapo agents. 'Is there trouble?'

'This Fräulein will not let me look inside her bag, Herr Inspector.'

'Then I must insist, Fräulein,' the agent said.

Anna opened her shoulder bag again and took out the carte blanche. The agent unfolded it, gazed at the contents, and gulped. 'I apologize, Fräulein. If there is anything . . .'

'I do not require assistance at this time,' Anna said.

'Yes. Yes, of course. You'll forgive me. Come along, you fool,' he said to the bewildered policeman, almost pushing him out of the compartment.

The other two passengers stared at Anna, who smiled at them. 'They are really very reasonable,' she explained.

The train reached Geneva at eight, and Anna was in her hotel room by a quarter to nine. It was a double, and had a well-appointed bathroom. She ordered a late supper and a bottle of wine, undressed, had a shower, and put on her dressing gown. A waiter arrived with her meal a few minutes later, and she poured a glass of wine and settled herself in front of the table, suddenly becoming conscious of how tired she was.

She found herself staring at the attaché case. She was still absorbing all that its contents implied, both for Germany, for

Himmler, and for herself; and then found herself wondering where the OSS involvement came in, and whether the two could possibly be connected. She had something to eat, her thoughts drifting to who was going to come knocking on her door, possibly in a few minutes' time . . . and was taken by surprise when the door suddenly opened: the waiter had apparently taken it off the latch after serving her meal.

She found herself looking at two men, whose belted trench coats and fedoras could leave her in no doubt that they were policemen. One was fairly large, with a moon-like face; she had never seen him before. But the other . . . She regarded the short, slight body, the ferret-like features, the piercing eyes . . . 'What in the name of God are you doing here?'

Joachim Feutlanger snapped his fingers, and his aide closed the door, this time locking it. 'I am here in the name of the Reich, Countess.'

'I see.' Anna did some calculations. She realized that if she did not do something about the situation she was in danger of at the very least being manhandled. Nor did she doubt that Feutlanger's sidekick was armed, and her pistol was still in her shoulder bag, which was lying on the bed. As for dealing with them without a weapon, she did not suppose Feutlanger would be a problem, but his companion might be, certainly as, in whatever happened, he would be backed up by his superior. She would have to bide her time and use all her assets: Feutlanger had never actually seen her in action, although from that earlier Prague episode he knew of her prowess with a gun. On the other hand, she felt sure that his desire to deal with her as a policeman was subordinate to his desire for her as a woman – her secret weapon, time and again. 'And you are stationed in Geneva, now?' she asked pleasantly.

'I am Commandant of the Gestapo Office in Munich,' Feutlanger announced, importantly. 'But when my people at the border reported that they had encountered you in the act of fleeing Germany, I considered it my duty to come down here and investigate personally.'

'Your people reported me by name?' Anna asked, interested.

'They did not recognize you, if that is what you mean. But they found your behaviour suspicious, and thought it necessary to report it. And when I asked for a description – well, I knew immediately who it had to be, *Fräulein* O'Brien.'

'And how did you know where I was staying?'

'I did not know where you were staying, Countess. As soon as I received the news from the border I telephoned our local office here and told them to put a tail on you until I could get here. They picked you up at the station.'

'And I never noticed. I am a silly woman.' Because I was in a daydream, she thought. The same thing had happened once before, in Washington, when she had carelessly walked into that NKVD trap. That had cost six lives. Well, she thought, there are only two involved here. 'Oh, do sit down, Herr Feutlanger. I'm afraid there is only the one chair, but your friend can sit on the bed, if he likes.' She crossed her legs, allowing the dressing gown to drop away from above her knees.

The agent gulped, and remained standing, staring at her. Feutlanger sat down, facing her.

'Would you like a glass of wine?' Anna asked. 'There is only the one glass, and I have already drunk from it, but I do assure you that I am not diseased.'

'Your effrontery never ceases to amaze me,' Feutlanger said. 'But this time I have caught you red-handed.'

'Have you? I am sure your man at the frontier told you why he did not attempt to arrest me.'

'Some document. No doubt forged.'

'I think you should look at it, before you make a judgement which may be gravely mistaken.'

'That will not be necessary. I wish to look at the contents of that attaché case.'

'And I cannot permit you to do that.'

'But there is no one going to burst in here and rescue you, as that swine Essermann did in Prague last year. There is just you, me, and Otto here. No one knows we are here, save the waiter who let us in, and he is in my pay. And I know all about your little tricks. Otto.'

Otto produced a Luger fitted with a silencer, levelled it.

'If she attempts to attack us,' Feutlanger said, 'shoot her in the belly. It will be a shame to destroy so much beauty, but at least we will have the pleasure of watching her die, slowly, and in agony. Do you want to die like that, Countess?'

Anna permitted herself a shudder. 'I should hate that, Herr Feutlanger. The case is locked.'

'But you have a key.'

While exposing her legs, Anna had carefully kept the dressing gown closed across her breasts. Now she sighed in apparent defeat. 'It is in my bag.'

'Very good. Empty the bag on to that table. Watch her, Otto, and if she does anything you do not like, shoot her.'

Otto looked suitably determined; Anna supposed that was as good a way to die as any. She got up, went to the bed, picked up the bag, and turned towards the men. As she did so, she released the dressing gown and allowed it to swing open, exposing her naked body. Otto gaped, and Anna acted with her usual lightning speed, thrusting her hand into the bag, grasping the pistol, and firing through the material. She had not yet fitted the silencer, but the bag muffled the sound of the shot.

The first bullet smacked into the wall behind Otto's head, but Anna had fired twice before he could react. And the second bullet struck him in the thigh. He gave a little squeal and fell to his knees, blood pouring from the severed artery to soak his trousers. He did manage to get off a shot but it hit the wall well wide of his target. Then he dropped the pistol to grasp at his wound.

'Fucking bitch!' Feutlanger dived for the gun, but Anna had dropped the bag and her gun and was already moving forward to kick him on the side of the head and send him rolling across the floor. Then she knelt beside the stricken Otto and took the pistol from his hand; she needed the use of the silencer.

'Fräulein!' he gasped. 'Countess!'

Anna shot him through the heart and turned to face Feutlanger, who was slowly regaining his feet. 'We have unfinished business,' she reminded him. 'From last year.'

'You would not dare,' he snarled. 'You would not *dare*. I am—'

'One of nature's more serious mistakes,' she told him, and shot him three times.

Anna sat down and drank some wine. She no longer felt like eating, knew herself well enough to expect the waves of revulsion that were about to sweep over her. Numbers twenty-three and twenty-four. Easy to remind herself that she had had no choice. Himmler's express orders had been that no one other than the man Laurent should open the bag.

Equally easy to say that if ever a man had deserved execution Feutlanger was the one. She might feel sorry for Otto, but he had certainly been going to obey his instructions and shoot her in the stomach. Yet the fact remained that she had now killed twenty-four people, and she was only twenty-three herself. But she had been protecting not only herself, but her family and, in this instance, Himmler. There was a sick joke . . .

There was a knock on the door. Anna put down her wine glass. Number twenty-five? The adrenaline was still flowing, still transforming her from a normal woman into a killing machine. She picked up her bag and took out her own silencer, then screwed it into the muzzle of her gun.

There was another gentle tap. She pulled Feutlanger's body away from the door, closed her dressing gown and tied the cord, opened the door, gazed at the man who stood there, and gasped. 'Clive! Oh, my God, Clive!' She fell into his arms.

Clive half-carried her into the room, kicked the door shut behind them. 'My darling girl! What . . .' He looked around him even as he inhaled. 'Holy Jesus Christ! What happened?'

'It's a long story.'

'It generally is. But I'm here to listen.'

Anna put down the gun, poured herself another glass of wine, drank, and then handed it to him to drink in turn. 'They came to arrest me.'

'They being . . .?'

'Gestapo. That one' – she pointed at Feutlanger – 'is the bastard who tried to torture me in Prague.'

'The Gestapo came here to arrest you, in Geneva? You mean you're coming out, at last? Thank God for that! But if you'd just let us know, we'd have arranged it for you.'

'I am not coming out, Clive. I am here for the SD, for Himmler. Listen.'

She told him what her mission was and what had happened. He listened in silence, occasionally looking at the two bodies. He had known Anna long enough to accept that anyone who attempted to get in the way of what she conceived to be her duty, or even her allotted path, was choosing the short way to the nearest cemetery.

'What do you want me to do?' she asked.

'Well, in the first instance, we must get you out of here.'

'I cannot leave here, until tomorrow morning.'

'My dear Anna, you cannot stay here with two corpses.'

'As I do not believe in ghosts, they are unlikely to trouble me, and they are unlikely to become a nuisance in twelve hours.'

'But the police . . .'

'Tomorrow morning, I shall leave this room at half past eight, having hung a "Do Not Disturb" sign on the door. The maid will certainly not come in for another couple of hours, by which time I will be on a train for Germany. It leaves at ten.'

'They will close the border.'

'I do not think they can do that before I get there. Think. The police will have to be called, and they will spend some time checking things out. I am registered under the name of Anna O'Brien, and my passport is in that name. The passport was issued in Dublin, or so it says. There is no indication as to where I have come from or where I am going. Before I leave I shall also remove all identification from the pair of them. For the Swiss police to close all the borders to find an Irishwoman who might just have killed two unknown males would be an absurdity.'

'They'll track you to the station. You're not exactly easy to miss.'

'By the time they do that, I will have changed back into being the Countess von Widerstand, and will be in Germany.'

'They'll ask for extradition.'

'They won't get it. Once I am across the border, Anna O'Brien ceases to exist. The fact that this alleged murderess might bear a resemblance to the Countess von Widerstand will not be acceptable to the German government.'

Clive scratched his head. Her coolness never ceased to fascinate him – and terrify him. 'So you will deliver the money and go back to Berlin.'

'I must do that, or forfeit Himmler's confidence. What I need to know is whether you will use this information.'

'I will have to check with Billy. But if we do use it, won't that endanger you?'

'Not if you make it plain that your source is someone in Switzerland.'

'We shall certainly do that. You'll have to give me a week

or so to get home. Check with Bartoli next week. We'll have been in touch by then.'

'I do not wish Bartoli to know of this.'

'I know you don't like the man—'

'My personal feelings have nothing to do with it. I have an instinct that he, or certainly his wife, is getting set to betray us.'

'And you would like to take him out.'

'If necessary. But his wife is even more dangerous.'

'Are you as bloodthirsty as you sometimes appear?'

'I hate to think that I am bloodthirsty at all. But I am fighting a war. So are you, and millions of others. And it is a war we have to win. I do, anyway, or everything I have done these last five years has been a colossal crime.'

He squeezed her hands. 'I know, my darling girl. I'm on you side, to the bitter end. It's just that I find your so-clinical approach a little startling, from time to time. Especially when I am looking at you. Well . . .' Another squeeze.

Anna freed herself and poured the last of the wine. 'There is another matter we need to discuss. And this, I feel, does endanger me.'

'Oh shit! What?'

Anna related her conversation with Johannsson. Now Clive stroked his chin. 'They obviously have some devious scheme on their minds.'

'And you have no idea what it might be?'

'Not a clue. I'll see what I can find out. But . . . When are you meeting this bloke Steinberg?'

'At dawn a week tomorrow.'

'That's a bit soon for me to make any headway. It's going to take me at least the week to get back to London. But you'll probably be able to discover what's up from this chap.'

'Clive,' Anna said, 'I am sure I will find out. What is bothering me is that down to a couple of days ago my identity as a double agent was known only to two people in Germany: Bartoli and his wife. And I've never been too happy about that. Now this Swede knows who I am.'

'But you tell me he said that Steinberg does not.'

'Steinberg certainly knows I work for Himmler. Yet apparently he has been persuaded that I will lend a sympathetic ear to whatever he, and the OSS, have dreamed up. That virtually puts me in Ravensbrück, at the very least, if anything goes wrong.'

Clive looked at her, then at the two dead bodies. 'You reckon it may be necessary . . .' He gulped.

'This whole thing could be a trap.'

'I cannot believe that Joe Andrews, or Wild Bill Donovan, would sell you out. I mean, did not you and Joe – well . . .'

'Does that still rankle?'

Clive sighed. 'I am not going to let it. Joe is an old friend, and you – well, you are just Anna. And I know you felt you owed him.'

'You say the sweetest things. Yes, I owed him my life. And I also do not think that either Joe or Wild Bill would ever dream of betraying me. But I can't say the same for everyone they have working for them. Listen, I can handle the situation, for a while. If it is a set-up, I can always tell Himmler that I went along with it to find out what these people are after.'

'And he'll believe you?'

'He always does. Or I wouldn't have been given this mission.'

'Do you and he – well . . .'

'He likes to touch me, from time to time. But he has never done anything more.'

'The man needs his head examined.'

'Absolutely. And not only as regards sex. But he happens to be the second most powerful man in Europe, at this moment. So I suppose he is entitled to have his foibles. On the other hand, as he does regard me as his private property, the last man I had sex with was Reinhard Heydrich, the night before he was blown up.'

Clive frowned at her. 'But . . . he was blown up on his way from his house outside Prague to the Hradcany Castle. Early in the morning.'

'That's right.'

'And you had spent the night with him?'

'His wife and daughter had already returned to Germany. He was going to follow them a day or two later, as he supposed; I am certain he would then have been officially appointed Hitler's heir and virtual co-Führer. He was on Cloud Nine that night. So much so that, believe it or not, he told me he was going to divorce his wife and marry me. That was the only time I ever felt sorry for him.'

'Because you knew the assassination had been arranged for the next morning?'

'Partly that.'

'What did you think when you saw him drive off?'

'He didn't drive off, Clive. I went with him.'

Clive released her hand. 'You were in that car? You were told not to endanger yourself.'

'So many previous attempts had failed, I realized I would have to adopt a hands-on approach. I had to persuade him to take the short cut down the side road where I had told the assassins to wait.'

'You could have been killed.'

'Not really. As I knew what was going to happen, I hit the floor of the car just before the grenade was thrown.'

'That was still going above and beyond.'

The temptation to tell him just how far above and beyond she had gone was enormous, but she resisted it. 'The assassination squad took a far greater risk, and paid for it with their lives.'

'And no one suspected your involvement?'

'Oh, yes.' Anna pointed. 'That piece of carrion. He was the Gestapo commander in Prague. He had me in his torture chamber, and was about to start . . . doing things to me, when an envoy from Himmler arrived to take me back to Berlin.'

'And Himmler never suspected?'

'He was just happy to have seen the back of a monster he had created and who was now scheming to displace him.'

'Shit! And you never told us before.'

'Well, I was just doing my job. You told me to set it up, and that is what I did. The point I am making is that it was fourteen months ago, and since then there are several parts of me that have become very lonely, if not atrophied, so . . . But we don't want to be interrupted.' She opened the door, checked that the corridor was empty, then wheeled the trolley out and stationed it against the wall. She returned into the room, locked the door and took off her dressing gown.

'For God's sake,' Clive protested. 'We can't do it here.'

'It's my bedroom.'

'Yes, but . . .' He gazed at the two bodies.

'I don't think they are going to interfere. But if they bother you . . .' She stripped the bed, draped the top sheet over Feutlanger, the bottom sheet over Otto. 'There we are. Now we can just forget them.'

'Can't we put them in the bath?'

'Well, no. I will want to have a bath tomorrow morning.' She lay on the mattress, her head on the pillow.

Clive sat beside her. 'Anna . . . God, I don' know what to say.'

She held his hand. 'Those two men belong to the organization, the society, that taught me how to kill, how never to feel remorse – never to blink, if you like. Is there not a biblical saying, that those who sew the wind must reap the whirlwind? They created the Countess von Widerstand. They must accept the consequences.'

'But me . . . MI6 . . . Joe Andrews . . .'

'You taught me that there might just be a calm when the wind dies down.' She put her arm round him to draw him against her. 'For you, the Countess von Widerstand does not exist. There is only Anna.'

The Conspiracy

To Anna's surprise, the address she had been given was not a bank but an ordinary office block. She presented herself before the desk in the front hall. 'My name is Anna O'Brien. I have an appointment with Herr Laurent.'

'Seventh floor,' he said, looking her up and down. She was again wearing her black dress and her black cloche. Well, she thought, she now had a reason to wear mourning. But, as always, he clearly liked what he was looking at. 'The elevator is over there.'

'Thank you.' She went to the lift, pressed number seven and looked at her watch; the car seemed to be moving with agonizing slowness. It was three minutes to nine. She had actually left the Gustav at a quarter to, having been awake since Clive's departure just before dawn.

They had loved with almost frantic desire. She always loved like that: physical sex was the only time she could give way to the passion that was always lurking in her mind, and so often threatening to overwhelm it – because the rest of the time that mind had to be so carefully controlled, so icy calm, so utterly sure of what she was doing and what she had to do to stay alive. She remembered that in her early days in this job she had thought of herself as swimming in a sea of sharks, all awaiting the opportunity to take a bite. Well, Feutlanger had felt his opportunity had come. Poor Feutlanger.

But Clive had not been relaxed. Well, she supposed, for all his years of experience, he had never spent the night in a room with two corpses, much less most of it making love. His obvious awareness of his surroundings had been inhibiting; she had been almost relieved when he had had to leave. When next they got together, she had told herself, it would be without any hang-ups. Supposing that was ever going to happen.

But from then on she had been working, with no margin for error. When she had left the room at eight thirty, having not eaten breakfast – she would eat on the train – the dinner trolley had been removed and the maid was already in the corridor, working on the room three numbers away. Anna had smiled at her, but just in case she had seen her leaving her room, she said, 'Please let my husband sleep for a few hours. He has had a busy night.'

The girl had not looked very pleased, and there was no telling how long she would wait; presumably she went off duty about noon. Anna had paid the bill, smiled at the clerk, and left the hotel to merge into the crowds hurrying to work. Walking a busy street which entirely lacked craters, in the midst of ebullient people who had never been bombed and presumably never would be, carried her back to Berlin three years ago or, better yet, her girlhood in Vienna . . . save that for as long as she could remember the people in Vienna had suggested strain and uncertainty, with the ever-looming menace of Nazi Germany dominating their thoughts. These people were happy.

Which was not to say that they would not hang her, or at least lock her up for life, were they to discover that she was the most recent occupant of the hotel room in which there were two dead men. And this lift was still ascending with damnable slowness. But at last it was stopping. It was two minutes past nine.

She stepped into a lobby, and through a swing door to another, faced a rather severe looking middle-aged woman sitting behind a desk and a large typewriter, who, unlike most men, did not look the least pleased to see her. 'You have business?' She spoke German.

'My name is Anna O'Brien,' Anna said in the same language, 'and I have an appointment with Herr Laurent. It is to do with a donation.'

The woman checked her diary, and pressed her intercom. 'Fräulein O'Brien is here . . . Very good, sir.' She flicked the switch. 'You are to go right in.' She indicated the corridor, while looking even less approving than before. 'The third door on the left.'

'Thank you.' Anna proceeded along the corridor, gave a brief knock, and opened the door – to check in surprise. The man seated behind the desk was amazingly young; she would not have placed him as more than in his early thirties. He was also remarkably handsome, with aquiline features, very like her own, she supposed, carefully groomed black hair, and a body which was well displayed by a flawlessly cut dark three-piece suit.

For his part, Laurent appeared equally struck by what he was looking at. 'Miss O'Brien?' He spoke perfect English.

'That is correct,' Anna said in the same language, and advanced into the room, closing the door behind her, before placing the attaché case on his desk with some relief; it had been growing heavier by the minute.

He came round the desk to take her hand. 'It is a great pleasure. I hope I am going to be allowed to take you out to lunch.'

'I am catching the ten o'clock train,' Anna said. 'So I really am a little short of time.'

He regarded her for a moment, then released her hand and returned behind his desk. 'Well, at least sit down for five minutes.'

'You will need the key,' Anna said. 'Will you excuse me?'

He gazed at her in consternation as she reached behind

herself to unbutton her dress, and then pulled it forward from her shoulders to expose the straps of her camiknickers, her crucifix, and the key. She lifted the cord over her head and handed it to him. He looked at it, and then at her as she replaced her dress. His expression had not changed, but there was a faint flush in his cheeks. 'This cord is damp.'

Anna sat down and crossed her knees. 'I was told not to take it off until in your presence, and I had a bath this morning.'

He looked at the cord, and then at her. 'It has lived an exciting life.' He sat also, opening the case. 'Herr Himmler must trust you very much.'

'Thank you. I will need a receipt. He said it was to be in both dollars and Swiss francs.'

'Of course.' He pressed his intercom. 'Fleugel. Come in here will you, please.'

An even younger man appeared.

'Would you check the contents of this case, please, and bring me a receipt for the total. In US dollars as well as francs.'

'Of course, sir.' Fleugel closed the case and left the room.

'Will he be long?' Anna said.

'Ten minutes.'

Ann looked at her watch: nine fifteen. 'It really is important that I catch that train.'

'I will drive you to the station myself. It is only ten minutes away. But is Herr Himmler that hard a taskmaster?'

'He makes up schedules, which his staff are required to meet.'

'It is good to have such a willing staff. But then he is a very powerful man.' He studied her. 'How long have you worked for him?'

'Five years.'

'That is a long time to work for such an exacting boss. You must admire him very much.'

Anna returned his gaze. 'Don't you?'

'I have never met him. Although I have heard a great deal about him, his reputation.'

'Yet you accept his money.'

'In the money business, certainly here in Switzerland, our clients are essentially both faceless and blameless. We invest their funds for them, and our percentage keeps us in business. Do you find that very immoral?'

'How can I,' Anna asked, 'as I have worked for him for five years?'

'You are a very intelligent young woman.'

'Thank you.' Anna looked at her watch. 'It is half past nine.'

'And here is Fluegel.' He took the receipt, glanced at it, and then handed it to her. 'Is that satisfactory?'

It was in both Swiss francs and US dollars. Anna was more interested in the latter, which apparently worked out at $533, 474.62. 'From which you will take . . .?'

'We only charge five per cent for handling the money, but of course we also hope to make a profit on the exchange rate and the source of our investment.'

'Of course.' Anna put the receipt in her shoulder bag, and stood up. 'And now . . .'

'You are in a hurry. Thank you, Fleugel.'

'Before we leave, may I use your toilet?'

'Of course. It is through there.'

It took Anna just five minutes to remove her hat and dress, put on her other dress, which was pink with a knee-length skirt, fluff out her hair and let it lie on her shoulders, stow her discarded dress and hat in her bag, and return to the office.

Laurent stared at her. 'My God! Do you do that often?'

'Do I do what, often?'

'Completely change your appearance and, indeed, your personality.'

'Which one do you prefer?'

'I thought I was dealing with a woman; now I find that you are a girl.'

'I am a girl in a hurry.'

'Of course.' He held the door for her, and escorted her to the lift leading down to the basement garage. He continued to study her as they descended, standing facing each other. 'I cannot help but feel that I have seen you before,' he remarked. 'Or is it just that you are the dream of every man to have seen before? – and perhaps met?'

'You put that very nicely,' Anna conceded. 'But you do know that is the standard approach of every pick-up artist?'

'Touché.' He ushered her to the predictable Mercedes, and a moment later they were on the street. To Anna's dismay the route took them past the Gustav, and sure enough there were three police cars parked outside, with a cluster of spectators standing around them. The maid could have waited no more than half an hour before going in; Anna hoped she had had hysterics. Laurent slowed. 'I wonder what has happened here.'

'We really do not have the time to stop,' Anna reminded him.

'Of course.'

Five minutes later they were at the station. There were the usual policemen to be seen, and as usual they gave her a second and then a third look, as did most other people, but no one attempted to interfere with her departure. Laurent accompanied her to the door of her carriage. 'Will I see you again?'

'I suspect you will, Herr Laurent, if you wish to.'

He kissed her fingers. 'I shall be counting the days.'

Berlin was blacked out, and the streets were largely deserted, even at nine o'clock at night, and yet, as she stepped off the train Anna had a sense of tension. 'Something has happened,' she said.

Essermann bent over her hand. 'Of course you would not have heard, Countess. Yes, something has happened. Hamburg has been wiped off the map.'

'Say again?'

He escorted her to the waiting car. If he had to have noticed that the attaché case was no longer as heavy as yesterday, he did not comment. But then she had no idea whether or not he was in Himmler's confidence. 'The RAF, and the Yanks, bombed it for three consecutive nights as well as during the day. They are calling it the Battle of Hamburg. The last raid was mainly incendiaries, dropped where there were already many fires. They are still burning out of control, because the damage is so great the various services cannot reach the conflagration. As I say, the city is virtually destroyed.'

'My God!' Anna commented. 'When did this happen?'

'The final raid, the fire raid, was last night.'

While I was in bed with Clive, she thought, and wondered if he had known what was going to happen. If that were true, he had no business accusing her of having too clinical an approach. 'Were there many casualties?'

'It will take time to evaluate. So many bodies were consumed entirely by the fire storm, and numbers of others are too badly burned to be identified. But they are talking of more than fifty thousand dead.'

'My God!' Anna said again, and gazed out of the windows at the empty streets, the bomb craters. Supposing something like that was to happen here?

'The Reichsführer's instructions were that you were to be taken direct to him, no matter what time you got back,' Essermann said.

'He told me he wanted that. Is he very upset?'

'The Reichsführer conceals his feelings very well. Perhaps you have noticed this.' The car stopped outside the apartment building. 'I had better accompany you in.'

He opened the door for her and escorted her past the SS sentries on the door, having, despite his uniform and the fact that they obviously knew who he was, to show a pass. 'It is the third floor,' he explained. 'I will wait for you in the lobby to take you home.'

'Thank you. I hope I shall not be too long.'

Enigmatically, he did not reply. But one of the guards must have called up, because when she exited the lift on the third floor there was an obvious butler waiting for her. But he was also a bodyguard. 'Good evening, Countess,' he said. 'Will you place your bags on that table, please.'

'It is the contents of these bags that the Reichsführer wishes to see,' Anna pointed out.

'Of course, Countess. But I must see them first.'

Anna placed both the bags on the table, and he looked into the attaché case, then emptied the shoulder bag, picking up the Luger and looking at her.

'It was the Reichsführer's command that I carry a weapon,' Anna explained.

The butler opened the chamber and sniffed. 'This gun has been fired, recently.'

'Yes, it has. I have not had the time to clean it. But that is a matter for the Reichsführer and myself.'

'Of course. But I must require you to leave it here until instructed by the Reichsführer.'

Anna shrugged.

'And now, Countess, would you stand facing the wall, and place your hands on it, above your head.'

'You intend to search me?'

'It is my duty to do so.'

Anna considered, briefly. But she could not fault his manners and, like her, he was an employee of Himmler. She went to the wall and placed her hands on the wood. She knew he was standing immediately behind her, and a moment later he touched her shoulders, sliding his hands under her armpits and round the front of her dress. This was perfunctory, but he was more thorough as he moved lower, exploring the valley of her groin.

His hands moved away, but Anna knew what had to follow and remained standing still. 'Legs apart, if you will, Countess.'

She spread her legs and he raised her skirt. As she wore only camiknickers underneath he had to be able to see at a glance that there was no concealed weapon, but he still felt it necessary to stroke the inside of her thighs and move upwards to touch the silk. Then the hands moved away and the dress fell back into place. 'You understand that I am only doing my job, Countess.'

Anna stepped away from the wall; she left the attaché case, placed the Luger beside it, picked up her shoulder bag and refilled it. 'If I did not understand that, you would not still be here.'

His slight smile indicated that he did not know a great deal about her. He stepped past her and opened a door. 'The Countess von Widerstand, Herr Reichsführer.'

'Anna!' As usual she thought he was going to embrace her but, also as usual, he thought better of it, to her relief: in addition to the other physically repellent aspects of his appearance, he was wearing a mauve brocade dressing gown and matching slippers.

'Heil Hitler, Herr Reichsführer.'

'Indeed. Come in, come in. I hope Albrecht did not give you a hard time?'

'I suspect the hardness was all on his side.'

'Ah . . . oh, yes. Of course. Ha ha. Cognac?'

'Thank you, sir.'

He poured and gave her the balloon, taking one for himself. 'Sit down. Did you have a successful trip?'

Anna sat on the settee. 'Yes, and no.'

'Explain.'

'The goods were delivered.' She gave him the receipt.

He perused it. 'Splendid. You are a treasure. But . . .?'

'I was followed to Geneva by two Gestapo agents, who attempted to arrest me.'

'Good heavens! Gestapo agents? In Geneva? What were they doing there?'

'Apparently, despite my false papers, I was identified at the border, and the Munich office decided that I must be absconding.'

'And so they followed you to Geneva? I shall have to look into this. And you say they attempted to arrest you? Did you not use your carte blanche?'

'I did, and they chose to ignore it. One of them was the man Feutlanger, who gave us that trouble in Prague, last year.'

'I shall have to see about this. But you managed to talk your way out of it.'

'No, sir. It is very difficult to talk Herr Feutlanger out of anything when he gets a bee in his bonnet. And besides, he has always hated me, ever since that other incident in Prague, three years ago.'

'Then what did you do?'

'I had to shoot him. And his support.'

Himmler gazed at her for several moments. Then he said, 'You shot two Gestapo agents? What were they doing while this was going on?'

'They were trying to shoot me back, but they weren't very good.'

'And now they are in hospital?'

'No, sir. By now they are in the morgue.'

Himmler got up, somewhat unsteadily, and refilled his glass. He glanced at hers, but she had only taken one sip.

'I did not see that I had any alternative,' she explained. 'Herr Feutlanger was determined to see the contents of the attaché case, and you had instructed me that no one was to be allowed to do that.'

'My God! Of course you did the right thing. But when it comes out . . .'

'Neither you, nor I, nor the government of the Reich will be involved.' She opened her bag again, and took out the various documents 'I went through their pockets before leaving, and removed all identification. I left the room at eight thirty this morning, having attached a "Do Not Disturb" notice to the door. I delivered the case, completely changed my clothes and my appearance, and caught a train at ten o'clock. All that is known to the Swiss is that an Irish woman named Anna O'Brien arrived in Geneva last night, dressed all in black and with her hair invisible, and departed again this morning, leaving two unidentified dead men in her bedroom. They will not be able to find any trace of her leaving the country, as I used my German passport at the border. The investigation as to what happened will be at a dead end before it even begins.'

Himmler produced a coloured handkerchief to wipe his neck. 'The Gestapo office in Munich will know that Feutlanger paid a visit to Geneva yesterday. They may even know what he was after: you.'

'And he did not return. What he did was still illegal. What will they do? Try to explain it to the Swiss police? In any event, sir, surely you can kill any investigation?'

'Of course I can,' he agreed, as if he had forgotten his powers. 'But the next time . . .'

'We will have to arrange a different delivery point. I am sure Herr Laurent will be co-operative in that.'

To her consternation he put his hand on her neck, under her hair, and gently massaged the flesh. Almost she thought she could feel the hair standing on end. Then his hand slid away again. 'You are a treasure. Now go home and have a good night's sleep. I will see you tomorrow.'

'I hope the Reichsführer was pleased, Countess?' Essermann asked, as they sat together in the back of the car.

'He seemed to be.'

He stared into the darkness beyond the driver's head. 'I almost expected to be told that you had no further use for me tonight.'

'Are you mine to use?' Anna countered.

He still preferred not to look at her. 'I would be content to fill that role, as I think you know.'

'But we are both the Reichsführer's,' she reminded him, 'to be used as he sees fit.'

'Professionally. Surely, if it were otherwise, he would have invited you to stay. But he has never done that, has he?'

'I am his employee, and he intends that I should continue

in that role. I do not think he would care for either of us to develop a relationship out of his control.'

'He need never know.'

The car stopped and the chauffeur got out to open the door for her; Anna had no idea how much of the conversation he had overheard. As she made to step out, Essermann caught her hand.

She looked down at it. 'I am not going to invite you up, Hellmuth. It has been an exhausting two days, and I wish only to have a bath and go to bed.'

'I just want you to know that if there is ever anything I can do for you, you have but to say.'

'Anything?'

'Anything.'

She leaned over and kissed him on the cheek. 'I shall remember your promise. Auf Wiedersehen.'

She freed her hand, went into the lobby, smiled at the night concierge, and took the lift to the sixth floor.

'Countess!' Birgit was waiting for her. 'I am so glad you came back.'

'Weren't you expecting me to?' Anna went into the lounge. 'How did you get on with Stefan?'

'Oh, he was so upset that you were not here.'

'Did he photograph you?'

'Well . . . yes, he did. Oh, Countess! The things he made me do! The poses . . .'

'After you had taken off your clothes.'

Birgit blushed.'Well . . . yes. Countess, have you . . .?'

'I have posed for Stefan, yes. It gives him such pleasure. Now tell me, did he have sex with you?'

'Oh no, Countess. I couldn't allow that. Besides, I am not sure he wanted it. He wanted to wait for you to come in. When I told him you were not coming in until very late, he left. I think he was very angry.'

But also very faithful, Anna reflected, and wondered if she was, inadvertently, recruiting a private army of her own.

'Well,' she said. 'I have no doubt he will come to see us again, when we may be able to work something out.'

'Welcome home,' Baxter said. 'I trust your journey was rewarding? As you are here, I assume you had no trouble getting out?'

'It was both tedious and tiresome. I had to spend a night in the back of a vegetable truck. I am never going to eat cabbage again. Now tell me, did you know about Hamburg?' Clive asked, '– that it was going to happen?'

'As a matter of fact, no. As I told you, I did know that something very big was being planned, but it hardly came under the heading of Military Intelligence – at least our Military Intelligence. And Harris played his cards very close to his chest. You have not told me that your mission was as successful.'

'Yes, and no.'

Baxter reached for his pipe. 'You lady friend didn't show.'

'Oh, she showed. And she had some very interesting things to say.'

'Such as, she's getting married to Himmler or somebody and all bets are off.'

'You couldn't be more wrong.'

Baxter took out his tobacco pouch. 'So you got her between the sheets. And you're still unhappy. I can see it in your face. Some people are never satisfied.'

'It was a little crowded,' Clive said. 'There were four of us in the room.'

Baxter's fingers were delving into the pouch. 'You mean she goes in for gang-bangs as well? That woman is a monster.'

'It wasn't quite like that,' Clive explained. 'The other two were dead. They were dead when I got there,' he hastily added.

The pouch slipped from Baxter's fingers; tobacco scattered across the desk.

'And she couldn't get rid of them, because she wasn't supposed to be there, if you follow me.'

Baxter used his hand to sweep up tobacco. 'I do not follow you at all. I'm not sure I want to. So you arrive there and find Anna contemplating a couple of corpses, as is her wont . . . Whose corpses?'

'A pair of Gestapo heavies who had tracked her there, and with whom she seems to have had a long-standing feud.'

'Wait a moment. Doesn't she work for the Gestapo?'

'No, no. She works for the SD and Himmler.'

Baxter scratched his head, forgetting that his fingers were still full of tobacco strands. 'But doesn't Himmler command both the SD and the Gestapo, not to mention the SS?'

'There is some rivalry between the departments. Just as there is between us and MI5, or between us both and the Special Branch.'

'But we don't go around killing each other, thank God! OK, so you turn up and find her doing what she does best, so I suppose you pushed off. But you say she did have something to tell you, even if your night's entertainment was ruined.'

'I did not, as you put it, push off.'

'You mean you spent the night there with all that company? Weren't they a little inhibiting?'

'Anna does not suffer from inhibitions.'

'You mean you . . . Holy Jesus Christ.' Baxter had his matches in his hand. Now he laid them down. 'You mean, you *could*?'

'Well . . . we hadn't seen each other for eighteen months.'

Baxter laid down the pipe as well. 'So tell me what was on her mind – apart from sex and murder.'

'Two things: one interesting, the other disturbing.'

Baxter listened. 'As you say, interesting and disturbing. Number one: Himmler isn't going to try getting out of Germany on a few hundred thousand dollars.'

'Agreed. Anna more or less said that this was intended to be the first of many.'

'So he's not planning to do a bunk for a while. We'll sit on this one. I assume Anna will keep us informed?'

'In so far as she can. I'm coming to that in a moment. But this American thing . . . Quite apart from the fact that she is our baby, breaking her cover without reference to us is putting her in a hell of a spot.'

'It's also unethical,' Baxter pointed out. 'But I did warn you that they don't co-operate, they dictate. I agree that we need to do something about it. You have to get hold of your friend Andrews right away. And until you do, Anna must be kept on ice.'

Clive looked at his watch; it was six o'clock on Monday evening. 'In precisely twelve hours from now, Anna is going to be meeting this contact.'

'Oh, for Christ's sake. Didn't you tell her to sit tight until she hears from us?'

'Unfortunately, our record of responding promptly to her information is not impressive.'

'Well, can't you get a message through to Bartoli tonight? He's her couturier, isn't he? He's entitled to ring her up.'

'Anna doesn't trust Bartoli, or his wife. That's why she had to see me, personally, rather than just sending a message. In fact, she would like something done about him.'

'Now, wait a moment,' Baxter said.

'Oh, she won't do it herself. Unless we give her the green light.'

'Of course,' Baxter said bitterly. 'She only kills our people by mistake.'

'I think she has a point – about Bartoli.'

'This whole thing is setting up to be an intelligence disaster. So suppose we by-pass Bartoli. Have we got anyone in Basle who can take his place, and get in and out of Germany?'

'Unfortunately, no. You know how these things work, in neutrals, Billy. Our people in Basle have identified every German agent there, and the Germans have identified every one of ours. They don't do anything about each other, as a rule. Sometimes they even have a drink together. They certainly meet at cock-tail parties and what have you. All very civilized. But if one of our people tried to get into Germany they'd have him the moment he stepped off the train.'

'We parachuted those agents into Czechoslovakia without too much trouble, last year.'

'But we didn't get any of them back out, did we?' He had decided not to inform Billy how closely Anna had been involved in that business, and how close she had come to death.

'Well, then, it seems to me that we have reached an impasse. Anna won't deal with Bartoli on anything important, and we have nobody else *for* her to deal with, unless the Yanks will let us use this fellow Johannsson. You'd better make getting hold of Andrews top priority.'

'I intend to,' Clive agreed. 'But only to find out what they're at. If we hand Anna over to Johannsson as a controller, then we've lost her – to the Yanks.'

'You mean, you have lost her, to Andrews.'

'Same thing. But perhaps we could by-pass Bartoli, as we did with Judith, last year.'

'And she also wound up on a slab, poor girl.'

'I know. Her nerves weren't up to it. My fault. I should've spotted the symptoms earlier. But until she cracked, she and

Anna worked very well together, and Bartoli was totally unaware of her existence.'

'So where do you intend to find another Judith?'

'Ah . . . I was thinking about that on the flight home. Did you know that Belinda – I mean the real Belinda not the code word – has an Italian mother? Her father was Italian too.'

Baxter, who had been fiddling with his pipe, picked it up and put it down again.

'Her father was murdered by Mussolini's thugs, and so mother and daughter fled to England, where mother married again – that fellow Hoskin. Belinda was ten when this happened, and she adopted her stepfather's name, but she spent her childhood in Italy, remembers it well, and still speaks the language like a native. She also is fairly fluent in German. I suppose that background accounts for her somewhat volatile temper.'

'Are you out of your tiny mind?'

'Billy, she is, or could be, a natural. She hates Mussolini at least as much as Anna hates the Nazis.'

'And you would like to use her as a spy.'

'A go-between, Billy. Not a spy.'

'She is still your mistress. Isn't she?'

'When she's in the mood.'

'And you are prepared to risk her life.'

'I do not believe there is any risk involved. As I say, with the right papers she will be able to go in, and then out, of Germany as she chooses. And it'll be a one-off. All she has to do is contact Anna, hear the result of the meeting with the Steinberg character, and come home.'

'All very pat. I think you are overlooking one or two minor matters. One is that she is entirely untrained.'

'We can rush her through a training schedule. She has been my girlfriend for seven years and has garnered a fair knowledge of what I do and what it entails.'

'Remind me to have you arrested for breaching the Official Secrets Act. Point two: as you have just agreed, she has an extremely volatile temper. Judith was a depressive, and thus a disaster in the end. Belinda is an emotional bomb waiting to explode. Point three: she hates Anna's guts.'

'She doesn't really. They only met once, and then Anna saved her life.'

'And how did she get into a situation where she needed her

life saved? Because she walked in on you and the Honourable Mrs Ballantyne Bordman having an intimate discussion, took extreme umbrage, and departed for the Bordman flat to have it out with her rival the moment she came home . . .'

'Which does not alter the fact that when she was unlucky enough to run into Anna's controller, the woman Gehrig, she would have been for the high jump had Anna not intervened. Which cost *her* a bullet in the ribs and several weeks in hospital. Belinda hasn't forgotten that.'

'Is that why she walks out on you just about every time Anna's name is mentioned?'

'I told you, she's an Italian.'

'And you still expect her to risk her own life to be Anna's contact?'

'Again as I told you, she hates Musso and his Fascists, which by definition means that she also hates the Nazis. But there's more to it than that. I believe that much of Belinda's angst is caused less by the fact that I occasionally rush off to see Anna than by our having a rapport that is outside her reach. If we make her part of that rapport, I think she will not only be very enthusiastic but very useful.'

'And Anna's take on all this? I mean, she knows who, or what, Belinda is.'

'I have never seen Anna betray a trace of jealousy.'

'I sometimes wonder if you know as much about women as you think you do. All right, you have my permission to sign Belinda on, but whatever happens is on your own head. Meanwhile get on to Andrews just as soon as you can. Not that it appears you can do anything about Anna plunging in tomorrow morning.'

'I know,' Clive said, sadly.

There was a scrambled wireless link between MI6 and the OSS office in Washington, and as it was only two o'clock in the eastern States, Clive did not expect any difficulty in getting hold of Joseph Andrews. But . . . 'I'm sorry, Mr Bartley,' the telegrapher said, 'but Mr Andrews is out of town.'

'Did you tell them who it is calling?'

'Yes, sir. And they said they would inform Mr Andrews on his return, and that he would contact you.'

The bastard, Clive thought. He had no doubt that Joe was

right there in his office. But he would have been told by Johannsson that the meeting with Steinberg was set up for tomorrow morning and had no intention of sharing anything with MI6 until it was a fait accompli. 'Amy,' he said. 'Get hold of Miss Hoskin for me, will you.'

'Ah . . . now, sir?'

'Of course now. I imagine she'll have gone home by now.'

'Yes, sir. It's just that . . . Well, as you instructed me to do, I called her after you left last week and told her that you would be unable to make dinner that night.'

'I see. And she took umbrage.'

'I won't go into detail as to the language she used, but the gist of it was that she never wished to speak to you, or hear your name, again. Sir. And then she hung up so violently I was deaf for two days.'

'It's her Italian blood,' Clive explained. 'She doesn't really mean it.'

'Sir?' Amy was clearly doubtful.

'Believe me. Get her on the line. Tell her it's a matter of life and death, and that I will be with her in half an hour.'

He got up, opened the wardrobe for his coat, and contemplated the bulletproof vest that hung beside it. He had not worn that vest for some time, not even when rushing to Switzerland, but he wondered if it might be necessary this evening. Then he grinned, opened his desk drawer, and took out an Official Secrets Act form instead.

He had to ring the doorbell several times before it opened. Belinda had clearly not been in long, for she still wore her smart business suit and her high-heeled shoes. A small, dark, intense woman with attractively sharp features and crisply cut short black hair, she could be very intense indeed, and most attractively so, when in the mood. She had first swum into Clive's orbit seven years before. He had been entranced – so much so that he had very soon asked her to marry him.

Belinda had declined. She had just been appointed Fashion Editor of a prominent London weekly, and although giving up her job had not been an essential part of the proposal, she had felt that marriage would be a distraction. More importantly, she knew what he did for a living, even if she of course could have no idea of what it entailed. But that was the point.

Belinda was a control freak, in or out of the office, and she could not contemplate a husband whose work she could never discuss and who was liable to disappear, quite without warning, for days and even weeks at a time – and be unable to explain what he had been doing. But as she had found him the most attractive man she had ever met, she had never objected to being his mistress, and their relationship had proceeded on a reasonably civilized level until the appearance of the Honourable Mrs Ballantyne Bordman.

But as he had put to Baxter, Clive had always felt that the various upheavals that had followed Anna's involvement in his private life had been a result less of jealousy per se than of Belinda's feeling that she was being excluded from an aspect of that life. If she had always been excluded, as long as it had been purely work, she had been prepared to accept it, if grudgingly; when it included a relationship with an utterly beautiful glamour-puss, it had been too much. Now he could only hope he was right.

For the moment, at least, she seemed in a good mood. 'I assume you have come to apologize for standing me up,' she remarked.

'Of course.' He swept her from the ground to lift her for a kiss: she only came up to his shoulder. 'We need to talk.'

'Oh, yes?' she said warily. 'Then you had better pour me a drink. And take one for yourself.' She sat on the settee, waited until he joined her with the two tumblers of Scotch and water. 'Talk about what?'

'How would you like to work for MI6?'

Belinda appeared to choke on her drink.

'On a part-time basis.'

Belinda got her breath back. 'Have you gone mad?'

'The fact is, I – we – the department – the country – need you, because there's a job to be done that only you can do.'

'What job?'

Clive drew a deep breath. 'We will provide you with some essential training. Very briefly, but enough to ensure you do not make any mistakes. Then you will be given an Italian identity, passport, background – the lot. With that cover we will get you into Sweden and then Germany. You will be travelling in clothes, as that is your normal business. Your cover will be that you are on your way home to Italy from a business trip to Sweden, but that you are hoping to sell some new designs to a man named Luigi Bartoli, who runs a dress shop called Antoinette's Boutique.'

'This is the agent I would be going to see?'

'No. As it happens, he *is* an agent of ours, but there is no need to contact him unless for some reason you are unable to reach the person we want you to see. I will give you the address. You will make contact, listen to what information this agent has for you, and then make your way into France. The exact route will be given to you to memorize. Your contact will be a man called Jacques. His address you will also memorize. He will see that you are safely returned here.'

'Just like that.'

'I'm not going to pretend that there isn't a certain element of risk involved. But it is minimal, as long as you remember to keep calm, remember your training, and not do or say anything stupid. I mean, you *are* an Italian. That you happen to be a naturalized British citizen cannot possibly be known to anyone in Germany.'

'Is this how you normally recruit people?'

'No, it is not. But our usual channel of communication has broken down, and while we are setting up a fresh channel, it is imperative that we contact this agent. And,' he added winningly, 'you would be working for – I mean, with me.'

'I see. And if by any chance I am found out, what happens then?'

'Ah. In our business, the secret is not to get caught out. There is no reason why you should, as I have said, as long as you keep your head.'

'You haven't answered my question. Suppose something does go wrong, and I am arrested.'

'Just keep cool and they'll have to let you go. They'll have nothing to hold you for. You will be carrying nothing incriminating, and Bartoli is a well-respected couturier.'

'So I keep cool while having electrodes pushed up my fundament and turned on.'

'You are at liberty to decline.'

'Don't you give your agents a suicide capsule, to be bitten if they're taken?'

'We do, where their capture might endanger other agents or release secret information, or indeed, involve them in an unacceptably unpleasant situation. But as I have said, we do not believe that you will be in any danger, providing you simply remember that you are in Germany on business, that you are going to see our contact and listen to what you are told, and then leave again immediately. However, if you would like a capsule you can have one. But Belinda, my darling Belinda, I would hate to think of you using it.'

She got up, went to the sideboard and poured herself another whisky. 'If all this is so top secret, no one will ever know about it, so I will get no kudos.'

'You will get all the kudos you can stand, once the war is over.'

She drank, and mused, still standing at the sideboard. 'If I agree to help, would you say that I would be striking a blow at Musso?'

'Absolutely. He is tied to Hitler. When Hitler goes, he goes with him.'

'And this will help Hitler to go?'

'Absolutely.'

Belinda looked into her glass for a moment, then raised her head. 'OK. Who am I going to meet?'

Clive took another very deep breath. 'Anna Fehrbach.'

Belinda threw the whisky decanter at him.

Anna was up early, had a cup of ersatz coffee, dressed in shorts, a singlet and running shoes, tied her hair in a pony-tail, and left the apartment. Birgit watched her with her usual anxious expression.

At six in the morning there were few people about, but those who were all clearly enjoyed the view of those strikingly long legs, and even more the splendours that lay beneath the thin material, exposed to the casual gaze as she walked the few blocks to the park and began to run, not very fast, but covering the ground with long, even strides, her hair flopping up and down on her back. She had actually done a complete circuit, sweat trickling down her neck and dampening her vest, and was just deciding that she would do one more before going home, when she became aware of a man running beside her. 'You are late, Count,' she remarked.

'I have been here for some time, watching you, Countess. Making sure that you were not being followed.'

'Or that I had not brought along a couple of SD heavies to arrest you?'

'What have I done to be arrested for?' he countered. 'It is a privilege to train beside a beautiful woman. But do you think we could sit down? I am not as fit as you.'

He was certainly panting. Anna indicated a bench beside the path, and he sank on to it, continuing to breathe heavily for some moments. 'I think we need to be brief,' Anna suggested, studying him; although she had seen him before, and had indeed met him at SS receptions, she had never actually taken much notice of him. He was a young man, about thirty, she estimated, not as tall as her but with a well-developed body which, like hers, was displayed by his singlet and shorts; he had muscular legs. With his close-cropped hair and chunky features he was quite attractive . . . and she knew that, unlike her, he was a genuine aristocrat.

'It is a difficult subject,' he remarked.

'So I gathered. But you requested this meeting.'

'You were recommended to me, as someone who might be sympathetic to what I have to say.'

'By Herr Johannsson. Do you know him well?'

'We have been acquaintances for some time. He belongs to a . . . discussion group, in which I share.'

'I see.' She still could not be certain that Johannsson had not confided that he worked for the Americans. 'What do you discuss, in this group?'

'The state of affairs.'

'You work for the government,' Anna reminded him, 'as do I. I do not think it is our business to discuss the state of affairs – merely to do our jobs. Do you know what my job is?'

'You are the Reichsführer's Personal Assistant. I understand that I am taking a grave risk in approaching you, but Herr Johannsson said . . .'

'That I might be sympathetic to whatever matter is concerning you. I should tell you that Herr Johannsson is only a slight acquaintance of mine. He is not in a position to determine to what, or what not, I might be sympathetic.'

Steinberg's face was contorted with apprehension. 'You mean you will have me arrested?'

'As you have pointed out, there is nothing criminal in wishing to talk with me, Count. Or in what you have so far said.' Now she was almost certain that he knew nothing about her real purpose, Anna felt in command of the situation, as she liked to be.

'But you do not wish to continue the conversation. I understand, Countess. I will leave you now, and will not trouble you again. Thank you for your time.'

He made to rise, and Anna placed her hand on his arm to encourage him to remain seated. 'I do not think you can just walk away. I think you have to tell me what your group discusses.'

He stared at her. 'So that you can arrest me?'

'You are beginning to sound paranoid. I would prefer to think that I may be able to advise you.' She had a sudden inspiration. If he had no idea that she worked for the OSS, much less MI6, and knew only that she was Himmler's aide, there could be only one reason for him to approach her, even if encouraged to do so by Johannsson. 'And so that I may consider whether or not what you have to say should be conveyed to Herr Himmler.'

He swallowed. 'I am placing my life in your hands.'

'Yes, you are. But it was your decision to do so.'

'Will you hear me out?'

'Of course. But as I have already said, be brief.'

He took a deep breath. 'The war is lost, militarily. You must realize this. We can do no more than hold the Russians in the east. The Allies are in Sicily. And we know, from the reports of the immense build-up of American troops in England that a landing in France can only be months away. And in addition, the Allied air forces are pounding our cities. You know about Hamburg?'

'Certainly. Are you proposing that the Reich should surrender?'

'Of course I am not. But we must seek a negotiated peace.'

'Ah.'

'Only the Führer will never do that.'

'You mean that the Allies would never deal with him.'

Steinberg snapped his fingers. 'You understand.'

'I would like to hear your solution to the problem.'

'It is very simple. If the Führer were to be replaced by somebody else, somebody acceptable to the Allies . . .'

Anna felt breathless. 'When you say replaced . . .?'

'Deposed. There would have to be a *coup d'état*.'

'Deposed,' Anna said thoughtfully. 'And replaced by whom? The Reichsmarschall is generally regarded as second in the Party hierarchy, but I don't think he would be acceptable to the Allies either.'

'In any event, Göring would be quite impossible. He is a drug addict.'

'So?'

'Well . . . the Reichsführer is the obvious choice. He already controls nearly all the essential departments of state.'

And you seriously suppose, Anna thought, that Himmler could ever be acceptable to the Allies, especially after the reports I have been filing for the past two years? 'That is an enormous concept,' she said. 'Tell me: you have discussed this . . . project, in your group?'

'Of course.'

'And how many are in this group?'

'There are a dozen of us.'

'I see. You do realize that what you have just told me *is* treason?'

His jaw sagged open.

'I have promised that I will not betray you, in the present circumstances. But can you be certain none of these twelve men—'

'Four are women,' he muttered.

'That is worse. Can you be certain that all of them are utterly reliable?'

'I would stake my life on it.'

'My dear Count, you have already done that. Now, if I understand the situation, you would like me to approach the Reichsführer and ascertain if he would be willing to take over the government in the event that the Führer were to be deposed. Is this your idea, or the idea of your group?'

'It was suggested by Johannsson.'

'Before the group?'

'No. He thought it would be best if I took the risk of contacting you before revealing it to the others. But the group is unanimous in agreeing that something needs to be done.'

'So that the other members are not as yet actually involved. But you do realize that once the Gestapo got you into one of their cells you would very rapidly reveal all of their names.'

Steinberg licked his lips. 'Johannsson gave me to under-stand that you would be sympathetic.'

The crunch. 'Did he give you a reason *why* I should be sympathetic?'

'Well . . . he gave the impression that he knew you very well.'

'I see.' Johannsson at least appeared to be behaving respon-sibly. 'But as I have said, he was not telling the truth.'

'But will you help us?' Steinberg asked, anxiously. 'It would be helping Germany,' he added ingenuously.

Given her recent conversations with Himmler, Anna knew that to raise the subject of his replacing Hitler, even legiti-mately, and whether or not he would be prepared to negotiate with the Allies or they with him, would be futile and could well be fatal. On the other hand, the existence of such a move-ment in the heart of Germany and, indeed, the government, was too potentially important not to be reported. How that was going to be done was merely another problem to be solved. Meanwhile . . .

'Tell me about this group. I am not seeking their names, but are they people of influence?'

'I think so. They are all intellectuals.'

'That is hardly a recommendation when it comes to deci-sive action. Are any of them soldiers?'

'One of us is a colonel.'

'A colonel. With a command in Berlin?'

'Well . . . no.'

'Do you suppose that if this idea of yours comes to fruition, it will simply be a matter of entering the Führer's office and saying, "Sorry, old man, but it is time to go"? In the first place, how will you gain access to him? He is constantly surrounded by SS guards. Anyone who wishes to see him, and is accepted, is rigorously searched before being allowed into his presence. And several relative strangers would never be admitted at the same time.'

'Well . . .'

'You would have to use considerable force. That almost certainly means bloodshed. Are you and your friends prepared for this?'

'Well . . .'

'And to be successful, you will need military back-up. That means you must have some senior officers on your side, if possible from the SS, but failing that from the Wehrmacht, and stationed here in Germany, preferably close to Berlin. Have you considered these points?'

'I will do so now.'

'I see. I will consider them also, as I will consider whether it may be possible to approach the Reichsführer.'

'Oh, Countess!' He seized her hand. 'You will help us? You will earn the everlasting gratitude of all Germany. Of the world.'

'I do not wish the gratitude of either Germany or the world. Nor do I wish to be hanged by the neck, slowly. So listen very carefully. I have said that I will consider what you have said. Whether I help you or not will depend on the conclusions I draw from my considerations. But if you, or any of your associates, attempt to betray me, or to act hastily, just remember that I have the ear of the Reichsführer, and his entire confidence. He will believe me before any accusations against me. And I will not hesitate to denounce you, and your friends, if, as I say, you act without my agreement, or reveal to anyone, except Johannsson, that we have had this meeting.'

Steinberg's fingers twitched against her.

'There is one more thing,' Anna said. 'When will you be seeing Johannsson again?'

'I believe he has gone back to Sweden. But I anticipate that he will return here in a few weeks.'

'When he does, tell him that I wish to see him.'

'I will do that, Countess.'

Anna freed her hand and stood up. 'Now we must run in opposite directions. I imagine we will meet again.'

The Doctor

Anna returned to her apartment in preference to going to the gymnasium. She considered that she had made up for missing the photographic appointment by having after all allowed Stefan to snap her in a variety of poses while she trained. Certainly, if a little cold at first, he had seemed very happy by the end, and she never knew when his infatuation might be useful. Sometimes she felt like a juggler, trying to keep several balls in the air at the same time.

She showered and dressed. Her brain was still spinning. There were so many considerations to be taken into account. Had the OSS set out to instigate a plot against Hitler, or had Johannsson merely stumbled on it by chance? But to involve her without any previous briefing was unforgivable, and unprofessional. Yet now that she was involved, the possible implications were endless. Quite apart from the dangers for herself, even if she did honestly believe that she would always have Himmler's support . . . But if she became involved and Himmler were to fall!

She desperately needed advice and, indeed, orders, but there was nothing she could do until after she left Gestapo Headquarters that evening. Then she hurried to the boutique.

Edda was in a highly nervous state. 'Have you heard the news from Rome, Countess?' she whispered.

'Yes, I have.'

'But if Il Duce were to fall . . .'

'I doubt that is the least likely,' Anna said, without conviction, and went into the office.

'Have you—' Bartoli began.

'Yes, I have,' Anna said. 'I have an urgent message for London.'

'Urgent. Always urgent. Is it about Rome? The Duce?'

It was the quickest way to obtain full co-operation. 'It concerns him, certainly.'

'Tell me.'

'Just send the message. Contact urgently required.'

Bartoli frowned. 'Didn't you make contact in Geneva?'

'No,' Anna said, looking him in the eye.

'What a fuck-up. If you had let me handle it . . .'

'Will you just send the message, and let me know as soon as a reply comes in.'

As he did not produce one of his glares, she knew he was really agitated. 'What happens if the Duce does fall?'

'We have one less enemy.'

'But what happens to us? Edda believes that we are working for him.'

'That was your idea.'

'Of course, you would have had her executed when she found out that I was operating an agency. I couldn't do that.'

'Luigi,' Anna said, 'in our business it is a fatal mistake to fall in love, with anyone.' Which was too close to the pot calling the kettle black, so she added, 'Unless they are absolutely trustworthy.'

'She is so good in bed.' He paused to peer at her. 'I don't suppose you know about things like that.'

'I have been a married woman,' Anna pointed out, primly. 'Don't forget that I wish to know the moment you have a reply from London.'

She did not hear from him for a week, during which she felt even more isolated than usual, as there was no sign of Johannsson either. To think that she was sitting on what could be the decisive event of the war, and she did not know what to do about it . . .

'There it is,' Himmler announced on Monday morning, coming into her office. 'The Italians have gone stark, raving mad. They have put Mussolini in prison.'

'My God!' Anna was genuinely shocked. Whatever the rumours of a constitutional crisis coming out of Rome, she had not anticipated anything like that, and her thoughts immediately roamed to Bartoli's possible reaction, and even more that of Edda. 'What does it mean?'

'In the short term, very little. I know you understand that I do not share the Führer's high regard for that bloated bullfrog. And this fool Badoglio who has taken over the government has declared his intention of continuing the war as our ally, but I would not trust him further than I could kick him. I think we must prepare for the possibility – one could almost say the certainty – that Italy will drop out at some stage, probably fairly soon.'

'What will happen then?'

'Anyone who is not with us is against us. We will treat them as an enemy whose country we occupy.' He smiled. 'As I have said, this will actually make things easier for us.' He squeezed her shoulder. 'Do not worry your pretty little head about Italy. On the other hand . . . it may soon be time for you to take another trip.'

*   *   *

When Anna left Gestapo Headquarters that evening, she hurried to the boutique. Edda was not to be seen; Anna ignored the rest of the staff and went straight to the office. No one attempted to stop her.

'I was going to call you tonight,' Bartoli said. 'I have heard from London.'

'What has happened here? Where is Edda?'

'She has gone home. She is not feeling well.'

'Because of the news from Italy?'

'Well, it is a serious matter, would you not say?'

'I wouldn't have thought it was that serious for her. What are you going to do?'

'I will calm her down. I will convince her that the Duce may have been arrested, but that it is a political matter which may well be reversed, and that it is our duty to continue our work for him.'

'You think she will believe that?'

'She believes everything I tell her,' he said proudly. 'Aren't you interested in the news from London?'

'Of course I am. What is it?'

'Simply that a contact has been arranged. What do they mean by that? Any contact should come through me. I queried it, of course. But they confirmed. I would like an explanation.'

Anna smiled at him, as winningly as she could. 'Like you, Luigi, all I do is obey London, do what they tell me to.'

'They did not tell you to set up that meeting in Geneva. You insisted on it.'

'I possessed something that had to be handed personally to an MI6 agent. It would have been a waste of time giving it to you, as you would not have known what to do with it.'

'And you were unable to make contact. I still should have been told what it was. I am being treated like a messenger boy, not the lynchpin of the entire operation.'

Anna decided to put Clive, or certainly Baxter, in it: it was their refusal to get rid of this oaf that had created this situation. 'I agree with you entirely, Luigi. I think they are treating you abominably. You are fully entitled to complain. In fact, I should tell them that unless they take you more fully into their confidence, you are going to quit.'

Bartoli's jaw dropped in consternation. 'You think they would let me do that?'

'How could they stop you?'

He did not draw the obvious conclusion. 'But what would happen to you?'

'I would have to manage as best I can without you,' she said bravely. 'Ciao.'

Anna walked back to her apartment, feeling more relaxed than at any time since her return from Geneva. She had no idea who might be coming to take control of her situation – obviously it could not again be Clive here in Germany – but she remembered with a mixture of pleasure and regret that charming woman Judith, so-called Countess de Sotomayer, who, as a Spaniard, had been able to travel freely in Europe. They had taken to each other from the moment of their first meeting, under the very eyes of the unsuspecting Essermann, and their relationship had been both intense and rewarding, even if she had early identified the tell-tale signs of anxiety and indeed fear. She had been totally surprised when Judith had informed her that she was in charge, with the necessary assistance of herself, of overseeing the assassination of Heydrich. She had felt then that London was playing with fire, but she had been horrified when, after the failure of the first attempt, Judith, on being approached, quite inadvertently, by two Gestapo agents, had bitten her cyanide capsule.

So while she hoped for another good relationship, she also hoped that London would choose more carefully this time. But at least it would be interesting, and she was gradually freeing herself of Bartoli. She reached the swing doors, and found that a man had appeared on either side of her. 'Do you wish something?' she asked.

'We wish you, Countess.'

The alarm bells were muted: she was, after all, Anna Fehrbach. 'Do you know who I am?'

'Yes, we do. You are the Countess von Widerstand. We are here from Dr Goebbels. He wishes to have a word with you, in private.'

Anna looked at them each in turn. Neither man was of the belted-trench-coat variety; indeed, both were neatly and quietly dressed and looked harmless enough. But Goebbels?

'Could the Doctor not merely telephone me and ask me for a meeting?' she inquired. 'I mean, how long have you been here, waiting for me?'

'Not long. We were informed when you left Gestapo Headquarters – though it took you longer to get here than we expected.'

That needed dealing with immediately. 'That is because I stopped by my couturier to discuss a new outfit. And I am afraid you are going to have to wait for a while longer. I do not go out in the evening until I have bathed and changed.'

'The matter is most urgent, Countess – and could be of great importance to you. Dr Goebbels said to tell you that it will not take long.'

There was a car waiting, and Anna could see no point in making a scene on the street. Besides, she was suddenly curious. She had met Goebbels on several occasions, but always at official functions. She knew his reputation as an insatiable lecher, and he had certainly looked at her with devouring eyes, but as she had always been with either Heydrich or Himmler they had never done more than exchange pleasantries. She had no desire to know him better: he was quite the most unpleasant-looking man she had ever met, quite apart from his club foot. But he certainly knew that she was Himmler's aide. So what could he have to say to her . . . in private? That he had chosen this way of approaching her instead of telephoning her in her office indicated that he did not wish Himmler to know of their meeting – at least until after the event. In view of the intrigue with which she had suddenly become surrounded, she thought it might indeed be very important to find out just what was on his mind. 'Then I had better not keep the Doctor waiting,' she said.

The door was held open for her, and one of the men got in beside her. The other sat in front with the driver. Neither man spoke again on the short drive to the Propaganda Ministry, where there was a female secretary waiting to escort her up the stairs. Late in the day as it was, there were still quite a few people about, all of whom stopped to look at the striking young woman.

A door was opened for her and she was shown into one of those large offices so favoured by the Nazi leaders. There was the usual big desk, and the usual mammoth portrait of Hitler on the wall. But there was also one difference from the offices of either Hitler or Himmler: a large settee to one side.

Josef Goebbels stood in front of the desk. He was a little man, several inches shorter than Anna, and had arranged his features into a smile, which she did not find the least attractive. Now he extended his hands. 'Countess! It is good of you to visit me.'

She allowed him to squeeze her fingers, but anchored her feet when he attempted to draw her forward. 'I was told it was an urgent matter. The Reichsführer is always interested in urgent matters.'

The smile disappeared, but only for a moment. 'And you are, of course, the Reichsführer's faithful handmaiden. Except that I suspect you are not a maiden.'

'Of course I am not a maiden, Herr Doktor. I am, or was, a married woman.'

'Of course. The Honourable Mrs Bordman. I had forgotten. And now you are divorced. A divorcee always has so much more freedom of action, hasn't she? Please sit down.' He indicated the settee.

'Freedom to do what, Herr Doktor?' Anna sat down and crossed her knees.

'Whatever she wishes.' He sat beside her, regarded the slender black-stockinged legs. 'I think black silk stockings are almost the sexiest of all female garments. Almost. What colour is your underwear?'

'When dressed for the office, it also is black, Herr Doktor.'

'And silk, of course.'

'Of course. Did you invite me here so urgently to discuss my underwear?'

'Ha ha. You have a sharp tongue. Schnapps?'

'Thank you.' She could only be patient, humour him, at least up to a point, and wait for him to get to his point.

He got up, moving slowly, and limped to his desk, from a drawer in which he took a bottle and two glasses. These he filled before returning to sit beside her. 'Your health.'

'And yours, Herr Doktor.'

He remained sitting up, half-turned towards her. 'I enjoy the feel of silk. If I were to stroke your leg, would you scream for help?'

Anna remained perfectly cool; she was working. 'Would it do me any good, here in your office, in your building?'

'The thought does not disturb you. Perhaps you would enjoy it. Or perhaps you would dispose of me with one of your lethal blows to the neck.'

Anna raised her eyebrows, and he smiled.

'I know everything about you. I have a file on you. I have files on a great number of people. Is it true that you are a lesbian?'

'I am what I am required to be, in the course of my duties, Herr Doktor.'

'You are a cool one. Are you this cool when lying naked in the arms of a man? – or a woman?'

'That, Herr Doktor, depends upon the man or the woman.'

'Ha ha. You are a delight. Do you find me repulsive?'

Who wouldn't? she wondered. But she merely said, 'I do not know you well enough to form an opinion.'

'I meant physically. Some people find the concept of a man with a deformity difficult to accept. But then, did not the great Lord Byron have a club foot? And he was the most famous lover of his age.'

He was also the most handsome man of his age, Anna thought, whereas you are the ugliest man of yours. It was time to end this absurdity. She finished her drink. 'It has been very pleasant, to sit here, discussing sexual matters with you, Herr Doktor, but you see, I am required to report to the Reichsführer not only everyone whom I meet but the contents of our conversation, and I suspect he will find a discussion of my underwear somewhat boring. I think I had better leave. I assume there is a car to take me back to my apartment?'

He gazed at her for several seconds, then he said, 'As you wish. But before you go, tell me about Bartoli.'

Anna nearly dropped the glass she was holding.

'You do know Bartoli, Countess? He is your couturier, is he not?'

Think, think, think, think, think. But she had to go along with him again, until she learned how much he knew, how much he merely suspected – and how and by whom his suspicions had been aroused. That meant denying nothing that could be proved against her. 'Signor Bartoli is my dress-maker, yes.'

'And more than that?'

'Certainly not. He is . . .'

'A repulsive little man? I agree with you. But every time you go to see him – and you see him quite often – you are closeted in his office. What do you talk about? Is it Mussolini?'

Years of practice had enabled Anna to control her facial expressions no matter what was thrown at her. 'We have talked about Il Duce, yes.'

'Because in addition to your other duties, serving Herr Himmler, you also work for him, Il Duce.'

If only he would give her time to think, work out a plan of behaviour, work out what he was after. But she could only keep stalling. 'I have never met Il Duce. In fact, I have never even seen him.'

'That is not an answer.'

'Have you any right to ask me these questions?'

'My dear Anna – you do not mind if I call you Anna? It is such an evocative name. Anna of the black silk stockings and the black silk underwear. That should be the title of a play. But I was saying: I have the right to ask questions of anyone in Germany. I am the eyes and ears of the Führer.' He rested his hand on her calf and moved it up to her knee, pushing the skirt with it. Anna hastily uncrossed her legs, and he squeezed, gently. 'So you see, while you are required to report all your conversations to Herr Himmler, I am required to report all of *my* conversations to Herr Himmler's master, who is the master of all of us. But I understand that you are obliged to obey your immediate master in all things, and I respect that. All I require is that you do not lie to me, because that would be lying to the Führer.'

His hand left her knee, but only to slide higher, on to her thigh, again taking her skirt with it. Anna made herself keep very still; she knew she was on the edge of a crisis, but how personal it would be – apart from sexual – she could not yet estimate.

'I invited you to come to see me,' Goebbels continued, 'because I know how valuable you have been to the Reich, and will certainly be again, unless you do something very stupid, and I would hate to think of your doing that. So listen very carefully to what I have to say.'

The fingers were inching slowly onwards; her legs were

now totally exposed. Perhaps this was his way of reducing his female victims' ability to think. She was determined that he was not going to accomplish that with her. But she did need to know in which direction she should *be* thinking.

'This morning,' Goebbels said, 'I received a visit from Bartoli's wife, a woman named Edda.'

Anna could not prevent a sharp intake of breath, but he had to suppose that was because his fingers had reached her camiknickers.

'Perhaps,' he said, 'you would be more comfortable if you took your skirt right off. The tie and the shirt as well.' Anna looked at the door, and he gave another smile. 'I do assure you that no one is going to come in that door without a summons from me.'

Anna sighed, but she did not see she had much choice, and what he had just said had to be followed up. She stood up, pulled off her tie, unbuttoned her shirt and laid it on a chair, then slipped down her skirt. She made to step out of her shoes, but he said, 'No. Leave the shoes. Sit down.'

Anna obeyed.

'Frau Bartoli had a most interesting tale to tell. She said that Antoinette's Boutique is just a front for an agency her husband claims to be operating on behalf of Mussolini's government. Do you know of this?'

'Of course I do not, Herr Doktor. But I suspect that the woman is fantasizing.'

'Of course that is possible.' His finger left her crotch, to her relief, but began to draw little patterns on the bodice of the camiknickers. 'But actually she appears to agree with you.'

'I don't understand,' Anna said, fervently hoping that she did not, indeed.

'Frau Bartoli has made a deduction, from recent events, that her husband has not actually been working for Mussolini at all' – Anna found that she was holding her breath, and got it back under control; again, that could be put down to what he was doing to her nipples – 'but is actually working for the Badoglio clique, who have now taken over the Italian government.' He paused to peer at her.

'It all sounds very far-fetched to me,' Anna said.

'It is a woman's logic, perhaps a woman's intuition. She observed that, while he has always professed, at least to her, the most fervent loyalty to Il Duce, he showed not the slightest emotion when the news arrived of Mussolini's arrest. She found that disturbing.'

Oh, what a fool that man is, Anna thought. But if she had always known that, and tried time and again to convince London of it, he was now becoming a positive danger. 'Perhaps you are right. Perhaps she is right. But why is she so anxious to get her husband into trouble?'

'Oh, well, because of you.'

'Me?'

'She suspects you of conducting an affair with her husband.'

'She has got to be joking. Bartoli is—'

'A repulsive little man? And he does not even have a club foot.'

Anna swallowed. 'I did not mean . . .'

'Of course you did not. I think you should take this garment off as well.'

Anna pulled herself together. 'Do you intend to have sex with me, Herr Doktor?'

'Certainly. But in due course. Are you going to object?'

Shit, Anna thought. Shit, shit, shit. But she got up and slid the straps of her camiknickers from her shoulders and let the garment slip down her thighs to the floor. Then she unfastened her suspender belt.

'No, no,' Goebbels said. 'There is no more evocative sight in the world than a beautiful woman naked except for black silk stockings and black court shoes. And when she is blonde . . . Release your hair.'

Today she was wearing a bun. She reached up to pull out the pins and allow her hair to fall past her shoulders.

'Exquisite.'

'You were telling me about Frau Bartoli,' she reminded him. 'And her husband.'

'And you denied any involvement with him. But you were speaking sexually. What about as regards Mussolini or Badoglio?'

'I know nothing of Signor Bartoli's affairs, Herr Doktor.'

'Hm. As I told you, I have a file on you. I have kept a file on you since your marriage to Bordman. And according to that file, when you left England in May 1940, it was by an Italian ship bound for Naples. Why did you take that route, if you had no links with the Italian government?'

It never ceased to amaze Anna how these people lived in such an atmosphere of plot and counter-plot they could find something suspicious in the simplest of actions. 'I chose that route, Herr Doktor, because it was the only one available to me. I had been warned by the local Gestapo agents that the Special Branch were closing in on me. I had to be out of England within hours. And here was a neutral ship, as Italy then was, leaving Southampton that night. I seized the opportunity.'

'And the agents who warned you did not. And then just disappeared. Do you have any idea what happened to them?'

I left their bodies in my flat, Anna remembered. 'I'm afraid I do not, Herr Doktor.'

'They perhaps lacked your ability to make instant decisions,' Goebbels mused. 'Now tell me about your trip to Switzerland, last month.'

'Sir?'

'Oh, come now, Anna. No prevarication. We are both too adult for that. You went to Geneva, for one night, on the instructions, I presume, of Herr Himmler. What was it about?'

Anna felt that she was standing on ice which was cracking beneath her feet and about to send her plunging into a bottomless lake. But she kept both her voice and her expression under control. 'I was travelling on secret business for the SS.'

'Which involved the deaths of two Gestapo agents?'

'Sir?'

'Anna, when two of our agents are discovered in Geneva, lying dead on the floor of a hotel room, which had been occupied by a mysterious young woman named O'Brien . . . I assume that was your mother's maiden name?'

'My mother's maiden name was Haggerty.' At last he was giving her time to think.

'No matter. The coincidence was too great. I wish an explanation. The *Führer* will wish an explanation.'

Anna took a deep breath. 'I was sent to Geneva, as you say, to make contact with a top foreign agent.' Which, she reflected, was perfectly true. 'He was bringing information about Allied plans for a possible invasion of Europe. Unfortunately, he had apparently been tracked by these two Gestapo agents, who broke in upon us, and refused to accept my explanation that I was on official business for the Reich.

They appeared determined to shoot my contact, and me, so I had to make an instant decision.'

'As you are so good at doing. I suppose it is no bad thing for one's last moment on earth to be spent looking into your eyes above the barrel of a gun. What were you wearing?'

'I was wearing nothing, Herr Doktor. I had just had a bath.'

'Well, you see, they must have died happy. What was the reaction of this agent of yours?'

'He was . . . disturbed.'

'I can imagine. And what was his information?'

'I have no idea, sir. It was in code. I returned it to our cipher department, but have not seen the transcript.'

'Let us hope that it was worth two lives. Now, I think we have talked business long enough.' He stood up and began to undress. 'You must make me as happy as you did those two men you shot.'

You have told me nothing that I really want to know, Anna thought. And now she was stuck. Goebbels removed his drawers. 'Have you ever seen anything to compare?' he asked.

It was certainly the largest she had ever seen. And in a matter of moments that was going to be inside her! 'No, Herr Doktor,' she said faintly.

'I am unique.'

Anna supposed he might be telling the truth. He sat beside her, kissed her mouth, more gently than she had feared, massaged her breasts and then seized her legs to upend her so that she was lying on her back on the settee, and he was inside her, kneeling with one of his legs on the carpet. She had not been treated like this, at least on a one-to-one basis, since she had found herself in the back seat of Chalyapov's car, three years ago. Of course she had been both younger and less experienced then. But it was satisfying to recall that when the commissar had tried to stop her escaping from the Lubyanka, she had shot him dead.

Mercifully, Goebbels was very quick; she had felt he was splitting her in two. Then he was sitting down again, panting, stroking her calves. Anna let him get on with it for some moments; she also needed to get her breath back. 'We must do that again,' Goebbels said. 'I will send for you.'

Shit! Anna thought – and reminded herself that she was working. 'What are you – we, going to do about this woman?'

she asked, carefully freeing her legs and easing herself upwards.

'Does she worry you?'

'I do not like people making untrue assertions about me.'

'That is annoying, isn't it? I have told her that I will look into the matter.'

'And . . .?'

'So far I have found nothing to substantiate her claim.'

'Is she to continue working at the boutique?'

'Well, she is Bartoli's wife, is she not?' He handed her her camiknickers: an act of dismissal.

'And he knows nothing of her betrayal?'

'As far as I know. Are you going to tell him?'

Anna stood up, pulled on the camiknickers. 'Do you wish me to?'

'It might be amusing.'

Anna put on her shirt and skirt, knotted her tie. 'It would be catastrophic for their marriage. And perhaps even for her.'

Goebbels himself got up, and went behind his desk. 'That might solve every problem, and without the involvement of any state department, do you not agree? However, as an accusation has been made, even if with very little apparent substance apart from a woman's jealousy, I think it should be followed up. I intend to turn the matter over to Herr Himmler, but I felt you might like to see what you can find out, first.'

Anna opened her handbag and took out her compact; a quick look determined that there was very little she could do about her hair but it gave her time to consider her options. Was this wretched little man trying to help her out of a possibly dangerous situation, or was he laying a trap? 'Is that a directive, sir?'

'It is a recommendation.'

'Yes, sir. May I ask a question?'

'Certainly.'

'Am I now working for you?'

'Unofficially, and privately.'

'Herr Himmler is certain to find out.'

'Does he fuck you, Anna?'

'He does not.'

Goebbels shook his head. 'I always knew there was something odd about that man.'

'But he does regard me as his personal possession.'

'As I have explained, Anna, he, you, I are all the personal possessions of the Führer. And I can assure you that I am closer to the Führer than is Herr Himmler. Indeed, I intend to recommend you to him.'

'Sir?' Anna could not control a squeak.

'He has severe problems, you know. He works too hard, and he is in his fifties, an age when many men have personal problems. That quack Morell fills him full of pills so that he always appears in public in the best of health and vitality, but that is not the case in the privacy of his bedroom. Sometimes he nearly goes mad at his . . . incapacity.'

'But . . . Fräulein Braun . . .'

'Eva Braun is a very valuable, soothing companion, who manages to relax the Führer, make him laugh. However, she is not, unfortunately, a very highly sexed woman, and in any event he sees little of her nowadays, as he spends so much of his time in Rastenburg, directing military affairs. I think that you would be very good for him. I cannot imagine any man, save perhaps Herr Himmler, being unable to erect when in your intimate presence.'

Oh, God Almighty! Anna thought. She had the strongest impulse to rush straight to the boutique and send a message to Clive that she wanted out. If only she could do that.

'So you see,' Goebbels went on, 'if, or when, Herr Himmler inquires into our relationship, you will tell him that I am interested in you as a possible companion for the Führer. I do not think he will pursue the matter very closely. There will be a car waiting for you downstairs to take you home. And I will be interested to hear from you as to the state of affairs in the Bartoli household. Heil Hitler!'

'Countess?' Birgit was anxious as she peered at her mistress. 'Are you all right?'

'Draw me a very hot bath,' Anna told her. 'And then open a bottle of champagne.'

But getting drunk, even on champagne, was not the answer. In fact, she found it impossible to get drunk, even with a full bottle to herself while sitting in a hot tub. There were so many considerations leaping about her brain that she found it difficult to determine which was the most important. But that had

to be contacting London. Save that London was as usual drag-
ging its feet. 'Contact will be made.' When? For God's sake!
Everything was coming up very fast, and all she could do was
swim with the tide until someone threw her a lifebelt. But now
she couldn't even do that. She was not standing on ice any
more; she was sitting on a powder keg with the fuse burning.
If she was going to survive, there was only one course of action
she could take, whether London wanted it or not.

Birgit was hovering in the bathroom doorway. 'Would you
like to see the mail, Countess?'

'Mail?' She never received mail.

'It came this afternoon. By hand.'

'Give it to me.'

She slit the envelope, soaking it with her wet hand: *Countess!
I should be honoured if you would accompany me to the opera
on Thursday night. It is Wagner. I will call for you at seven
thirty. Friedrich von Steinberg.*

'Oh, for God's sake!'

'Countess?'

The bastard wasn't even giving her the opportunity to
decline. And as an Austrian she was no great admirer of
Wagner; he was far too loud. Steinberg would want to know
if she had reached a decision on approaching Himmler. So he
would have to be stalled yet again. On the other hand, he
might be bringing word of a meeting with Johannsson.

But first of all there was Bartoli to be seen, and taken care
of. As the matter could not wait, London would have to accept
whatever happened.

She visited the boutique the next morning before going to
work. Edda was there, looking totally surprised to see her.
Anna wondered if she had assumed her treachery would result
in her arrest? 'Good morning, Edda,' she said brightly. 'Will
you inform Luigi that I wish a word? Tell him that I shall be
in the office?'

'But—'

'Just do it.' Anna went into the office and closed the door,
but was soon joined by Bartoli.

'I wish you wouldn't upset Edda,' he complained. 'She is
in a very delicate frame of mind. She actually shouted at me
just now, in front of a client.'

'What do you intend to do about her?' Anna asked.

'She is my wife.'

'She is also trying to get you into a Gestapo interrogation cell.'

His head jerked. 'What? That is ridiculous.'

'Listen very carefully,' Anna suggested, and recounted the relevant parts of her conversation with Goebbels, while Bartoli's face gradually became more and more contorted with mingled anger and apprehension. 'Now,' she said at the end, 'I have tried to persuade Dr Goebbels that she is inspired simply by jealousy.'

'Well, then . . .'

'However, he refused to be diverted. Dr Goebbels has a hobby.' Apart from sex, she thought. 'He keeps files. He claims to have files on everyone in the Reich who is of the least importance, either socially or politically, and to have the ability to call any of their past actions into question whenever he wishes.'

'He has nothing to do with the Gestapo.'

'He does not *command* the Gestapo. Himmler does that. But Goebbels is very close to Hitler, closer than anyone else in Germany. If he wants something done, it *is* done. And now your name is in his files. He intends to hand the file over to Herr Himmler.'

Bartoli gulped.

'Thus I feel that you should do something about your wife.' She was giving him a last out. Much as she disliked the man, they had been colleagues for the past three years.

'But . . . if I confront her, she will beat me up.'

'Oh, really, Luigi, are you a man or a mouse? This woman has tried to have you locked up. At the very least.'

'I will divorce her. But I cannot divorce her. I am a good Catholic. Are you not a good Catholic, Anna?'

'I do not pretend to be a good anything,' Anna said, 'in a moral sense. I am fighting a war. So are you. Anyway, divorcing Edda will be more dangerous than having her around.'

Bartoli produced a handkerchief and wiped his neck. 'I know what you would like me to do. But I am not a killer, like you. They would hang me.'

'They are equally likely to hang you if it gets back to the Führer that you may have had a hand in the downfall of his great friend Mussolini.'

Bartoli stared at her, his face white. 'They would hang you too.'

'I have powerful friends,' Anna reminded him. 'Both Reichsführer Himmler and Dr Goebbels.'

'Then you will be able to protect me. If you do not, and I were to be arrested . . .' He paused to lick his lips.

Anna gazed at him. 'Are you threatening me, Luigi?'

'I . . . Of course I am not. But if the Gestapo arrested me, and subjected me to torture, I do not know what I might say.'

That was it. He had sealed his own fate. 'Then I recommend that you make sure the Gestapo do not arrest you,. You do have a capsule?'

'You . . . you . . .'

'I estimate that your file is at this moment on Herr Himmler's desk. That means that the Gestapo will be here in under an hour.'

'But you . . . I will have to tell them everything.'

'I thought you might say that. You understand that I cannot permit that to happen.'

His face seemed to freeze as she opened her shoulder bag and took her own capsule from the special compartment in which she kept it. She also took out the Luger she had placed in the bag before leaving her apartment. 'You may use my pill.'

'Are you mad?'

'It is the only way out.'

'You wish me to kill myself. Are you going to kill yourself?'

'I think one of us needs to survive, for the sake of MI6, and while I do not wish to appear arrogant, I cannot help feeling that I am more valuable to that organization than you.'

'And you do not think the Gestapo will arrest you also?'

'Not if you are not here to testify against me.'

'And what do you think Edda will do? Or do you intend to kill her too?'

'Edda is of no consequence to me. I have convinced Dr Goebbels that in accusing me of involvement in your treason she was acting from sheer jealousy.' She pushed the pill across the desk with her gun muzzle.

'I absolutely refuse to do such a thing. Kill myself? My God!'

'If you refuse,' Anna said, 'then as an SD officer I will place you under arrest, and we will sit here until the Gestapo arrive. Do you know what they will do to you, Luigi? They will attach an electrical clip to your penis and put another up your ass, and turn on the current. Believe me, it is the worst possible experience. I know. It happened to me once, if not exactly like that, of course, as I am not a man.'

Bartoli stared at her with his mouth open.

'But very briefly,' Anna explained, 'a matter of a few seconds. They were punishing me, you see – not attempting to get information. But I estimate that if it had lasted for even a minute I would have gone mad and said anything they wished me to say. And when you have done that, then they will hang you. There will not be a drop. You will be hoisted from the floor, slowly, and left to kick your life away, while they poke fun at you. You will be naked, you see, and you know what happens to a man when he is hanged. There is no possibility of you surviving arrest. Only the certainty of several hours of agony followed by a humiliating death. I am offering you a quick and painless alternative.'

Bartoli licked his lips. 'You can sit there and say things like that to me, after we have been comrades for so long?'

'I do not think we have ever been comrades. And you may recall that two years ago, when Edda got me embroiled with the Abwehr, I told you to get rid of her. Instead you married her. But for that stupid mistake, you would not be in the position you now find yourself. Now time is running out. Use the capsule, or I will take it back and hand you over to the Gestapo.'

A last stare, then he picked up the capsule. A tear trickled out of his eye as he placed it in his mouth. Then he took a long breath, his eyes dilated, and he fell forward across his desk. Number twenty-five! Anna waited a few moments, then replaced the gun in her bag, dried her hands on her handkerchief – she was dripping sweat – and picked up the phone. She gave the number of Gestapo Headquarters. 'This is the Countess von Widerstand. Put me through to Reichsführer Himmler.'

There was no hesitation nowadays; everyone knew who the Countess von Widerstand was.

'Anna? Is something the matter?'

'Herr Reichsführer,' Anna said. 'I have a problem.'

Just Good Friends

'What a terrible thing,' Himmler said, holding Anna's hand. 'A nest of vipers, in our very bosom! Do you know that when we searched Bartoli's house, we found some very sophisticated radio equipment? The man has been a spy for ages.'

'This equipment . . .' Anna held her breath.

'Oh, yes, we immediately monitored it. We didn't have a call sign, but we listened, and sure enough a message came through. It really was somewhat confusing. Our experts say it came from London, not Italy. That doesn't make sense, does it? On the other hand, when we decoded the transcript of the Morse message it was in English. But as for what it meant – all about someone named Belinda being contacted – have you ever heard of anyone named Belinda?'

'No, sir.'

'Well, no matter. He, or she, is not going to be contacted now. All thanks to you. You are a quite remarkable young woman.'

'I really had nothing to do with it,' Anna protested.

'You are too modest.'

'No, truly,' Anna said. 'Dr Goebbels suggested I go to see Bartoli, because he knew I was acquainted with him, and his wife had made this accusation against him. Dr Goebbels only said I should inform him of his wife's action and observe his reaction. Well, I was absolutely amazed when, no sooner had I finished speaking, he clapped his hand to his mouth, I thought he was coughing for a moment, then I realized what was happening. I tried to stop him, but it was too late. He never actually admitted anything.'

'But don't you see, Anna – the fact that the moment he learned of his wife's accusation he committed suicide is a confession of guilt?'

'Ah,' Anna said, 'yes. I never thought of that. But if the radio link is with London, it proves that Frau Bartoli's accusation *was* simply jealousy, as Dr Goebbels and I both suspected.'

'Absolutely. But it is amazing what can emerge from the most careless action. In her fit of jealousy, this woman uncovered a vast spy plot.'

'What will happen to her?'

'I think she had better go to Ravensbrück. She is obviously a troublemaker. I mean, accusing you of having had an affair with her husband . . .' He peered at her. 'You didn't, did you?'

'Of course I did not.' Anna bristled with indignation. 'Can you imagine me and that . . . that . . .'

'No, I cannot imagine it,' Himmler agreed. 'I apologize. Tell me, ah . . . Dr Goebbels didn't make any improper advances, did he?'

'Dr Goebbels behaved like a perfect gentleman when I was in his office.' Which, she reflected, he had done, according to his interpretation of the word.

'One hears these rumours . . . Well, Anna, you have done very well. As always. My congratulations. I think you could take the rest of today off. Yesterday must have been a considerable ordeal for you.'

'Thank you, sir.' And think about Belinda, she thought. But whoever was coming was surely going to be intelligent enough only to use the word to her. As for von Steinberg, tonight . . .

'Mr Andrews is here,' Amy said, disapprovingly. She was fully aware of Clive's futile attempts to contact his American opposite number.

'Here?!' Clive stood up. 'Bring him in.'

'Mr Bartley can see you now, Mr Andrews,' Amy announced, using her boom-boom voice.

'Joe!' Clive said. 'How good to see you. What brings you across the Atlantic?'

'Sarcasm never did become you.' Joseph Andrews's voice was a slow Southern drawl. His entire demeanour suggested a relaxed, contented view of life which fitted his tall, rather thin body and strongly aquiline features, but Clive had known him, and from time to time worked with him, for several years before the war, and had always had the highest regard for his ability and pragmatic determination. He also knew that when the famous Wild Bill Donovan had been charged by President Roosevelt with setting up the enigmatic and top secret Office of Strategic Services, Joe Andrews had been one of his first recruits, out of the FBI.

But he had never been particularly happy at having to share Anna. It had been forced on him, after Anna had had that confrontation with the NKVD operatives in Washington two years previously. That had made a complicated situation into a jigsaw puzzle with every player holding a different piece. To the Germans Anna was their prize agent, utterly loyal because of the hold they had on her family. To the Russians she was an international assassin employed by the SD, to be killed on sight. To the British she was *their* prize agent. But to the Americans, who had had to be informed of her MI6 connection to obtain their aid in getting her out of Russia, she was merely a double agent, with no guarantee which side was her favourite. And then she had gone and committed mass murder on American soil, her victims being nationals of a country that the United States, if not yet at war herself, had elected to support in every possible way short of war. For all his efforts, Clive had an idea that Anna could have wound up on Death Row had not Joe Andrews himself fallen head over heels in love with her while smuggling her out of Russia in 1941. Joe had persuaded Donovan that she would be more valuable working for the Stars and Stripes as well as the Union Jack rather than sitting in an electric chair. But there was a limit.

'Sorry I couldn't take your calls,' Joe said. 'We figured it'd be better to see you.'

'And it took you six weeks to get around to it. Sit down.'

'There were problems.' Andrews lowered his lanky frame into the chair before the desk. 'I'm not quite sure what's bugging you. Anna does work for us as well as you, you know.'

'What is bugging me,' Clive said, 'is that you have virtually blown her cover.'

'Oh, come now, old buddy. We put one of our most reliable people in touch with her. I would say that Johannsson is a hell of a lot safer than your Bartoli.'

'And this Steinberg, and his group?'

'Let me fill you in on that. We have had our agents planted in Germany since well before we got into this business, as I'm sure you understand. Their job was to watch, listen and report, but also to encourage anti-Nazi opinions. So Johannsson, using his cover as a Swedish journalist, joined a group of intellectuals who were meeting privately to discuss various situations as they arose.'

'Intellectuals,' Clive remarked, disparagingly. 'Don't you suppose one of them might have been a Gestapo spy?'

'If he was, or she, there has been no evidence of it. We're not going to get anywhere without taking the odd risk.'

'Not with Anna's life.'

'Anna risks her life every day she's in Germany.'

'And you're happy to shorten the odds.'

'No. But this could be too big to overlook. These people have come to the conclusion, obvious to you and me, maybe, but not to the average German, that the Reich can no longer win this war. But they are also aware of the declaration issued at Casablanca by Roosevelt and Churchill, that they will only accept unconditional surrender. However, this group feels it only applies to Hitler, and that if he were to be removed from office, the Allies might be more amenable.'

Clive gave a short laugh. 'As you say, Joe: intellectuals. And you have allowed them to involve Anna? As the person to do the job, I suppose. Regardless of what happens to her afterwards. You're still remembering the Lubyanka. Do you seriously suppose you can get her out of a Gestapo cell? Or even Ravensbrück?'

'Keep your shirt on. No one's talking about assassinating Hitler. He is simply to be forced to resign his position as Führer.'

'For God's sake. Do you or your intellectual friends have any idea of what you are playing with? So why is Anna involved, if it is not a killing job?'

'She is involved because the idea is to replace Hitler with Himmler. Don't you see: the adherence of Himmler, commander of all the German police and secret services, would guarantee the success of the coup. And Anna works for Himmler, and is, as we understand it, just about his closest and most trusted aide. Believe me, no one in that group has the slightest idea that Anna is anything more than a dedicated member of Himmler's staff, but Johannsson has suggested that she is also a dedicated German, who can be persuaded that the country can be saved from the worst by her boss, with her at his side.'

'And you have allowed this farce to develop?'

'Well . . . it could be dynamite.'

'Oh, certainly. And result in an explosion that could blow Anna out of sight. Have you had a response from her?'

'No, that's the point. We know she has seen Steinberg, but according to Johannsson the best he could get out of her was that she would consider his proposal. That was some time ago. She did say that she would like a further meeting with Johannsson, who of course identified himself to her as one of our people, but he wanted a further directive from us before agreeing to see her again. As I say, these people know nothing about her, and they are terrified of betrayal.'

'Simply because she didn't jump up and down and clap her hands and shout "I'll do it, I'll do it"? Anna is too sensible for that.'

'But from your messages I gather she's referred the matter to you.'

'When last we were in contact, she knew nothing more than that your man Johannsson wanted her to meet with Steinberg.'

'But they met five weeks ago.'

'That's right. But she doesn't trust Bartoli any more than you do. She's asked for a private contact. We first of all had to find such a person, then give her some rudimentary training, and then arrange for a safe entry into Germany.'

'Did you say "her"?'

'Anna is more inclined to trust women than men. Anyway, she already knows this agent.'

'And when does this woman get to Germany?'

'Actually, she should arrive today.'

'With what instructions?'

'Simply that she should contact Anna, hear what she has to say, and come straight back to England.'

'And what do you suppose Anna *is* going to say?'

'I have absolutely no idea. But I don't think she is going to be happy with the situation. Just as I am not happy. With respect, Joe, you guys are amateurs. This isn't a game, what-ever the novelists pretend. This is life and death, and the death can be extremely unpleasant. To have put Anna in such a position is both diabolical and unethical and, above all, unprofessional.'

'OK, OK. As you keep telling me, we're fighting a war. And we're not really risking her. We have a couple of their people under lock and key back home. If something were to go wrong we'd simply do a swap. We'd lose her as an agent, but she would be out of it.'

'Oh, good God Almighty. You simply don't have a clue, do you? You people are living in some romantic Hollywood-inspired never-never land where the good guys always come out on top. Joseph, don't you realize that whenever she regards the situation as unacceptably risky, Anna has a cyanide capsule in her mouth and if she ever feels she is in a position that cannot be resolved by either force or charm she will bite the capsule and be dead in thirty seconds.'

Andrews stared at him with his mouth open. 'You can't be serious.'

'I am always serious where Anna is concerned.'

'Holy shit! What are we to do?'

Clive looked at his watch. 'Go and have lunch. There is nothing we can do, until Belinda gets back.'

Belinda was on deck as the ferry from Malmö rounded the headland and entered Lübeck Harbour. She was both excited and apprehensive. Of course, her adventure hadn't actually started yet; it would not begin until she set foot on German soil. But just to be a part of what she had always heard described as the Great Game was exhilarating. And she was actually looking forward to meeting Anna again, and as an equal. Obviously she was aware that she lacked Anna's beauty and charisma, not to mention her lethal skills, but always in the past she had felt that Anna had regarded her as nothing more than a necessary appendage, to keep Clive's bed warm when she wasn't available. But now she would have to accord her the respect due to another agent, and one vital to her own success.

She gazed at the considerable amount of bomb damage done to the seaport, particularly it seemed in the docks area, as the ferry nosed alongside the wharf. Warps were thrown and secured, and the gangway was run out. Belinda picked up her valise – she was only planning to spend two nights in Germany – and joined the queue, her shoulder bag nestling against her side. It was her business to be as inconspicuous as possible, so she wore a quiet blue suit over a white blouse, low-heeled shoes, and a slouch hat. The line moved slowly forward, the head of it crossing the dock to disappear into the Customs and Immigration building, where the windows, obviously shattered, were boarded up. There were two policemen on the dock, but they looked utterly bored.

Belinda followed the line into the doorway and the gloomy interior lit by dim electric bulbs, where inevitably there was a long, low counter, on which each set of bags was being placed, while at the far end of the room there were two men, wearing lounge suits but very obviously also policemen. They watched the line of new arrivals, but equally without great interest.

Belinda arrived before one of the immigration officials and presented her passport. She was aware that her pulse had quickened, but did not feel that it was showing in her face. 'Claudia Ratosi,' the officer said. 'Italy is in the south, Fräulein.' He had noticed the absence of a wedding ring.

'I have been in Sweden on business,' Belinda said, pleased with the evenness of her voice.

'What is your business?'

'Clothes.'

'You have come to Germany to buy clothes?' He seemed surprised.

'I am actually on my way home,' Belinda explained. 'But I am going to Berlin for a few days.'

'To buy clothes.'

'No, to sell clothes. I am a saleswoman for an Italian couturier. So I am going to see Signor Bartoli, of Antoinette's Boutique. Perhaps you have heard of him? Then I am going on to Milan.'

The officer nodded, and stamped her passport. 'I will wish you good business, Fräulein.'

Belinda passed down the line to Customs, opened her valise. She had no doubt that the customs officer had overheard the exchange, but she was not concerned: MI6 had fitted her out with a folder of dress designs, and another of material samples.

'You say these are for Antoinette's Boutique in Berlin?' He had a somewhat loud voice.

'No, no,' Belinda said. 'They are for Signor Bartoli to look at, and hopefully place an order.'

He nodded, closed the case, and scribbled on it with a piece of chalk. 'Next.'

Belinda could not suppress a faint sigh of relief as she turned towards the door. She glanced at the two plain-clothes policemen, looked away, and one of them said. 'Excuse me, Fräulein, will you step into the office a moment.'

Belinda raised her head. 'What for?'

'Because I asked you to,' he pointed out, and showed her his wallet.

Gestapo! Belinda took a deep breath. Heads were turning, and then hastily turned away again. None of the other passengers, several of whom she had spoken with on the voyage, wanted to know anyone who was being questioned by the Gestapo. But these thugs could not possibly know anything about her. 'Am I allowed to ask what this is about?' She was still pleased at the evenness of her voice.

'We will discuss that in the office.'

Was she being arrested? But that was impossible. She had done nothing to be arrested for. The capsule! But it was in her shoulder bag. Anyway, she could not possibly commit suicide just because she was being questioned by the Gestapo.

The other agent was holding the door open for her. She stepped through. The room contained a desk, two chairs, a filing cabinet and a table against the far wall. There was no window. Both men followed her, and the door was closed. 'Sit down,' the first man said.

Belinda sat in the straight chair before the desk; he went behind it. The other agent stood against the wall, arms folded.

'My name is Werter,' the man behind the desk said. 'You may call me sir. And you are Signorina Claudia Ratosi.' He raised his head to look at her.

'That is correct,' Belinda said. 'Am I under arrest? I would like to know the charge.'

'Why should you be under arrest, signorina? Have you committed a crime?'

'Of course I have not. I have only been in your country fifteen minutes. You mean I can leave?' She stood up.

'Sit down,' Werter said. 'Give me your bag.'

Belinda hesitated, then sat down. Now she could be in

trouble. She simply had to brazen it out. 'You have no right to search my bag, unless you are arresting me. If you are arresting me, I wish to call a lawyer.'

'You have a lawyer in Germany?'

'Of course I do not. I will telephone the Italian embassy, and they will take care of the matter.'

'The Italian embassy,' Werter said thoughtfully. 'The shoulder bag, signorina.'

'I have said—'

'You talk too much. Wilhelm!'

Before Belinda could grasp what was happening, the shoulder bag had been ripped off, pulled over her head, dislodging her hat, and placed on the desk.

'You bastard!' Belinda cried.

In response, Wilhelm's hand closed on her shoulder, with such strength she thought his fingers might be eating into her flesh. She gave a squeal of agony.

'Do not antagonize Wilhelm,' Werter advised. 'He can be very brutal.' He emptied the contents of the bag on to the desk

'You have no right,' Belinda gasped.

'No, no, signorina: you are the one with no right. Remember this.'

Belinda panted, but Wilhelm's hand was still resting on her shoulder, although he was no longer actually squeezing. Werter opened his drawer and took out a magnifying glass to peer at the back of her compact. 'Max Factor,' he remarked. 'Is that not an English name?'

'I think it is American,' Belinda snapped.

'Then how did you obtain it? Italy is at war with America?'

'I bought it in Rome, ten years ago,' Belinda said, refusing to allow herself to panic.

'I see.' He sifted the rest of the contents of the bag, held up the pill box. 'What is this?'

'A digestive tablet.'

He regarded her for several seconds, then swept the contents back into the bag, higgledy-piggledy. 'Undress.'

'What did you say?'

'I wish you to take off your clothing, signorina. Strip!'

'You have no—' Belinda bit her lip as she felt Wilhelm's fingers tighten. 'You wish to search me?'

'That is correct.'

'You cannot ask me to submit to this except in the presence of a woman officer and a doctor.'

'You keep telling me what I can and cannot do.' Werter leaned across the desk. 'I can do anything I like to anyone I suspect of acting against the best interests of the Reich. You come into that category.'

'But why? How?' Belinda realized she was wailing. 'What am I supposed to have done? I am on my way back to Italy from a business trip to Sweden.'

'You are going to Berlin to see a man named Bartoli.'

Oh, my God! Belinda thought. What can have happened?

'His name was given to me by one of my customers in Sweden, as someone who might be interested in the line I am selling.'

'I do not believe you. Now take off your clothes. If you refuse to do so, I will have Wilhelm take them off for you. I must tell you that he will almost certainly tear the material, and probably bruise you as well.'

Belinda took a deep breath. Then she stood up and unbuttoned her jacket.

Anna wore a pale-green sheath evening gown with a deep décolletage, and replaced her crucifix with her pearl choker, but remained staring at the gold accessory while Birgit piled her hair on the top of her head and secured it with pins. Was she being the ultimate hypocrite in wearing such a Christian symbol at all, when only twenty-four hours ago she had condemned a man to death, and sat before him to watch him die?

He was number twenty-five but the first she had executed in cold blood since Heydrich in Prague a year ago. Nearly all the others, before and since Heydrich, had been in combat, against people who had been armed and determined on her destruction. Before Heydrich there had really only been Marlene Gehrig, in Moscow, two years ago, in cold blood. But Marlene had been intending to betray her. In fact, the little witch had already betrayed her, although she had been unaware of it. Bartoli was different. She did not know if he had truly ever considered betraying her, but because of his weakness he had become too vulnerable, and once the Gestapo had him in their sights, whether or not they had actually intended to arrest him at that time, he had become too much of a risk. So, she thought, I have become accuser, judge, jury and executioner.

Only the crucifix, and the thought of Clive, offered the slightest hope of salvation.

'Is that satisfactory, Countess?' Birgit asked, as anxious as ever.

'Very. If you ever leave my service, Birgit, I recommend that you set up as a hairdresser.'

Birgit's expression became more anxious yet. 'Am I ever going to leave your service, Countess?'

'I hope not, Birgit. I sincerely hope not. There is the bell. Let the gentleman in, and give him a drink. I will be out in a moment.'

Remarkably, she was nervous. Simply because she was uncertain. If only Belinda – whoever Belinda turned out to be – had got here before tonight to give her a lead. Surely Clive would have been able to get hold of Joe by now and find out the score. The unfortunate thing was, if their decision was to drop the idea, the obvious concomitant was that Steinberg, and his entire group, would have to be turned over to the Gestapo with all that that entailed. Right this minute she had no wish to play judge and executioner, even by remote control, ever again. And Steinberg was such a nice young man. Whereas, if London were to say go for it . . .

'Countess! May I say how beautiful you look.' Steinberg bent over her glove.

'Of course you may say it, Count. Even if you do not mean it.'

'I do mean it.' He straightened. 'Can we . . .?'

'Go to the opera,' Anna said. 'We may be late returning, Birgit. Do not wait up.'

'Yes, Countess.' Birgit gave a brief curtsey and withdrew.

'You do not trust her,' Steinberg suggested as they rode down in the lift.

'I do not trust anybody, entirely, Count. Birgit is a good and faithful servant of Anna, Countess von Widerstand, whom she only knows as a devoted servant of the Reich. I would not like to confuse her. She will be in bed by the time we return tonight, and I will invite you in for a nightcap. Just remember to play it my way, without question. The apartment is bugged.'

He clearly found the mental intimacy they were sharing almost as exciting as the mere fact of having such a beautiful woman on his arm, the envious and admiring glances cast his way by the other theatre-goers, most of whom knew Anna at least by sight. She tried to relax him by allowing him to hold her hand when the lights went down, but she doubted he saw or heard much of *Lohengrin*.

'I should like to kiss you,' he whispered in the taxi on their way back to the apartment.

'Most men want more,' she breathed into his mouth.

'Ah, well . . .'

'You will have to be patient.'

He possessed himself until they were in the lift, then took her in his arms. She put her hands on his chest. 'We are working. When I am working, I am working. Afterwards, perhaps. But remember that my apartment is bugged, so I will permit you some intimacies. But what you have to say is more important.'

He released her, reluctantly. 'Then you really are what they say of you.'

'What do they say of me?'

'Two things, really: that emotionally you are a block of ice, and that sexually you prefer women to men.'

'Well, you will have to make your own judgement.' The lift stopped, and she led him into the apartment. 'There is cognac on the sideboard,' she said. 'I will put the gramophone on.' She put some soft music on the turntable, then sat beside him on the settee. 'Now snuggle up close and keep your voice down.'

'This is a splendid apartment.'

'Yes,' she agreed. 'It was given to me by Reichsführer Himmler.'

He had been nestling his cheek against hers. Now he pulled his head back. 'You mean you . . .'

'Have you forgotten that I work for him? Is that not why you are here? But perhaps you did not realize that I do whatever he wishes me to.'

He licked his lips. 'You know how to floor a man.'

'Actually, I do. But if I choose, I allow them to recover. Now hold me close, and tell me what you have to say.'

He took her in his arms again, his lips against her ear. 'I

considered what you told me when we met in the park, and decided you were correct in your judgement as to what we might need. So I went to see Field Marshal von Beck.'

It was Anna's turn to jerk her head back. 'What did you say?'

Steinberg pulled her against him. 'Have you ever met the Field Marshal?'

'Yes, I have. When he was commander-in-chief of the Wehrmacht.'

'Before Hitler fired him.'

'And you have taken this crackpot idea to Germany's senior living soldier? Now I know you are mad.'

'I have known the Field Marshal since I was a little boy. He was – is, a friend of my family. And it may interest you to know that he listened to me, and agreed with much of what I had to say.'

'Well of course he would,' Anna pointed out. 'He resents having been dismissed. But the man I said you needed was one with an active command, preferably close to or in Berlin. Beck commands nothing.'

'He is still looked up to by many of the generals and field marshals. They respect his judgement.'

He was now caressing her breast, but she was too agitated to notice. 'And you told him about me?'

'No, I did not. I told him that we had a contact high in the SS who was of the opinion that Himmler might be prepared to take over were we to remove the Führer.'

'And what did he say to that?'

'He refused to accept that idea. He does not trust Himmler.'

Anna moved his hand. 'Well, then . . .?'

'I think he would prefer to be the new Führer himself.'

'I'm sure he would. Then he is prepared to commit himself to your project?'

'There is a caveat. Well, two, actually.'

'I had no doubt that there would be.'

'He will only commit if we obtain a guarantee from the Allies that they will withdraw their demand for unconditional surrender and negotiate with whichever government succeeds the Führer.'

'How are you supposed to obtain such a guarantee?' She held her breath.

'I know it will be difficult,' Steinberg said. 'I am thinking of approaching Johannsson.'

Anna breathed slowly and carefully. 'Do you think he has any connection with the Allies?'

'I don't know. But he is a Swede, and presumably can contact the British or American embassy in Stockholm.'

'And increase the risk of your betrayal.'

'It is a risk we have to take. But the Field Marshal said something else that is far more important. An echo of your own opinion. He said that we could not simply depose Hitler, that we would have to kill him. His reason is not any fear of a shoot-out but simply, as he pointed out, that when Hitler assumed supreme power on the death of Hindenburg in 1935, he made every soldier in the Wehrmacht, the Luftwaffe, and every sailor in the Navy, take a personal oath of allegiance to him, as Führer. Were he deposed but still alive, that oath would still have effect on the hearts and minds of most of the troops. But if he were dead – well, they would have to look to his successor.'

'So now you contemplate murder,' Anna said. 'Have you thought about what it will entail? Have you ever killed a man?'

'Well, no. I have never served in the Wehrmacht.'

'It is not necessary to have fought in a war to have killed somebody,' Anna pointed out. '*Could* you kill somebody?'

'I don't know. Could you?'

Anna was grateful that with their cheeks pressed together he could not see her eyes. 'That is not the question. I am a woman. If you are not sure you can do it, then you can't. Certainly not the Führer. Certainly if by doing so, or attempting to do so, you would be risking death yourself.'

'You almost speak as if you have had such an experience.'

'Let's say that I have a very close friend who has had such an experience.'

'Well, I know I am not the man for the job. He will have to be recruited.'

'You mean you have no one in mind. None of your group who might be able to do it.'

'I don't think so. As I told you—'

'You are all intellectuals. Yes, you told me. Well, I will wish you good fortune.'

'But will you be on our side? May I tell the Field Marshal this?'

'Certainly not, Friedrich. My terms are the same as before. If you ever tell a soul that you have even spoken with me on this subject, I will turn you over to the Gestapo.'

'But Himmler . . . We need . . .'

'I understand this. But now a new factor has been introduced. You are asking him to accept the command of Beck. I do not know if he will be prepared to do this. In any event, even more than the Field Marshal he will need to be certain of your success before he will commit himself.'

'But he has told you that he *will* commit himself.'

'I did not say that, and I will not have you putting words into my mouth. Go away, find your assassin, make out a plan of campaign, in your head, please, not on paper, and then come back to me. If it is at all viable, I may put it before the Reichsführer. Just remember that the word is "may".'

'And once you have our plan, you can turn the whole thing over to the Gestapo.'

'Why, that is a risk you have to take. If you are not prepared to do that, I suggest you leave now.'

He moved back to stare at her, his expression a mixture of longing and apprehension. She leaned forward and kissed him on the mouth. 'But I think you would rather stay.' She held his hand and stood up. 'Let us go to bed for a while.'

He gasped. She wondered if he would make it. But she felt it was important to make him her slave, at least until she knew for certain whether this hare-brained plot was going to get anywhere and, more importantly, whether London wanted it to get anywhere. Besides, she felt like being sexually dominant, just for a change.

'Anna!' Himmler announced, entering her office, which was sufficiently surprising to have her head jerk: he usually sent for her. 'You will never guess what has happened.'

Oh, shit! she thought. She had been feeling deliciously relaxed. On the one hand, she had bought herself some time, quite a lot of time, as she did not suppose Friedrich would find his assassin very rapidly. And on the other, he had proved himself a very acceptable lover, so terribly anxious to indulge her every whim just as he had been so very clean and well groomed. Though she could not escape the feeling that he was doomed, he might prove a very satisfying companion for a while. But to have Himmler marching into her office . . . On the other hand, the Reichsführer did not look either disturbed or angry. 'I am sure I cannot, sir,' she said.

'Your coup,' he said. 'The man Bartoli.'

Anna's stomach muscles tightened. 'Sir?'

Himmler actually sat on the desk. 'I told you that when we raided his house we found all that radio equipment, and received a message from London that a contact was on his way.'

'Ye-es,' Anna said cautiously.

'Well, it would seem that the contact may have turned up.'

Oh, my God! She thought. 'Can it be possible?'

'That is what I want you to find out, because it is your baby, eh?'

'Yes, sir. This contact—'

Himmler held up his finger. 'I don't want you to go jumping to conclusions. You must keep an open mind. The woman may be entirely innocent. It is just such a coincidence.'

'Woman?'

'Some Italian. Named . . .' He thought for a moment. 'Claudia Ratosi.'

'Claudia Ratosi.'

'Do you know of her?'

'I have never heard the name before. And you say she has been arrested . . .?'

'In Lübeck, after getting off the Malmö ferry. I telephoned you last night as soon as I received the report. But your maid said that you had gone to the opera.'

And she never thought to tell me you had called, Anna thought. 'Yes, sir.'

'*Lohengrin*, was it? I didn't know you were a Wagner fan?'

'Isn't everyone?' Anna asked, innocently.

'Oh, absolutely. But . . . You went alone?'

'No, sir.' She did not know how many of the people she had encountered at the theatre were Gestapo employees. 'I was escorted by Count von Steinberg.'

'Freddie? Such a nice lad. And talented, too. He has a great future in front of him, you know. But' – Himmler frowned – 'I wouldn't have thought he was your type.'

'I wouldn't have thought so either, Herr Reichsführer. But he invited me. I do not get many invitations,' she added a trifle wistfully. 'About this woman . . .'

'I think that is terrible,' Himmler said. 'An attractive young woman like you. Do you know who you should take up with? Hellmuth Essermann. He is very fond of you, you know, and I am sure he is more to your taste than Freddie von Steinberg.'

Anna laid down the pencil she had been holding just before she snapped it in two. 'I have no doubt of it, sir. This woman . . .'

'Would you like me to have a word with him? Tell him you are, or might be, receptive.'

'No, I would not,' Anna all but shouted. 'You say this woman was arrested yesterday. Where is she now?'

'Oh, she is still in Lübeck. I told them to keep her there for the time being.'

'May I ask why she was arrested?'

'Well, obviously, after Bartoli's suicide, and the message from London, his name was circulated to all our agencies, with instructions to hold for interrogation anyone attempting to contact him. Frankly, I never expected anyone just to walk into our arms like that, which is why I have a feeling that she may be an innocent coincidence. Still, there it is, she has to be investigated.'

'Yes, sir.' Anna took a deep breath. 'And you say she has been in the hands of the Gestapo in Lübeck for twenty-four hours? Under interrogation?' In which case, she thought, she has either gone mad or told them everything they wish to know.

'No, no. I only told them to hold her, but not to begin inter-rogation until someone arrived from Berlin. This business is potentially too important to be handled by some flat-footed policeman.'

Anna managed to suppress a sigh of relief. 'I entirely agree with you, sir. I will go up there now. Supposing I encounter opposition . . . I am not the Gestapo's favourite person.'

'And they don't even know the truth about Feutlanger, eh? Ha ha. I will telephone Lübeck now and tell them that the Countess von Widerstand, a senior officer in the SD, is coming to take over the investigation, and that she is to be obeyed in everything without question. You will use an official car. Does that satisfy you?'

'Entirely, sir. With your permission, I will leave immediately.'

Anna knew that Lübeck had been heavily bombed by the RAF just about the time of the Hamburg raid in July. Indeed, as it was only a few kilometres north of the devastated city, the whole countryside seemed in a state of febrile collapse; her car had to stop at several roadblocks to reach the Baltic seaport. But her driver's SD pass eased her journey.

She had carefully placed her mind on hold, as she had no idea what to expect. She actually knew very little about Bartoli's business, where he had obtained his stock; it would make sense for him to deal with an Italian wholesaler. In which case this unfortunate female had innocently walked into a situation she could not possibly understand. At the same time, *she* was expecting an English contact, and as London could not possibly yet know that Bartoli was dead, it would make logical sense for them to have given their messenger the boutique as a cover. Or did it? When, the previous year, she had first expressed her doubts as to Bartoli's reliability and they had sent Judith de Sotomayer as a back-up contact, they had deliberately told Bartoli nothing about it.

But now she was here, and the car was drawing to a halt before Gestapo Headquarters. 'I have no idea how long I shall be, Klaeger,' she said as she opened the door. 'But I will require to be taken back to Berlin, some time this afternoon or tonight.'

'My instructions are to wait for you, Countess.'

'Thank you.'

'Your business?' barked the armed guard on the door.

'I am the Countess von Widerstand,' Anna told him. 'I am here to see your commanding officer.'

The man looked at her pass and gulped, then clicked to attention before opening the door. 'The Countess von Widerstand,' he said to the corrridor within. 'To see Herr Werter.'

Anna entered, nostrils dilating as she inhaled the stale but familiar air. A hard-faced woman secretary was just emerging from an office, but there was no one else about; it was in fact a small building with an obviously limited establishment. 'I think you are expecting me,' Anna said.

The young woman looked her up and down. Before leaving Berlin Anna had gone home and changed into a frock, adding her jewellery but leaving her hair loose. This was because of her mischievous sense of humour: she knew, as Laurent had pointed out, that with her hair drifting past her shoulders she looked no more than eighteen. 'From Berlin?' the secretary asked, incredulously.

'That is correct.'

'The message said the Countess von Widerstand?'

'That is also correct. Are you going to keep me standing here all day?'

The secretary gulped, and turned to the door as Werter emerged. Anna was congenitally conditioned to disliking all Gestapo agents on sight, and she saw no reason to change her opinion now. 'What is the trouble, Gertrude?' he inquired.

'This young lady—'

'I am Anna von Widerstand,' Anna announced. 'And I dislike being kept waiting. Were you not informed by the Reichsführer's office that I was coming?'

'We were informed' – he also looked her up and down – 'that a senior SD officer was coming to take charge of the prisoner Ratosi.'

'Where is she?'

'*You* are a senior SD officer?'

'Listen very carefully,' Anna recommended. 'I am the most senior SD officer you are ever likely to meet. I have been sent here, by Herr Himmler personally, to take charge of this prisoner of yours. I wish to see her – *now*. Or would you like me to telephone the Reichsführer and tell him that you are being entirely uncooperative?'

Werter considered for a moment, then looked at Gertrude and waggled his eyebrows. She returned to her office, no doubt, Anna supposed, to telephone Berlin and obtain confirmation and a description. 'If you will come with me, Fräulein,' Werter said.

'You will address me as Countess.' Anna told him. 'I would first of all like to see the prisoner's effects.'

'Yes, ah . . . Countess.' He ushered her into his office. 'Her shoulder bag, and her valise. She was travelling very light.'

Anna pointed. 'And what are those?'

'Those are her clothes, Countess.'

'Her clothes? What is she wearing now?'

'Nothing.'

'She is naked in her cell? How long has she been in that condition?'

'Since she was searched, yesterday morning.'

'I see. Is she a good-looking woman?'

'Attractive, Countess.'

'So she was abused.'

'She was not abused, Countess. She was searched.'

Anna knew exactly what that would have entailed, but it could keep, for the moment. 'And since then you have kept her naked for your personal gratification.'

'By no means, Countess,' he protested. 'Keeping a prisoner naked is an essential part of discovering the truth about them. It robs them of their self-esteem, their confidence. Also, when they have no clothes, it is impossible for them to commit suicide. It is in the manual.'

'You mean she has been given no bedclothes either.'

'It is in the manual.'

'I am sure it is. But no doubt you have looked at her from time to time.'

'It is my duty to do so, Countess. To make sure—'

'That she has not committed suicide. Having taken steps to make sure that she could not commit suicide even if she wished to. Don't tell me: that also is in the manual.' She emptied the shoulder bag on to the desk.

'In that pill box,' Werter said, 'there is a cyanide capsule.'

Oh, the fool, Anna thought. 'Which she did not use?'

'I think we surprised her.'

'Hm.' Anna picked up the passport, flicked it open, and could not prevent herself from drawing a sharp breath.

'Countess? You know this woman?'

Do I know this woman? Anna thought. She had only met Belinda Hoskin on one occasion, and that had been three years ago, but as it was an occasion she would never forget, so Belinda's was a face she would never forget either. But Belinda, here, in a Gestapo cell . . . What in the name of God could Clive be playing at? But one thing was overwhelmingly certain: *she* had to play her end of the game with absolute accuracy and absolute certainty. She certainly could not allow Belinda to see *her* face until she could be put in the picture. 'No, I do not know her,' she said. 'But she is certainly attractive. There is nothing incriminating here.' She opened the valise, flicked through the clothing, took out the sample charts, giving her heart time to settle down. 'She appears to be a travelling saleswoman.'

'That is what she claims, certainly.'

'And you found that suspicious.'

'I was acting on instructions, Countess, that I should place under restraint anyone who attempted to enter or leave the country, with any connection to the man Bartoli, who recently committed suicide. Perhaps you do not know of this.'

Anna had determined how this should be handled. 'I watched him die,' she said.

Werter's mouth opened, and then snapped shut again. 'She was also carrying a suicide pill.'

'So you say. I think I will have to take this woman to Berlin. But I will carry out a preliminary investigation now.'

'Because she is a good-looking woman?' Werter suggested, slyly.

'Why, yes,' Anna agreed. 'It is always more amusing to interrogate an attractive woman than an ugly one. Very good. She is in your cell downstairs. You have an interrogation room?'

'Yes.'

'Then place her in there. Secure her for a flogging. And see that she is blindfolded.'

'Countess?'

'Is that not in the manual? Being blindfolded is far more disconcerting than being naked, Herr Werter. If one does not know who is interrogating one, or what is about to be done to one, one cannot prepare oneself to resist.'

'That is a very interesting point,' Werter agreed.

'Then, as I say, prepare her, and let me know when she is ready. You have a radio down there?'

'Of course.'

'When she is ready for me, switch it on full volume.'

'Of course.'

'Very good. I am waiting.'

Anna put the pill box in her own bag, then sat in Werter's chair behind the desk, keeping absolutely still; Gertrude looked in on her once, and hastily went away again. Anna hardly noticed her. She was composing herself for what lay ahead. She had no doubt that she could extricate Belinda from the mess into which she had been dumped, either by Clive or by her own carelessness, but it could only be done if Belinda was prepared to co-operate entirely and accept whatever was going to happen, whatever was going to be done to her. Anna wondered if she could, if her essentially positive personality and the sense of security that had been instilled into her by living in so civilized a country as England could yield as entirely as was going to be required. While she . . . she had known this feeling before, and always endeavoured to reject it. But she had never entirely succeeded. She could not deny that physical mastery, physical dominance, powerfully appealed to her subconscious. What was even more sinister, she knew that if Belinda would not fully cooperate, she would have to be eliminated as ruthlessly as Bartoli had been. Had she, as Werter claimed, been too surprised to take the pill? or had she not been sufficiently trained? or had she simply lacked the courage? On their very brief acquaintance, Anna had not felt that she lacked courage.

Werter appeared in the doorway. 'She is ready for you, Countess.'

Anna drew a deep breath and stood up. The time for brooding was past. 'Well, then, take me to her.'

He led her to the inevitable flight of stairs leading down. 'You understand that we have a limited facility here.'

'Are you telling me that this woman has been sharing a cell?' That could have been catastrophic.

'No, no. But we only have two cells. We do not have many subversives here.'

'Then you are to be congratulated.' Anna followed him along the corridor, so redolent of past horrors, and checked beside the table on which was the radio, playing a selection of, inevitably, Wagner. 'That is not loud enough.'

Werter raised his eyebrows. 'Actually, Countess, she has not screamed at all. She complains all the time. She keeps telling me that I have no right to treat her so.'

'But she has not yet been interrogated by me,' Anna pointed out.

Werter swallowed and turned up the volume. If Belinda could shriek as loudly as Brunhilde, Anna thought, she could well crack one of the bulbs. Werter opened the door of the interrogation cell.

Anna was well acquainted with such rooms, having suffered in one herself. She was more interested in the woman standing in the centre of the floor than in the various unpleasant instruments hanging on the walls, although she also noted the security camera mounted just under the ceiling. There could be no faking.

Belinda's arms had been carried above her head, her wrists secured to iron rings suspended from the ceiling. There were no marks on her body, which was sufficiently voluptuous to allow Anna to feel that Clive must be a very contented man, in his domestic life. And she was alert; her head turned as the door opened.

'Here we are, Countess,' Werter said. 'She is all yours.'

Belinda's head turned more sharply yet, and her mouth opened. 'A—'

Anna stepped up to her and hit her in the stomach. 'Bitch! Speak when you are spoken to.'

Belinda gasped, her body sagging, her mouth hanging open as she gasped for breath.

'Now leave us,' Anna told Werter.

'Leave you? But . . .'

'It is not in the manual? But I am conducting this interrogation, and there are things I may wish to do to this woman for which I would prefer you to be absent.' Werter did another of his gulps, and Anna smiled at him. 'But you can play the film over afterwards. I am sure you intend to do that anyway. Now out.'

He hesitated, then clicked his heels and left, closing the door behind him. Anna stood close to Belinda, who was just recovering her breath, and pulled the hood from her head. Belinda gasped again as Anna slid her hands over her body. 'I am sorry about this,' she said into Belinda's ear, her voice lost in the booming music. 'But it is the only way I can talk to you and at the same time get you out of here. Do you understand?'

'Oh, Anna, is it really you? I have been so afraid.'

'It is really me. Now listen, I am going to play with you

for a little while. While I do that we will talk. Then I am going to have to whip you. When I do that, you must scream as loudly as you can. Do you understand?'

'Whip me? Oh, Anna . . .'

'They are filming us. I have to interrogate you. It is a choice between being whipped, suffering electric shocks in your genitals, or having your nails pulled out. Believe me, the whipping is the least painful and you will recover from it more quickly than the others, both mentally and physically.'

'But you will not hit me too hard, Anna.'

'These people are not fools. I must mark your body.'

'And you say you can get me out afterwards?'

'Yes, if you obey me. Now gasp and wriggle.'

Belinda was doing that anyway as Anna stroked her breasts and buttocks.

'Clive sent you. Did he not give you my address?'

'He made me memorize it.'

'And he told you to go to Bartoli?'

'As a back-up if I needed it.'

'Then how did they connect you?'

Belinda licked her lips. 'I suppose I mentioned that I was going to the boutique, to the customs officer. He seemed so friendly.'

'In other words you just about dug your own grave. In our profession, our business is to listen, never to offer gratuitous information. Now we have talked long enough. I am going to whip you.'

'Oh, God! But Clive said that you had information to give me.'

'I do. But it can wait until afterwards. Jut remember, do not attempt to talk until I tell you it is safe to do so. Disobey me in this and I will kill you.'

Belinda's eyes had been half-shut as her breathing had become heavier. Now they opened very wide. 'You—'

'In this business, and for the sake of our ultimate victory, my life is more important than yours. Remember this.'

The Directive

'Ah, Anna,' Himmler said. 'Did you have success?'
Anna stood before his desk. The capsule now rested in her own pill pouch; she did not see that there was any way that Werter, essentially a subordinate officer, and having surrendered his prisoner to her superior authority, could ever find out what had happened to her, or to the evidence against her. 'Yes I did, Herr Reichsführer. But I am afraid that it is negative. The woman Ratosi is entirely innocent of any treasonable or subversive connection with Bartoli.'

He frowned. 'She was properly interrogated?'

'I questioned her personally, sir. The session was recorded on film, if you wish to see it.'

Himmler took off his glasses to polish them; Anna could tell that he was wondering if she had given way to the lesbian tendencies he was sure she possessed. Well, she thought, he would not be disappointed if he watched the film. But it was the surest way to distract him.

'And you found nothing suspicious?'

'She is a travelling saleswoman who has had no previous connection with Signor Bartoli. I was able to ascertain this by a couple of questions to which she did not know the answers. She was apparently given Bartoli's name as a possible customer by one of her Swedish clients. Everything she had with her bore out this claim, and her story never wavered even when she was being flogged.'

'You attended to that personally?'

'Yes, sir, I did.'

'Then I am sure you are right in your judgement. What did you do with her?'

'I also ascertained,' Anna went on, 'that she is a profound Fascist and a believer in our regime, as well as being a fanatical supporter of Mussolini.'

'You are sure these were not just claims?'

'It is hard to make such claims, coherently, when one's buttocks are being torn to pieces.'

This time he used the handkerchief to wipe his neck.

'She was, however, somewhat upset by her treatment, so I brought her to Berlin with me, let her spend the night in my apartment, and this morning put her on a train for Milan. That is where she lives.'

'She spent the night in your apartment?'

'Yes, sir. I considered it important to – shall I say, smooth her ruffled feathers.'

'And did you succeed?'

'I think so, sir,' Anna said modestly.

'Miss Hoskin is here, sir,' Amy Barstow said, apprehensively. Belinda had never visited MI6 before.

'Thank God for that.' Clive hurried round his desk. 'Belinda! I had almost given you up for lost. Belinda?'

It was definitely Belinda, well dressed as always and well groomed as always . . . and yet he had a sudden sensation that this was not, actually, Belinda. Or, at least, not the Belinda with whom he had been sharing part of his life for the last seven years. Now she came into the office without speaking. Clive looked past her at Amy, whose eyebrows were arched so high as almost to merge with her hairline.

'Thank you, Miss Barstow. Close the door, will you, please?'

Amy looked almost inclined to disobey, if only to protect her boss. Then she left the room and closed the door.

'Belinda!' Clive took her in his arms, but to his surprise she wriggled free without offering her mouth, and sat before the desk, carefully. Clive returned behind it and also sat down. 'Am I to understand that you encountered problems?'

'That depends upon your definition of the word "problem".' Belinda opened her handbag and took out a packet of cigarettes, at which Clive stared in consternation: Belinda had never smoked.

'But you're here,' he said brightly. 'You're back. God, I was so worried when you didn't turn up at Jacques's on schedule.'

'There were delays.'

'So it seems. But you got into Germany all right. And you saw Anna?'

Belinda looked at him through a cloud of smoke, and he felt distinctly uncomfortable. 'How well do you know Anna?' she asked.

'I would say I know her as well as anyone. As well as it is possible to know Anna. She has hidden depths.'

'I know.'

'Ah . . .' Just what did she mean by that? 'But anyway, you got to her without difficulty. You didn't have to use Bartoli?'

'Bartoli is dead.'

'*What?*'

'Officially, he committed suicide, minutes before being arrested by the Gestapo.'

'But . . . what went wrong?'

'He was betrayed by his wife.'

'Damnation. Anna always said that she didn't trust that woman. But Anna . . .'

'Anna is perfectly well. She killed Bartoli.'

'She . . .?!'

'She said it was to prevent his being arrested, which would have involved her.'

'Holy smoke! But it was always likely to happen. The important thing is that she is all right.'

'Yes,' Belinda said. 'I assume you know that she is very high up in the SD? – Himmler's right-hand woman.'

'That is why she is so important to us.'

'She seems to have unlimited power.' Belinda looked around the desk, could not see an ashtray, and flicked ash on to the floor. 'Are you sure you know *all* about her?'

'You mean, do I know that she can kill without hesitation or compunction when she feels threatened? Yes. And so do you. You saw her do it, once.'

'The Gehrig woman. I shall never forget that.'

'She was saving your life.'

'I know. I still don't think you know her as well as you think you do. Anyway, you may be pleased to know that she saved my life again, two weeks ago.'

'My God! What went wrong?'

'She got me out of a Gestapo cell, as they were about to start torturing me. So she took over torturing me herself. She said it was the only way.'

She related what had happened, and Clive listened in

consternation. 'I know it was my fault,' Belinda admitted when she finished. 'I should not have mentioned Bartoli's name. As Anna said, a spy's business is to listen, not to talk.'

'She is right. But this whipping . . .'

'It was genuine, Clive. It had to be, because apparently we were being filmed. And it wasn't half as bad as being searched, having them put their fingers into me . . . ugh! But she enjoyed it. Whipping me, I mean.'

'She didn't search you herself?'

'No, the men did that, before her arrival. They took away my clothes, and left me naked, for a whole day.'

It was impossible, from the way neither her expression nor her voice had altered while she was speaking, to determine what she really felt about what had happened. 'But this was all a part of Anna's plan for getting you out of the hands of the Gestapo.'

'That's what she said, yes.'

'But you don't believe her.'

'Oh, I do. I mean . . . there was no other way.' Her expression was almost defiant.

'And you had the guts not to use the capsule. My dear girl—'

'I didn't use the capsule because I didn't expect to be arrested almost the moment I stepped off the ferry.'

'Jesus! All I can say is, thank God for Anna, even if she did have to rough you up a little.'

'Yes,' Belinda said. 'Thank God for Anna. Will you want me to go back again?'

'You mean you would be prepared to risk all that again?'

'Well . . .' Her tongue emerged and circled her lips. 'The way Anna arranged things, I am now entirely in the clear. I mean, they accept my cover that I am a travelling saleswoman. From Italy.'

'Despite the fact that you were caught in possession of a capsule? Or didn't they find it?'

'Oh, they found it. But Anna took care of that too. As I said, she seems to have an awful lot of clout. I think she would like me to be her regular contact.'

'It would still be very dangerous.'

'I know. But if it will help to win the war . . .'

'I'll have to talk to Billy. Now you'd better tell me what Anna had to say. I hope it was important.'

Baxter filled his pipe. 'Do you believe any of it?'

'Anna has never invented information in the past. This could be the decisive moment of the war, Billy. If there is any one man who is the driving force behind the Nazi ethos, the Nazi war machine, it is Adolf Hitler. If he disappears, who have they got left? Göring? Himmler? Goebbels? None of those is a leader of men.'

'Is Beck?'

'He was once. He could be again.'

'It is still all airy-fairy. According to Anna, they don't even have a plan as to how it is to be done, yet. Much less an assassin prepared to do it. Unless . . .'

'No way,' Clive said. 'You can just forget that.'

'But you must admit she'd be useful in setting it up. I mean, she set up the Heydrich business.'

'Ah . . .' Once again Clive considered telling his boss the truth about that. But involving Anna in what more and more appeared to be a hare-brained plot would be too risky. 'Yes, she did. But she came under suspicion, and but for Himmler's support, she could well have been done.'

'Strange bedfellows,' Baxter commented, leaving Clive unsure as to just what he was referring. 'Well, we can do nothing further until I can put Beck's terms to the big boys. You say that Belinda survived her ordeal pretty well?'

Clive considered. 'She survived the ordeal,' he said at last.

'Sounds like there could be a but in there.'

'There is. At this moment, she is not the Belinda I have known for the past seven years.'

'Well, there's nothing surprising in that. I mean, she's a well-brought-up young woman. Having her knickers torn off by a couple of thugs so that they could shove their fingers up her ass is tantamount to being raped. And then to be whipped by someone you were told to regard as a friend . . . well! And yet you say that she's willing to go back. That woman has a lot of guts. You really should marry her.'

'I don't think she'd go for that, right now,' Clive said, thoughtfully.

'Well, I'd better get on.' Baxter picked up his house phone.

'Miss Lucas, get me an appointment with the boss. Tell him it's an extremely urgent matter.' He replaced the phone and grinned at Clive. 'Wish me luck.'

Baxter felt exactly as he had done some thirty years before when he had been facing his first job interview. He sat in a straight chair facing a long desk and three men, not one of whom looked the least pleased to see him. The General he knew. The Foreign Office minister he had met. The third man was unknown to him, but he gathered he was a cabinet secretary.

The FO minister began proceedings. 'This is a very remarkable situation, Mr Baxter. I gather that you are prepared to vouch, absolutely, for the accuracy of the information that you have placed before us.'

Baxter looked at the General; he had gone through all of this the previous week. 'I am, sir. It comes from our most reliable agent in Germany.'

'And how did this agent obtain it?'

Baxter had already prepared his reply; the less these people knew about the links between the OSS and MI6 the better. 'She was approached, quite inadvertently, by one of the conspirators, who thought she might be sympathetic. She holds a high position within the Nazi hierarchy.'

'Are you telling us that your principal agent in Germany is a *woman*?' The minister looked at the General in turn, in search of an explanation.

Here we go again, Baxter thought: a case of rampant misogyny. He reflected with some satisfaction that none of these gentlemen, or indeed, all three together, would last a moment in Anna's company if they encountered her when she was in a bad mood.

The General was prepared to support him. 'Mr Baxter has every confidence in this – ah, lady. And I have every confidence in Mr Baxter's judgement.'

'I see. And when you say that she is well placed within the Nazi hierarchy, exactly what do you mean?'

'The lady is Reichsführer Himmler's Personal Assistant.'

'Good heavens! Therefore we must conclude that not only is she a German, but that she is a Nazi herself. Yet she is prepared to be involved in this project?'

'She is prepared to become involved, minister, if we tell her to,' Baxter said. 'And she is not a German. She was born in Vienna, and has an Irish mother.'

'Ulster or Eire?'

'I'm afraid, Eire.'

'Good God!'

'I should point out that not all Irish republicans are IRA terrorists,' the General said.

'And this creature has been worming her way up the Nazi tree. How long has she been doing this?'

'She has been working for us since the spring of 1939.'

'After growing up in the Nazi Youth Movement, no doubt. Working for us, you say. Has it occurred to you that she could be a double agent?'

'She *is* a double agent,' the General agreed. 'But she is our double agent. As for growing up in the Nazi Youth, as Mr Baxter said, she was born and grew up in Vienna. She had nothing to do with the Nazi Youth. She was only eighteen when we recruited her.'

The minister stared at him with his mouth open, while Baxter held his breath. As this man worked in the Foreign Office, he would almost certainly have known Ballantyne Bordman, and his wife, who was still considered, even by certain people in the government who lacked the requisite information, as a German arch-spy. But the General did not let him down by saying anything further. The minister was amazed in any event. 'You recruited an eighteen-year-old girl as a spy?'

'As an agent,' the General corrected.

'And now you say that she is Himmler's PA? How old is she now?'

'Well, as that was in March 1939, she is now twenty-three. She was born in May,' the General added, helpfully.

The minister scratched his head and turned to the secretary, who was looking somewhat impatient: he dealt in facts, not personalities.

'I have, of course, placed the matter before the Prime Minister,' the secretary said. 'He was sufficiently interested to refer it to President Roosevelt. But before it is carried any further, there is one thing he wishes made abundantly clear: there can be no restatement, or watering down, of the

Casablanca Declaration. If these people are prepared to go ahead with their plot, and they succeed, we shall of course be very pleased, as it should definitely shorten the war. But the only aim they can have, as regards the western democracies, is to expedite the unconditional surrender that we require.'

Baxter opened his mouth, but the General beat him to it. 'You would not consider that to be somewhat counterproductive?'

'What I, or you, may consider, is of no importance. That is a directive from the Prime Minister, and he has no doubt that it will also be the point of view of the President. However, as I have said, he fully understands that such a coup, if it were to be successful, would greatly help the Allied cause. Now, this agent . . .' He paused to look at the minister. 'I hope you understand, sir, that whatever is said here today is absolutely confidential, and is to be repeated to no one. No one at all.'

'Well, of course I understand that,' the minister snapped, bridling.

'Well, then . . .' Now the secretary looked from the General to Baxter. 'I am assuming that we are talking about the woman Anna Fehrbach?'

The General gulped, and Baxter reached for his pipe, only he hadn't brought it with him.

'Alias the Countess von Widerstand, alias the Honourable Mrs Ballantyne Bordman.'

The minister turned in his chair. 'What did you say? That bitch is—'

'Our leading agent in Germany,' the secretary said smoothly. 'Don't look so horrified, gentlemen. The Prime Minister has a file on the glamorous Countess. He is very interested in her. After all, was she not sent here to assassinate him?'

'She was already working for us,' the General muttered.

'Of course. But these things create a bond, do they not? Mr Churchill remembers meeting her at an official function, and being impressed.'

'But . . . this woman . . . Bordman . . .' the minister was spluttering.

'How is the poor fellow?' the secretary inquired, solicitously.

'Well . . . he's never recovered. He's in a state of permanent decline.'

'Remembering, no doubt,' the secretary said with an unexpected touch of black humour. 'He did share her bed for a year.'

'He'll never work again,' the minister grumbled.

'Very sad,' the secretary agreed. 'But as I recall, he did bring it on himself by falling hopelessly in love with a girl less than half his age. These things never turn out well. We are drifting away from the point. As I was saying, the Prime Minister, while unable to offer these conspirators any terms, is well aware that the elimination of Hitler, and his replacement by someone who might be willing to surrender, would be greatly to the advantage of us all and would enable us to regard them, and possibly the German people as a whole, in a more favourable light. And when I put the information before him, he said immediately, Fehrbach!'

Both the General and Baxter stiffened. 'Just what are you proposing?' the General asked.

'Well, you claim that she is Himmler's PA. Frankly we were unaware that she had risen so high . . .' He paused, censoriously, to indicate that the PM might well wish to know *why* he had not been kept up to date on Anna's progress. 'However, if this is true, then she must move in the highest Nazi circles, with ready access to all the Party leaders, including the Führer. Now, he understands that you will be reluctant to risk compromising such a valuable asset, and he is content that she should remain on the sidelines if that is possible. However, should this conspiracy collapse or come to nought, he directs that you should tell your agent definitely to become involved and carry the project to a successful conclusion.'

'Are you telling us that you wish Fehrbach to attempt the assassination of the Führer herself?'

'That is her profession, is it not?'

'Then do you understand that you are asking me to sentence our best agent to death?'

'As she is our agent, is her life not in extreme danger in any event?'

'Not so long as she maintains her position as a faithful servant of the regime, and confines her activities to relaying information to us.'

'I appreciate your concern, Mr Baxter, but this is too big a subject for us to take personalities, or their sex, into consideration. We could be talking about the saving of hundreds of thousands of lives. But as I have explained, we are not requiring Fehrbach to risk herself, except as a last resort. If she, or the conspirators, can find someone else to carry out the actual assassination, well and good. If not . . . as I say, we are fighting a war. However, we would like the business completed by the end of this year. That gives her three months to set things in motion.'

'That is a directive from the PM?' the General asked.

'It is.' The secretary stood up. 'The Prime Minister would like to be informed as to the progress of this venture. Good morning, gentlemen.'

The General accompanied Baxter into the lobby. 'I am sorry, Billy. I know you regard Fehrbach as a prize, but she is there to serve a purpose, and now this has come up . . .'

'I am very inclined to hand you my resignation here and now.'

'My dear fellow, what good would that do? She would still receive the orders, and from a less sympathetic source.'

'Do you have any idea what they will do to her if she's caught trying to assassinate Hitler?'

'Yes, I do. But she has her capsule.'

The two men gazed at each other. 'If this goes wrong,' Baxter said, 'may the Devil have mercy on our souls. God certainly will not.'

Clive stared across the desk at his boss. 'Are they mad?'

'Just desperate.'

'Aren't we winning the war, with or without Hitler?'

'Perhaps we are. But it is still costing several thousand lives a day. And if we have to carry out an invasion of the continent, that cost is going to go up tenfold. While if Germany is truly on the verge of developing secret weapons of mass destruction – well, perhaps then a victorious end would not be quite as guaranteed as it presently appears.'

'You are asking me to condemn Anna to death.'

'I understand what *we* are being asked to do, Clive. And I hate it as much as you do. But as the man says, it is her profession, and she must long ago have realized that the day would come when she would not be able to shoot or charm or love her way out of trouble. In any event, we have received a direct order from the very top, and we are going to carry it out. The first thing we need to do is contact Anna.'

Clive sighed. 'Belinda indicated that she might be willing to go back.'

'That's out.'

'She volunteered.'

'Maybe. But things have changed.'

'You mean because Badoglio has declared neutrality? Belinda's cover is that she is a fervent supporter of Mussolini, and now that Hitler's boy Skorzeny has got Musso out of hock . . .'

'That may be, but – and this is top secret – Badoglio is about to declare Italy's re-entry into the war as a member of the Allies. The date of the announcement is, as I say, being kept secret for the moment, to allow the Allies to get a good grip on the Toe while the Germans are unsure who are their friends and who are their enemies. We don't know exactly what their reaction will be when Italy becomes an active enemy, but we can be pretty sure it is going to be drastic, and it will encompass every Italian they can lay hands on, whether or not they declare allegiance to Il Duce. After all, right this moment he is just a problem. What do they do with an ex-dictator who has no one to dictate to? No, I'm sorry to say we are going to have to use Johannsson.'

'But that will mean—'

'Bringing the OSS into full partnership. But that's going to happen anyway, when Winston puts the situation fully to the President. Andrews is still here, isn't he?'

Clive nodded.

'Then get on to him right away.'

'I don't imagine he will be any happier than we are, at having to put Anna in such a spot.'

'But if I know my Americans, he'll do it. But listen: I have an idea.'

'I'm glad of that.'

'Whether Anna can find a substitute, or whether she has to do it herself, I am not thinking in terms of an old-fashioned bullet in the gut or knife in the back. That is not necessary.'

'You have an alternative?'

'Come with me.'

The two men descended the several flights of stairs to the

basement, watched by curious staff members: Baxter and Clive did not often go anywhere together. The cellars beneath the building were not used only for file storage, but also as research laboratories. In one of these there was a little man, bald and somewhat overweight, wearing white overalls and sitting at a cluttered desk studying a sheet of paper.

'James!' Baxter announced enthusiastically. 'Hard at work, as always.'

'Someone has to do it.'

'Absolutely. You know Clive Bartley?'

'Well, of course I know Clive. What's on your mind?'

'We would like to commit a murder.'

'You have my blessing.'

'But we don't want to be present when our subject dies.'

'I assume you have some access to the victim. Pop a pill in his milk.'

'Won't work. This man is very carefully protected, and all his food is tasted before he eats or drinks it.'

'You'll be making me think you are talking about someone named Adolf.' He raised his head as there was no immediate reply.

'Just don't think about it,' Baxter recommended. 'We believe we can obtain access to our target. We want our man to be able to place an explosive device close enough to blow the target to bits, but we also want him to have sufficient time to leave the scene before the bang.'

'You are thinking of a timer.'

'But it obviously can't be something that ticks,' Clive said. 'Nor can it be an obvious explosive. Anyone approaching the target is carefully searched.'

James considered for a few seconds. 'I don't see a problem.'

'You don't?' Baxter asked in surprise.

'Your man will need a good-sized bag, or an attaché case.'

'We can manage that. But you do realize that the bag will also be searched?'

James ignored what he clearly regarded as an unnecessary interjection. 'He should also be vain enough to touch up his hair from time to time.'

'Can do.'

'I will give you a bottle of what appears to be hydrogen peroxide, but into which I will introduce a certain catalyst.

This is not detectable by anything less than a complete chemical analysis. Now, this liquid is, by itself, entirely harmless in an explosive sense. If you spill it on your clothing, it will probably rot the material. It wouldn't do your hair any good either, if you actually used it. However, if a certain acid is introduced to it, there will be a very big bang indeed.'

'How big?' Baxter asked.

'The bottle I will give you would, if it went off here, destroy this room and everything in it.'

'Sounds perfect. But how is our agent to introduce the acid without going up with everything, and everyone, else?'

'This is the secret,' James said. 'The acid attacks glass, but cannot penetrate metal, and its penetration of glass is a slow and regular process. So it is carried in a metal container. The screw top has a pin. When your agent is ready to go, he presses on the top, the pin pierces the container, and the acid leaks. Please note that to avoid the risk of an accident, the pin must be pressed in very hard. Now, once this is done, if the container is placed next to the bottle, the acid will eat through the glass and, as I say, once it reaches the explosive liquid, it will go off. The carrier bag has to be written off, of course. I will give you an exact calculation, but off the top of my head, I would say it would take about half an hour to complete the penetration. If, as soon as the bag is placed, your man found it necessary to leave the room, say to go to the toilet, he would have that amount of time to remove himself far enough away from the scene to be safe, and indeed to remove himself from the area.'

Baxter looked at Clive. 'What do you think?'

'It sounds ingenious. But there is a caveat. As we told you, James, our man will be thoroughly searched – certainly any bag he may be carrying – before he will be admitted. The container for the acid will have to be commonplace and unremarkable.'

'That is hardly a problem,' James said, somewhat contemptuously. 'Just about every man carries a cigarette lighter.'

'And that will contain enough of the acid?' Baxter asked.

'Certainly.'

Again Baxter looked at Clive.

'Tell you what,' Clive said. 'Make it a lipstick and you're on.'

* * *

'You can't be serious,' Joe said, sipping wine. The two men were lunching together at the Café Royal. 'I thought you had something going for that girl.'

'I have more going for Anna than for anyone else in the world,' Clive said. 'But this is an order from the top. I have an idea you are going to be told to cooperate.'

'In writing her off.'

'That may not be unavoidable,' Clive said, and told him what James was preparing.

'That is still asking her to take one hell of a risk.'

'It's the best we can do. What I need is the use of your man Johannsson. Our communication chain has broken down, and Johannsson is already involved.'

'We don't aim to lose him.'

'There is no reason why you should. Didn't he make contact with Anna once before?'

'Yeah.' Joe played with his wine glass. 'You know, old buddy, if I told you that Johannsson wasn't available, you'd have no means of getting in touch with Anna; she wouldn't receive any instructions, or the bomb, therefore . . .' He gazed at his friend. 'But you won't buy that.'

'I'd hate to have to go over your head to Wild Bill. Anyway, she's already involved. If we don't give her positive instructions, and the necessary means to carry them out, God alone knows what she'll do, how far she'll stick her neck out.'

'Yeah.' Joe said. 'OK, you got him. Give me the stuff, and I'll take it across to Sweden personally.'

'Just remember not to fiddle with it,' Clive advised.

'There,' Himmler said. 'What did I tell you, Anna. Not content with dropping out, the Italians have now declared war on us. The effrontery of these people is amazing.' He raised his head as Anna, standing in front of his desk, made no reply. 'Is something the matter?'

'Ah . . . no, Herr Reichsführer. But is this not serious news?'

'As I said before, this will make it easier to deal with them.' He pointed with his pencil. 'I know what's bothering you: that your little friend Ratosi is now an enemy of the Reich.'

'Well,' Anna said. 'I am disappointed, of course.' There goes another contact, she thought. And Belinda, once she had recovered from her ordeal, had proved stimulating company.

'You are incorrigible. And a very naughty girl. But you may well be able to see her again. Did you not say she is a supporter of Il Duce?'

'Yes, she is. But Il Duce—'

'I know. At the moment he is a completely broken man. But you do not suppose that the Führer went to all the trouble of sending Skorzeny and a picked squad of commandos to pull him out of that mountain prison just for the sake of old comradeship. It is our intention to set him up in northern Italy with a new Fascist state. Frankly, I don't expect it to amount to much, or be of much value, but if Ratosi is an honest Fascist, I see no reason why she should not be welcome here.'

'It would be nice to see her again,' Anna said, wondering if Clive would be prepared to take the risk. But if he was not, she was completely cut off from any communication with London, while as she had heard nothing from Johannsson since their single meeting, she had no means of communicating with Washington either.

'Now,' Himmler said, 'it is time for you to go on your travels again.'

Oh, Lord, Anna thought. At such a time! 'To Geneva, sir?'

'No. We agreed that might be a little risky. You will go to Lucerne. The hotel is the Lakeview. I assume it overlooks the lake. Laurent will contact you there.'

'Will I again be Anna O'Brien?'

'No, no. That would be far too risky. This time you will be a Swedish lady. Anna Borkman.'

'Laurent will know who I am when he sees me.'

'Laurent is my agent, and absolutely trustworthy. The important thing is that no one, either inside or outside Germany, should know that you are the Countess von Widerstand, my PA. Or they might draw the obvious conclusion.'

How little you know, Anna thought. Neither that, to Laurent, you are just another client, not exclusive, nor that Goebbels is watching, and aware of, your every movement. But she said, 'Yes, sir. When will this be?'

'You will leave tomorrow, and he should come to you on Wednesday. But you are booked in for two days, just in case he is delayed. You will return here on Friday. Here are your passport, your tickets and your carte blanche. And, of course, the case.'

'Yes, sir.' Anna took the case; it seemed even heavier than the last. 'May I ask a question, sir?'

'Certainly.'

'It is only two months since my trip to Geneva. Where does all this money come from in so short a space of time?'

'Ah, well, we have greatly increased our arrests of Jews and undesirables. We have extended our net to cover all of Europe we control. That fellow Eichmann . . . Have you ever met him?'

'Yes,' Anna said, unenthusiastically. 'Here in this building.'

'Of course. And you did not like him. Few people do. But he is doing a splendid job of ferreting these people out. And getting hold of their money, eh?'

'Which is always brought here.'

'Well, of course. It is our responsibility.'

'Yes, but doesn't it belong to the state?'

Himmler regarded her for several seconds. Then he said, 'I would never like to think that you and I do not operate with one mind, Anna.'

I am a spy, and an assassin, Anna thought. Those may both be reprehensible professions. But I am not a common thief. 'I should like that also, sir.'

'Well, then, we understand each other, and you understand why this operation has to be carried out in the utmost secrecy. Always remember that you have a share in this. I am protecting your future.'

'I do understand that, sir. And I appreciate it.'

'Good girl. Now, take the rest of the day off and prepare for your trip. Essermann will pick you up at eight tomorrow morning. And I will see you on Friday night.'

'Yes, Herr Reichsführer. Heil Hitler.'

Anna took a taxi to her apartment building, the attaché case resting against her side. She paid the driver, stepped on to the pavement, and a voice said, 'Countess! How very nice to see you again. May I offer you a cup of coffee?'

She turned her head, feeling an immediate tension. 'Why, Herr Johannsson, I thought you had forgotten my existence.'

'No man could ever do that,' he said gallantly.

'Then I would love to have a cup of coffee.'

They sat together, and were served by Franz.

'What have you got there?' he asked. 'It looks big enough, and heavy enough, to hold all the secrets of the Reich.'

'Perhaps it does,' she agreed. 'Have you seen Steinberg?'

'Yes. He has a prospect. Do you know of this?'

'I have not seen him for a couple of weeks. I understand that he has been away from Berlin.' Or he would certainly have tried to return to my bed, she reflected.

'Yes. And as I say, he has come up with a prospective candidate. As to whether anything will come of it, I cannot say. But we are not going to wait.'

'Uncle Sam is getting impatient? I think I should remind you that I have two employers. And frankly, the other is the more important. Until I hear from them, I cannot become involved.'

'At this moment, Countess, you have only one employer.'

Anna gave him her most imperious stare. 'Then I think we had better terminate this conversation, and you can tell Joe that unilateral control was not part of the deal.'

She put down her coffee cup and started to rise, and he said. 'Belinda agrees with you.'

Anna sank back into her seat.

'It has been decided,' Johannsson went on, 'that this project is too big for rivalry. Thus from this moment, and until the project is completed, Belinda and Joe are as one.'

Anna continued to regard him for some seconds. Then she said, 'I am afraid I must ask for proof of that.'

'Suppose I were to say that Belinda's best friend is named Clive, who is now in charge of the project, and who sends you his everlasting love.'

Breath rushed through Anna's nostrils, and she knew she was flushing.

'Joe sends his as well,' Johannsson added.

'Herr Johannsson, you could grow on me. May I therefore presume that Belinda got back safely?'

Franz was hovering 'Two more coffees, please,' Johannsson said, and he went away again. 'Do you think he was listening?'

'I doubt it,' Anna said. 'Anyway, we haven't said anything incriminating yet.'

'And you reported our earlier meeting to your superiors.'

'Of course. I reported that I had been approached by a correspondent from the *Stockholm Gazette* for an interview, but that I refused. Now you are trying again.' She smiled. 'With no more success. They will suppose that you are falling in love with me.'

'That would not be difficult to do,' he said, seriously.

'Business before pleasure, Herr Johannsson. Tell me the reaction to Belinda's information.'

'It caused quite a stir. But they went for it. Especially as you are involved.'

Franz brought the coffee, and Anna stirred, slowly. 'What exactly are you telling me?'

'It seems that they did not realize that you might have access to the subject.'

'The word is "might", Herr Johannsson. I cannot guarantee it.'

'They have tremendous faith in you. They want you to take control, and carry the project through. I understand you have done this kind of thing before.'

Anna sipped; the initial tension was being replaced by a curious feeling of lightness spreading through her body. 'They wish me to join this group?'

'They do not wish you to become involved in the conspiracy until its success is guaranteed. But you need to communicate with Steinberg, certainly.'

'Yes,' Anna said thoughtfully.

'This link is important, because it is necessary to have the succession arranged before the event. Belinda will accept the Field Marshal as head of state, but this must be certain.'

'The Field Marshal laid down certain conditions.'

'I am sorry, Countess. They will accept no preconditions.'

'Not even a promise to negotiate with a non-Nazi government? They have done a deal with Badoglio.'

'Badoglio also was required to surrender unconditionally. This he did. Then he was offered terms. The people here will have to take the same risk.'

'And if they decide they cannot do that?'

Johannsson looked into his coffee cup. 'Then Belinda requires the task to be carried out without their assistance. In fact, they are placing the successful completion of this project in your hands, should the conspiracy fail.'

Anna was aware of a sudden chill. 'They never required this before. It was I who put the idea into their heads.'

'I know. Perhaps you should not have done that. Their information has always been that it is impossible to get to Hitler. But if you can . . .'

'So now they wish me to commit suicide,' she said bitterly.

'They do not believe it will come to that.'

'Tell me about it.'

'I have a present for you.' From his coat pocket he took a small parcel and placed it on the table.

'What is that?'

'It is simply a packet of – shall we say, feminine accessories. Now listen very carefully, because if you make a mistake, it could well be fatal.'

Anna listened as he told her the properties of the bomb, and how it was to be detonated. 'It could work,' she said, when he finished.

'It cannot fail, as long as you can access the Führer.'

'I told you, the word is "might".'

He frowned 'Are you not intimate with him?'

'I have never had sex with Hitler. As he values my services, we have been alone together on occasions in the past, but the last time was several months ago.'

'You do not have to be alone with him – just in an enclosed space with him, to magnify the effects of the explosion.'

Anna remembered her conversation with Goebbels. It was an obscenely unpleasant path to go down, but . . . 'It might be possible,' she said. 'I will need a little time to arrange it.'

'We accept that. But obviously the sooner it can be done, the better.'

Anna picked up the parcel and put it into her bag. 'And it was Joe and Belinda gave me this assignment.'

'Neither one likes what they have had to do, but they were obeying orders from the very top. However, if Steinberg does succeed in organizing something – well, you can give him this device.'

'How soon will we know if Steinberg has actually found someone?'

'I will see him before I return to Sweden. But you understand again that whoever it is will also have to be someone who can gain access to the Führer. That means a staff officer, or something like that. Finding one willing to take the risk may be a lengthy business.'

'So how long have I got?'

'They would like the job done by the end of the year.'

'Eight weeks. Are they that tied up with conventional dating?'

'I do not think so. It is just that there are very big plans for next year, and they feel that these plans would have more chance of success if Hitler were not about.'

'You are talking about the invasion.'

'I am not competent to discuss that, Countess.'

'Then tell me something else: what happens afterwards, supposing I succeed? The people around Hitler are not fools. No matter how many people are in the room when the bomb goes off, those who are not in the room will realize that I am the only survivor.'

'Yes, but with Hitler dead there will be utter chaos for several hours. That will give Beck time to take over.'

Once again, cloud cuckoo land, Anna thought. I am only to take executive action myself if Steinberg cannot provide someone else. But if Steinberg cannot provide someone else, the plot – his plot – will collapse. In any event, if I have to operate on my own, it would be even more suicidal for me to tell him in advance, so that he could notify Beck to stand by. At this moment she was a shadowy fringe figure, known only to Steinberg, and then only as a possible go-between to persuade Himmler to cooperate. Once she stepped out of the shadows, if anything went wrong . . .

Johannsson had been studying her expression. Now his hand moved across the table to hold hers. 'I will dream of your success. As I will dream of you, for the rest of my life.'

'You say the sweetest things. But I am not dead yet. And if this thing works, I may even survive. Ciao.'

The Summons

I f, she thought as she rode up in the lift. What a huge word. And time! She had been given two months. She had never been in this position before, and she didn't like being in it now. When the SD had planted her in London, in 1938, she had been told it was simply to gather information through her well-placed husband, Ballantyne Bordman, and the social circle in which he moved and into which she had been welcomed. When, in April 1940, she had suddenly been informed that it was necessary that Winston Churchill, who, the Nazi Government had felt, correctly, was their most dangerous enemy in Britain, should die, she had been told that it had to be done in a week. There had been little time to think about it. Fortunately, by then she had already joined forces with Clive and MI6, and they had sorted it out . . . just.

When she had been sent to Moscow, in the summer of 1940, as Personal Assistant to the Chief Secretary of the German embassy, her appointed task had been to seduce a prominent member of the Soviet government, again in search of information. And when, in the middle of June the following year, she had been told that her real task was the elimination of Stalin immediately before the German invasion began, she had been given just four days.

MI6 worked differently. They had given her several months to organize the death of Heydrich . . . but that had been with definite instructions that she was not to be personally involved. This time . . . And the ifs were far more numerous than even Clive, much less Johannsson, imagined. She could now have no doubt that Himmler would prove a broken reed in any violent change of government. But she also didn't know what his reaction might be, or, supposing the plot was successful, what might be the attitude of Beck to the Gestapo chief, who had to be about the most hated man in Germany. And only he and Hitler, amongst the Party leaders at any rate, knew of her parents' situation, and why they were there. If Himmler were to disappear, or die in a palace coup, her parents' fate might then rest in the hands of some obscure and fanatical SS officer . . . unless she could get to the Polish prison camp before news of what had happened in Berlin leaked out. As for Katherine . . .

Of course she had been given an out. She had always been given an out, save that the outs had always been theoretical. Not one of them had ever actually worked. Yet she had had to believe that they would. One had to hope. Therefore . . . empty her mind of what lay ahead until she had seen Steinberg again, and discovered if he really did have a volunteer for the mission. And meanwhile, listen to the two explosives clinking in her bag and wonder when she would be blown to pieces.

She couldn't take them with her to Lucerne. She locked them in her dressing-table drawer. It would have been too out of character for her to tell Birgit not to attempt to open the drawer, but she felt safe there because if Birgit did try to see what was inside, supposing she wasn't blown up, she would know that her mistress would spot the forced entry as soon as she returned.

'I hope to be back on Friday night,' she told the maid. 'Please try to behave yourself.'

'Oh, Countess,' Birgit protested.

Anna chucked her under the chin. 'I am only joking.'

Essermann was as always on time; she wondered if his whole life was so regimented, if his sex was a matter of twelve thrusts and then out, because that was all the time he would allot to that particular activity. But he was also as gallant as always. 'Seeing you always brightens the day, Countess.'

'You say the sweetest things,' Anna said. But as it was a dull day, she thought he might be right. As the only reasonable description the Swiss police could have of Anna O'Brien was that of a tall, handsome woman in a black dress – she had never revealed her hair outside of the hotel room until she had changed in Laurent's office, and she did not think the floor waiter would have wanted to become involved in what had, after all, been an illegal activity on the part of his Gestapo friends – she had today opted for the complete change she had adopted after meeting Laurent, wore a pink suit with deep side pockets in which a pistol would be entirely concealed, over a white blouse and a smart matching hat together with a cloth coat; this ensemble exposed her hair, but it certainly was a total contrast to how she had appeared on her last visit.

'I understand that I am to meet Friday night's train,' Essermann remarked, as they drove to the station.

'That is the idea.'

'So, will you be free on Saturday night?'

'As far as I know, yes. Is something happening on Saturday night?'

'I would like to take you to the opera. I saw you at *Lohengrin* last month, with Count von Steinberg.'

'Were you there?' One can't do anything in this goddamned city, she thought, without everyone knowing about it. But thank God she had already told Himmler. 'I never saw you.'

'I was in the gallery.'

'With your mistress?'

'With someone I would willingly have exchanged for you.'

'Ah! And Saturday is . . .?'

'*Rienzi.*'

'The would-be dictator of fourteenth-century Rome who was torn to pieces by a mob.'

'Ah . . . yes. I didn't know you were that up on Wagner.'

'I'm not. I'm that up on history. I wouldn't have thought that was an entirely appropriate subject, right this minute.'

'Oh, well, I don't suppose Il Duce will attend the performance. And it is one of the Führer's favourites. I believe it was the first opera he ever saw. Will you come?'

'Do you know,' Anna said, 'I think I will.'

Was he growing on her? she wondered, as she sat in the train heading south. He was both good-looking and admiring. So he was a Nazi, and as a member of the SD as guilty as herself of all their crimes. They had a great deal in common. But the main reason, she knew, was that she was becoming fed up with the repeated assumption of her superiors that she was a lesbian . . . and perhaps with the fact that, when she had to act that part, she enjoyed it.

This time her journey was uneventful. As the days were now drawing in quite rapidly, it was dark when she arrived in Lucerne, but the Lakeview was more comfortable than the Gustav. She had a late dinner and slept soundly, enjoying a lie-in the next morning, even if she wondered when Laurent would turn up. Until he did, her movements were hampered, as it would have been distinctly odd, for example, for her to go down to the bar or the terrace overlooking the lake carrying a very heavy attaché case – and she was not prepared to let it out of her sight. So she told the maid that she had a headache and would not be leaving her room that morning, but allowed her to make the bed anyway. That brought a visit from the housekeeper, who arrived with a bottle of aspirin. Anna accepted this, but said she would take the medication later. Then she sat and read a book, but at eleven o'clock there came a tap on the door.

After her experience in Geneva she was not prepared to take any risks. She placed her Luger in the pocket of her suit and left her right hand in the pocket, forefinger curled round the trigger, as she opened the door.

But it was Laurent, as flawlessly dressed and groomed as she remembered, carrying a briefcase and looking her up and down; she wasn't wearing her hat and her hair was loose. 'Fräulein Borkman, I believe,' he said. 'Or should I address you properly, as the Countess von Widerstand?'

Almost Anna's finger closed on the trigger. But it was the wrong place and the wrong time. And besides, Himmler had said this man was to be trusted, and was, indeed, trusting him with his life. So she stepped back, leaving her hand in her pocket. Laurent entered the room and closed the door. 'I apologize, Countess. It was too great a temptation to resist.'

'It was a very dangerous thing to do,' Anna pointed out.

'You mean you might have attacked me?'

'I mean I might have killed you.' She took her hand from her pocket, still holding the Luger.

He gazed at it, and then at her. 'Then it is all true.'

'I do not know what "it" is. But I would like you to tell me.'

'May I sit down?'

'Of course.' She indicated the settee, and he sat on it, his briefcase by his side. Anna sat in a chair opposite, next to the table, on which she rested the pistol, her hand beside it.

'And if you do not like what I say,' he suggested, 'you *will* shoot me.'

'Very possibly. I do not know what you are carrying in that case, or in your pockets.'

'I do not travel with a gun, if that is what you mean.'

'You have something to tell me,' Anna reminded him.

'The last time we met, your voice was soft. And you had just killed two men.'

'The last time we met I was prepared to regard you as a friend.'

'And you're not prepared to do that now?'

'I need to be convinced. Tell me how you discovered who I am, and what you have done with the information.'

'Well, if I may recapitulate: of course it was obvious to everyone who had done the shooting at the Hotel Gustav, even

if it was difficult to reconcile a double murder with a strikingly good-looking young woman – which was all anyone
knew about you – who had entirely disappeared. There was
not even a worthwhile description of you – just a name. But
there was a reported sighting of someone who could have
been you boarding a train for Germany. I believe the police
did make contact with their German counterparts, but they
got nowhere. Well, of course, they would not, would they?'

'You were with me at the station.'

'Who would look twice at me when they could look once
at you, Anna?'

'You have still not told me anything that I need to know.'

'I have friends in Germany, and I was fascinated. Well, you
know that. You fascinated me from the moment I saw you.
You fascinate me now, looking so much like the Angel of
Death, waiting to pounce. And with your hair like that – just
as on the platform in Geneva – you don't look a day over
eighteen.'

'You say the sweetest things. But you know, one of my
superiors once told me that it was an asset for a woman to
look older than her age, up to twenty-five. After that, it
becomes increasingly important to look younger, as long as
possible. Apparently one should aim to be permanently
twenty-three.'

'So how old are you, if I am not being impertinent?'

'You are being impertinent, but I shall forgive you. I am,
actually, twenty-three. Unfortunately, come next May, I shall
be twenty-four. There is not a damn thing anyone can do about
that, or about all the other Mays to come, supposing I am still
around to see any of them. But you have still not told me how
you found out my name.'

'Herr Himmler is not my only . . . associate in Germany. I
made inquiries. I mean, I knew you were a trusted emissary
for the Reichsführer, but that a young girl could calmly shoot
two men with two shots . . .'

'Actually,' Anna said, 'there were six shots, but the last two
were unnecessary.'

'And then to appear calmly immaculate in both dress and
demeanour in my office on schedule the next morning . . .'

'I was working,' Anna said, modestly.

'But where did you spend the night? I mean, you obviously

couldn't get rid of the bodies, and the police placed time of death at before midnight.'

'I slept in my bed, Herr Laurent. I do not like sleeping rough.'

'You . . .' He licked his lips. 'I don't suppose you have anything to drink?'

'Not handy. But I can have something sent up.' She picked up the phone, pressed 'Room Service'. 'Champagne suit you?'

'Thank you.'

Anna ordered a bottle of Veuve Clicquot. 'I am still waiting to be told something of importance, other than that you have studied the facts of that case.'

'Well, as I said, I have various friends in Germany apart from Herr Himmler, one or two in the Gestapo, and when I asked one of them if he knew anything of a quite beautiful young woman with lethal capabilities, he said without hesitation, "You are speaking of the Countess von Widerstand."'

'I see,' Anna said. 'What else did he say?'

'Only that you are a legend in the Secret Service. He said you had killed several times, for the Reich. He didn't know about the two men in Geneva, of course.' He paused. 'Can that be true?'

'Several times,' Anna mused, wondering if twenty-five came into the category of 'several'. 'I really have not kept count, Herr Laurent.'

There was a knock on the door, and she got up to admit the floor waiter. The bottle in the ice bucket was already uncorked, so Anna tipped him and herself poured, handing Laurent his glass.

'This is a new experience for me,' he remarked.

She raised her eyebrows. 'You have never drunk champagne before?'

'Not with a self-confessed murderess.'

Anna gazed at him, and he flushed. 'I do apologize. That was unforgivable. I should have said assassin. Or should it be executioner?'

Anna sat down again. 'I suppose it depends on whether you are looking at the subject from the point of view of victim or executive. Tell me what you propose to do with your knowledge.'

'Become your friend. Try to understand you – your motivation.'

Anna sipped. 'My motivation is that I serve the Reich. Once one has done that, at least in my profession, one cannot merely retire.'

'Are you saying that your profession is killing people?'

'I'm afraid it is – when I am told to do so; or when, as in Geneva, I have no choice. So, wouldn't you say that wishing to be my friend could be a highly dangerous thing to attempt?'

'Touché. But you know, Anna . . . May I call you Anna?'

'I can think of no reason why not.'

'And you must call me Henri. I would cheerfully risk my life just to – well . . .'

'Have sex with me.'

'Ah . . .' He flushed.

'Business before pleasure, Henri. There is a great deal of money to be counted, and converted. I think you should begin with that.'

Himmler studied the receipt. 'This is very satisfactory. This means there is more than a million US dollars in that account. Is that not splendid, Anna?'

'Indeed it is, Herr Reichsführer. Is the account in your name?' Anna asked, using her most innocent voice.

'No, no. You know nothing about international finance, my dear girl. One does not use names. One uses numbers.'

'But you know what the number is.'

'Well, of course I do.'

'And so does Herr Laurent?'

'Naturally.'

'And no one else?'

'Well, I suppose one or two of his most trusted clerks also know the number. But they don't know to whom it belongs. Only Laurent and I know that. And you, of course.'

'But I do not know the number.'

'You will, when the time is right. Now tell me, you had no trouble, this time, I hope?'

'No trouble at all, sir.'

'And did Laurent bring up the matter of the Geneva affair?'

'We concentrated on the business in hand, sir.'

'Excellent. I told you he was an utterly reliable fellow. Now you go home to bed. In all the circumstances, I think you

could take the weekend off. Spend tomorrow in bed. I will
see you on Monday.'

'Thank you, sir.'

Anna left the apartment, smiled at Albrecht – they were
getting to know each other quite well – and rode down in the
lift. She was, in fact, quite tired. Laurent had been in no hurry
to leave. In fact, as he had an office in Lucerne, into which
he had been able to pay the money immediately, and a flat in
which there was a complete change of clothes as well as
toiletries, he had stayed the whole two days. They had lunched
together, then made love all afternoon, then dined together.
Then she had gone with him to his flat and spent the night,
and the same pattern had been repeated. He had been quite
insatiable in his desire, almost reminiscent of Ewfim
Chalyapov in Moscow over the winter of 1940–41; the difference was that where Chalyapov's love-making had been all
aggressive, and often painful, masculinity, Henri had been a
perfect gentleman from beginning to end. He had been in awe
of her, certainly, as much, she felt, for her reputation as for
her beauty and sexuality when aroused, but he had never let
it get in the way of their essential equality, at least in bed.

In this he had reminded her of Joe Andrews, and had
been totally unlike Freddie von Steinberg, who knew nothing
of her true background – so far as she was aware – and yet
had been a trembling emotional mess. She refused to
compare any of them with Clive, because that was something entirely different. Clive was her psychological haven
far more than a sexual partner. But the fact was that seeing
Clive once in two years was not enough when her life was
being lived on an ever-increasing level of tension and potential catastrophe. So, after all, she was turning to her sex for
relief, something that would once have been unthinkable
for a convent schoolgirl.

Or was she actually, cold-bloodedly, creating that elite band
of supporters who would die for her? They all claimed that
they would, but did she dare believe any of them? And waiting
outside the door of the lift was another would-be Romeo, perhaps
the most dangerous of them all, but also possibly the most valuable. 'I assume the Reichsführer is pleased?' he inquired as he
escorted her to the car.

'I think so.'

'And I would be completely out of court if I asked what is it you do on these missions?'

Anna settled herself on the cushions. 'Yes, you would. But, seeing as how it is you, Hellmuth, I can tell you that I meet people and receive certain information, and bring it back to the Reichsführer. As the information is in code, and I do not have the key, I'm afraid I cannot tell you more than that. So you see, it is all very boring.'

'And never dangerous, I hope.'

'This last trip certainly was not.'

'And may I ask if you have decided to accept my invitation for tomorrow night?'

'I thought I had already done that. I am looking forward to it.'

'Excellent.' The car had stopped. 'Then may I come up for a nightcap?'

Anna considered. She really was very tired. And she had agreed to go out with him tomorrow night. But having adopted this course of action, she had no intention of offending him in any way: she had put him off too often in the past. 'A nightcap,' she said. 'If I am to be at all bright tomorrow, I must get to bed.'

'Ten minutes more of your company, Anna, and I will be a happy man.'

She led him into the lift, and he took her in his arms. She allowed him that, and a kiss, which was reassuringly tender. She wondered if he knew what she really did. But it seemed that everyone in the Secret Service knew that.

'Do you realize that you are every man's dream?' he whispered.

'But not all at the same time.' She disengaged herself as the lift stopped, and led him across the floor to her door. But she had only just inserted her latchkey when the door opened for her. She stared at Birgit, who had obviously been waiting on the other side.

'Oh, Countess,' Birgit said, and looked past her at Essermann's black uniform. 'Oh, Countess! Ohhh . . .' her gasp ended in a sigh and her knees gave way.

'Birgit!' Anna cried, catching her just before she hit the floor. Her brain raced. Birgit had never had a moment's ill health since coming to work for her, nor was she given to fainting fits. And that this was not real was instantly revealed by Birgit's fingers on her arm; the first squeeze could have been convulsive, but the next two were a signal.

Essermann knelt beside them. 'What is the matter with her?'

'I do not know. She has these fainting fits . . .'

'We had better take her inside. Let me help you.'

Another surreptitious squeeze.

'I think she needs seeing to,' Anna said. 'Hellmuth, would you go back down and tell the concierge to ring for an ambulance?'

Essermann hesitated. 'You mean to leave her lying there?'

'I think it may be best. We are always being told at first-aid class that it is often dangerous to cart people about when they suddenly collapse. It could be something internal.'

'Oh. Ah.'

'I will stay with her until you get back.'

'I'll be as quick as I can.'

He returned to the lift and the door closed. 'Tell me,' Anna said.

Birgit's eyes opened. 'Count von Steinberg . . .'

'Oh, my God! Here?'

'He insisted upon waiting for you, Countess. I didn't know what to do.'

'So you gave him a drink, I suppose. All right, Birgit. Thank you for warning me.' She frowned. But it would just have been a case of one boy friend running into another.

'The Count seems very agitated, Countess. And the Colonel is SD, like you. I didn't know if – well . . .'

Anna kissed her. 'You are very thoughtful, Birgit. You and I must have a little chat.'

They had had a little chat once before, when Joe Andrews had engineered things so that she and Clive could have a weekend together in his Virginia home. She had explained that Clive was really another SD agent who she had been sent to the States to contact and receive information from. Birgit had become wildly excited about being allowed to share such a secret. Now her instincts had made her feel that Anna would not like these two men to meet, at least in her apartment. Was that loyalty, intuition, or presumption . . . or something far more sinister?

She realized that the prevailing paranoia of Nazi society

was beginning to rub off on her, and stood up. 'In the mean-
time, stay just like that until Colonel Essermann returns.'

'What is the matter with me, Countess?'

'You just came over faint. Lots of people do, from time to
time. It may have been something you ate. You will have to
let the ambulance people poke you around for a little while;
then you can make a complete recovery.'

She squeezed Birgit's hand, and went into the drawing
room, where Steinberg was looking anxious. 'I heard a man's
voice . . .'

'Yes, you did,' Anna told him. 'He is a colonel in the SD,
and he is coming back.'

'He is your lover!' It was an accusation.

'Of course he is not' – yet, at any rate. 'Now tell me what
in the name of God are you doing here?'

'I had to see you. Something has happened.'

'Shit!' She could hear Essermann's voice. 'Get in the
bedroom, quickly.' She pushed him through the door, held him
close for a moment. 'Into the wardrobe,' she whispered. 'And
stay there until I let you out.' She closed the door and ran
into the bathroom, delving into the cupboard above the basin
to find a bottle of smelling salts, and returned to the drawing
room as Essermann entered.

'Anna?'

'I was looking for this.' Anna waved the bottle at him.

'I think she is coming to. This is a lovely room. But . . .'
He pointed at the obviously used glass: there was still a trace
of liquid in the bottom. He picked it up and sniffed. 'Schnapps!
I think your maid was drinking while you were away.'

Anna snapped her fingers. 'Of course! The little wretch! I
shall whip her.'

'I would like to help you. I have called an ambulance for
no reason.'

'Oh, Hellmuth . . .' She rested her hand on his arm. 'I am
so sorry. Believe me, I will make her squeal. You had better
go down and cancel the call.'

'I can do that from here. You have a telephone.'

'Yes, but the ambulance will already be on its way. You
will have to meet the men in the lobby and tell them it is a
false alarm.'

'Oh. Ah. Yes, I suppose you're right. I will come back up.'

'Hellmuth!' She was still holding his arm. 'You are a dear, sweet man. And I would love you to come back up. But I am absolutely exhausted, and I so want to enjoy tomorrow night. Could we leave it until then?'

'Leave what?'

'Whatever you wanted to do tonight.'

He gazed at her for several seconds. 'Is that a promise?'

'Of course it is a promise.'

He took her in his arms and kissed her on the mouth. 'I adore you.'

'You will adore me more after tomorrow night,' she promised.

Another kiss, then he released her and returned to the lobby. 'And this?' He nudged Birgit with the toe of his boot. She gave a little squeal and sat up.

'Oh, I am going to deal with her,' Anna said. 'I will beat her till she bleeds.'

'Countess?!' Birgit rose to her knees in alarm.

Anna pointed at the lounge. 'Get in there!'

Birgit gulped, scrambled to her feet, and hurried through the door.

Essermann kissed Anna again. 'You are even more beautiful when you are angry. Terrifying, but beautiful. Will you ever be angry with me?'

'I should hope not,' Anna assured him.

Birgit was shivering as Anna closed the door. 'Countess? Are you really going to beat me?'

'Of course I am not. It was necessary to get rid of him. But when he comes tomorrow night, be sure to limp and act as if you are in pain. Believe me, Birgit, I am enormously grateful to you. Now go to bed.'

'But . . . the Count . . .?'

'I am going to deal with him now.'

She returned to the bedroom, opened the wardrobe door. He almost fell into her arms. 'Anna—'

'Ssh.' She held him close, whispered into his ear. 'Don't speak. Take off your shoes and your jacket.'

He obeyed, started to release his tie.

Anna shook her head.

'But . . . aren't we . . .?'

'No, we are not. Get into bed.'

He slid beneath the sheet. Anna took off her own pink jacket, kicked off her shoes, and got in beside him. His arms went round her to hold her close. 'Anna—'

'I am not in the mood for sex,' she pointed out. 'Tell me what you are doing here, uninvited.'

'While you are bringing an SD officer home to your bed,' he said bitterly.

'What I do, and who I do it with, is none of your business. I happen to sleep with an SD officer every night of the year: me. Now tell me why you are here.'

'We have had a setback, which could be serious.'

She refused to allow herself to be agitated. 'Tell me.'

'I told you I thought I had found someone who would be prepared to act for us.'

'And you were mistaken.'

'Not in the man. He was prepared to commit murder. But when I told him who his target was to be, he refused. He is a staff officer in the Luftwaffe, and frequently takes reports to the Führer. He agrees with us that the situation is serious, but then said he could not consider breaking his oath of fealty.'

'Who did he think you were after?'

'Göring. He, and I gather many other Luftwaffe personnel, regard Göring as responsible for our defeats in the air, especially the Hamburg catastrophe in July.'

'And he supposed that assassinating Göring could change that?'

'I think there is a personal element involved.'

'So what happened when he declined?'

'When I mentioned Hitler, he became quite agitated. He said he did not wish to speak with me again, and went off.'

'You mean you let him go, after confiding your plans to him?'

'Well, what was I to do?'

My God! Anna thought. Now what am *I* to do? She had been becoming quite fond of this man, who was really only a boy stumbling through an adult world he did not understand. 'I need to know this man's name.'

'Conrad Freiling.'

'And you say he is a discontented Luftwaffe officer. What rank?'

'Major.'

'Why is he discontented?'

'He was recently passed over for promotion to colonel. He is sure the recommendation was quashed by Göring personally. They apparently were once at a party together and had a public difference of opinion.'

'Hm. All right. Now, you told him there was a plot to assassinate Hitler. Did you tell him who was in the plot?'

'Of course I did not. I am not a fool.'

You could have fooled me, Anna thought. 'But you must have given him some idea that the plot would succeed – after Hitler's death, I mean.'

'I told him we had the support of two very senior and important figures in the Reich.'

'But no names and no sexes?'

'Good God, no.'

'I see. Now Freddie, you do realize that you have taken a very grave risk. You must now have the courage to see it through.'

'I am not afraid.'

'I am sure you are not. But if this man betrays you to the Gestapo and they interrogate you, courage will not come into it, because you will soon be unable to tell right from wrong, good from bad, truth from falsehood. Please believe me.'

'What are you saying?'

Anna swung her legs out of bed, went to her shoulder bag, and took out the cyanide capsule she had taken from Belinda's bag. She knew that, much as she liked him, she should do a Bartoli and end it now. But she had never executed a man with whom she had had willing sex, and anyway . . . there was a chance . . .

She lay beside him again. 'Listen very carefully. You have made a very serious mistake. I am going to see if I can sort it out. If I cannot, and this man Freiling goes to the Gestapo and tells them what you proposed, you cannot afford to be arrested. As I warned you, mere strength, whether mental or physical, will not be sufficient to sustain you.'

'You think Freiling may do that?'

'Yes, I do. We can only hope that he has not yet done it. In which case I may be in time.'

'But . . . if they arrest me . . .'

'I have said, you cannot allow that to happen, or every one of your associates will be executed.' Including me, she thought.

'But . . . how do I avoid arrest?'

'You take this.'

She placed the capsule in his hand, and he raised it to look at it. 'This . . .'

'It would be unfortunate. But at least you will know that once you bite that you will never feel pain again. Nor will you betray your friends.'

He raised his head to stare at her. 'How did you get this?'

'I am an SD agent. I sometimes have to travel on secret business. Thus I am issued with a capsule. I understand what I have to do if I am ever captured by the other side.'

'But . . . we are working for them.'

'I work for the Reich, Freddie, and so do you. I have said I am going to do everything I can to sort out this mess. But if I fail, you must not let your people down.'

'Oh, Anna . . .'

'Promise me.'

'Yes. Yes, I promise. But Anna, as we are here, together, for perhaps the last time—'

She kissed him. 'Do you seriously think you could get it up? Listen, as soon as it is safe to do so we will get together again. Until then, trust me. As I am going to trust you.'

So, Anna reflected, as had been the case with Heydrich, everything was again sitting in her lap and, again as with Heydrich, there was no one to whom she could turn for either assistance or advice. She had to rely entirely on her skill at manipulating men. Even those men who considered themselves to be super-intelligent.

'Why, Anna!' Goebbels exclaimed. 'How very nice to see you. Do you know, I was just considering sending for you.'

Anna sat on that so-well-remembered settee and crossed her knees. 'I had expected you to send for me before, Herr Doktor. Or did I disappoint you?'

'You could never disappoint any man.' He sat beside her, his hand immediately resting on her knee, his fingers seeping under her skirt. 'But I have been so terribly busy, touring the country, talking with people . . . These air raids are becoming quite unacceptable. Every night! It seems as if they are trying to wipe Berlin off the map.'

Anna, who, like everyone else, had been forced to spend most of those nights in the cellar beneath her apartment block, was inclined to feel they were succeeding. The miracle was that her building had not yet been hit. But what a stupid situation, that the Allies should be trying to destroy the woman on whom rested most of their hopes for shortening the war!

'If we could reciprocate in kind it would be different,' Goebbels grumbled. 'But there are so many calls on the Luftwaffe, what we can do over England is nothing more than a pinprick.'

'Are you suggesting we could be losing the war, Herr Doktor?'

'Oh, good heavens no. Things will change as soon as our new secret weapons are operational. But I do not wish to talk shop. What brings you here? Or is it simply an insatiable desire again to have me inside you?' He pushed her skirt up to her hips to caress her thighs.

'Well, of course I wish you inside me, Herr Doktor. It was an unforgettable experience. But it so happens that something has come up, and I do not know who I can turn to, except you.'

'Do you not work for the Reichsführer?'

'Yes, I do. But . . .'

'You prefer to bring your personal problems to me. I appreciate that. And of course I will assist you in every way possible.'

'Thank you, Herr Doktor.'

'But while we talk, I would like to play with you. Take off your clothes.'

Anna obeyed. Now we can discover who has the greater powers of concentration, she thought.

Naked, she sat beside him and he began to stroke her. 'Now tell me your problem.'

'I have an acquaintance: Freddie von Steinberg.'

'Ah, yes, Freddie. An unstable young man. Do you sleep with him?'

'I have done so,' Anna said, cautiously, keeping her breathing under control as the fingers continued their exploration.

'Is he any good?'

'Not really.'

'I hope you do not confide any state secrets to him. As I say, he is an unstable fellow.'

'I have not confided in him, Herr Doktor. But he has confided in me. Men seem to like to do that,' she added ingenuously.

'I can believe that,' Goebbels agreed, playing with her nipples. 'What did he have to confide?'

'Something quite terrifying. He has a friend, or, I suppose I should say, had a friend, Conrad Freiling, a major in the Luftwaffe, who has approached him – you will not believe this – with a plan to assassinate the Reichsmarschall. Ow!'

The fingers had suddenly changed from stroking to pinching. 'Forgive me,' Goebbels said. 'You took me by surprise. I assume this Freiling has a reason for wishing to remove the Reichsmarschall?'

'There is apparently a long-standing feud between them, and Freiling feels that his failure to gain the promotion he thinks he deserves is because of the Reichsmarschall's dislike of him.'

'Plausible. I seem to remember that one or two American presidents were assassinated by disgruntled place-seekers.'

'Lincoln, possibly, Arthur, very likely, and McKinley, definitely. Someone also tried to do Roosevelt, a few years ago.'

'Good heavens! I had forgotten that you are a genius. Tell me, are you the least bit interested in what I am doing to you?'

Anna felt that she could allow herself a pant. 'Of course I am, Herr Doktor. My heart is pounding.'

Which was not actually a lie, as Goebbels ascertained by resuming holding her breasts. 'And what was Freddie's reaction to this plan?'

'Well, obviously he refused to have anything to do with it. But he is terrified. Freiling apparently told him that if he went down, he would carry Freddie with him by accusing him of everything he could think of, even of planning to assassinate the Führer.'

'He does sound a nasty piece of work. Anna, I can wait no longer. Go and bend over the desk.'

Shit! she thought. She had not yet reached the point she was after. But there was nothing for it, and he was, as before, mercifully quick.

'God,' he panted. 'Your ass is something to dream about.'

Anna was also indulging in some heavy breathing, mainly because her stomach had been repeatedly forced into the desk edge. But she had also moaned appreciatively, and not altogether falsely: she never faked her sexual responses. 'You say the sweetest things, Herr Doktor. May I straighten?'

'Of course.' He moved away from her and virtually collapsed on the settee. 'Did you . . .?'

What a question for a womanizer like Goebbels to ask. 'Don't you think I did, Herr Doktor? – with that huge weapon you possess.'

'I try to please. I will look into this Freiling fellow. He might just be dangerous.'

'Thank you, sir. I would not like Freddie to get into trouble. He is a harmless little man.'

'I will bear that in mind. Now, Anna . . .'

'Of course, Herr Doktor.' Anna picked up her camiknickers. Had she missed her opportunity? But she could not afford to do that. 'I trust the Führer is well?' she asked conversationally as she pulled on the garment.

'Now, you know he is not, Anna.'

'Oh. Yes. You said once that I might be able to help him.'

Without warning he seized her wrist and turned her round, pulling her down across his lap. She had to resist an overwhelming impulse to react violently and lethally; instead took refuge in a feminine squawk. 'What . . .'

She made to rise and he placed one hand on her back to hold her in place, while with the other he slapped her hard on the buttocks. 'Ow!' she cried.

'Are you that insatiable? For sex? Or is it really ambition?'

He hit her again, and Anna gave a cry of genuine pain. 'I only wish to serve the Reich,' she panted.

Another slap. 'Perhaps by replacing Fräulein Braun.'

'No,' Anna moaned. 'I would not dream of that. I only wish to serve the Führer.'

Goebbels took his hand away from her back and heaved her off his lap. She rolled over and sat heavily on the floor, immediately to gasp with pain and rise to her knees. 'If you went to the Führer, you would have to give him whatever he wanted,' he said. 'You might not enjoy that. Or do you enjoy sex in any form?'

Anna got to her feet. 'Does he also like to spank women?'

'I do not know what he likes. I do know that all men like different things. I think you *might* just be good for him. I will find out if he would like to receive you.'

'Will it be any time soon?'

'I cannot say. When I am with the Führer we usually discuss business, not sexual matters. Are you that impatient?'

'Well,' Anna said, 'it would be the greatest event of my life.'

'Indeed?'

'Oh,' she added hastily, 'I am sure the actual sex could not possibly compare with yours, Herr Doktor, but—'

'You are nothing but a whore, Anna. But a most delightful whore. I will get you into bed with the Führer, if you so earnestly desire it, and I hope you do not regret it. There is one condition.'

'Sir?'

'That you tell me everything that happens between you.'

'So that you can put it in your files? Do you keep a file on the Führer?'

'I think you should leave now, or I will give you another spanking.'

'Have you heard anything about this business?' Himmler asked, pushing the report across his desk.

Anna, standing in front of the desk, took the sheet of paper, and scanned it. 'Good Lord!' she commented. 'Can it be true?'

'This fellow Freiling must obviously be mad. What defeats me is that the Gestapo launched an investigation without reference to me, and "on information received". How can information on such an important matter as the assassination of the Reichsmarschall be "received" and I know nothing about it?'

'I would say, sir, that, like you, they regarded it as the idea of a madman and did not take it seriously enough.'

'They have taken it seriously enough to arrest this fellow.'

'Well, yes, sir, they would have to do that. I meant they did not take it seriously enough to refer it to you. Everyone knows how busy you are.'

'Yes,' he mused. 'I suppose you are right. Still, I would like you to look into it. Liaise with Essermann.'

'Certainly, sir.'

Himmler regarded her. 'I understand you and he are getting on well together.'

'Sir?'

'He takes you to the opera, does he not?'

'He has done so, sir.'

Himmler glanced at a note on his desk. 'Every week for the past month.'

'Good heavens. Is it that often?'

'And what do you do after the opera?'

'We generally have a late supper, then he takes me home.'

'And stays. Sometimes he stays the night.'

Anna assumed her imperious expression. 'Are you having me watched, Herr Reichsführer?'

'I would not like you to become excessively attached to anyone.'

Save you, she thought. 'May I remind you, sir, that it was you recommended we get together in the first place.'

'Certainly I did. I think every attractive young woman should have a beau, or at least an escort. But I also think that she should be circumspect. Have you slept with him?'

If I didn't loathe this man, Anna thought, I would worry about him. What does he suppose we do when Hellmuth spends the night? Play tiddlywinks? 'He is an attractive man, sir.'

'I despair of you, Anna. You are a complete wanton. Well, go and find him and see what you can discover about this business.'

Anna returned to her office and sent out a message for Essermann to come up to her. She was becoming increasingly agitated, as yet again she was completely cut off, not only from her English and American employers but now from Goebbels. It was a month since they had had their last meeting, and there had been no word from him. In another fortnight it would be Christmas, and her instructions from London had been to organize the death of Hitler by the end of the year. Organize, she thought bitterly. If they had no means of knowing that it had come down to her . . . She would have supposed that at least Johannsson would have been in touch, if not with her then with Steinberg, to discover how things were progressing. Of course he might have been, and been discouraged by what Freddie had had to tell him. But then, even more, London should have chased her up to find out what she was now planning.

Instead she was committed to keeping Freddie out of trouble. His name had not been on the brief report given to the Reichsführer. Perhaps that was Goebbels's doing – oddly, however unpleasant a character he was, she trusted Goebbels to keep his word more than anyone else in the government – and now that she had been placed in charge of the investigation herself, as she had been with Belinda, she should be able to bury Freddie's part in it . . . but not if she had to associate Hellmuth in her investigation. And she had received a direct order.

'I have looked into the matter,' he said, after receiving his briefing and returning the following day. 'As you suggested, the fellow is undoubtedly deranged. He has been locked up and is undergoing interrogation. Would you like to attend?'

Anna shuddered. 'God forbid.'

'I quite understand. But – well, you could just be involved.'

'How can I be involved? I have never met the man. I don't think I have ever seen him.'

'He is claiming that he is innocent, and that he was approached by Count von Steinberg to assassinate the Führer.'

'Freddie? He has accused Freddie? The bastard!' It did not appear that Goebbels had passed on the information that she suspected this was going to happen.

'You date him, don't you? – Steinberg?'

'I have dated him,' Anna said carefully. 'And I can assure you that he is the least likely person in Germany to wish to assassinate the Führer. Not only is he a profound Nazi, but he is afraid of his own shadow.'

'I entirely agree with you, certainly as regards the latter. I cannot imagine what you ever saw in him.'

'I did not *see* anything in him,' Anna said coldly. 'He invited me to the opera one night, some time ago, and I accepted. Are you by any chance attempting to claim proprietorial rights?'

'Of course not, Countess,' Essermnann said hastily 'It is just that, as he has been named, he will have to be investigated – however much you, and I, may regard the accusation as ridiculous. I would not like your name to come into it.'

'Then keep my name out of it. Freddie regards himself as

a man about town. If you intend to follow up on every woman he has ever dated, this investigation is going to take a very long time.' Her telephone jangled, and she picked up the receiver. 'Yes?'

'Are you alone?'

Oh, my God! she thought. Oh, my *God*! 'No, Herr . . . ah, sir.'

'Well, listen very carefully. Be at Rangsdorf Airport at six o'clock. Pack for one night. You will be returning tomorrow. Tell no one where you are going. Understood?'

Anna swallowed. 'Yes, sir.' What was he saying? How was she going to travel? 'Did you say "airport", sir?' She had never flown in her life, and she wasn't sure she wanted to start now. 'Cannot I go by train?'

'Train? Anna, you are not going to Berchtesgaden. The Führer is at Rastenburg, That is several hundred miles away, in Poland. Good fortune.' The phone went dead.

Essermann was gazing at her. 'Was that bad news?'

'Why should there be bad news?'

'I have no idea. But your cheeks went quite pale for a moment then. And now they are flushed. You are being sent somewhere.'

'Your powers of observation never cease to amaze me.' And alarm me, she thought. 'I was thinking. Perhaps I should have a word with Freddie before you or any of your heavies do so.'

'With what in mind?'

'There are two reasons. One would be to warn him against trying to involve me in any foolish plots into which he might have been sucked. And the other is that I think I can discover if there *is* a plot. I believe I can do this better than any of your people. He trusts me.'

Essermann stroked his chin. 'You will, of course, do as you think best, Anna. I think you may be taking a risk . . .'

'I do not take risks,' Anna pointed out. 'I am Personal Assistant to the Reichsführer and have his complete confidence. I am telling you what I propose simply because I wish you to understand. I wish you to trust me, as well, Hellmuth,' she added in her most winning tone.

'Of course I trust you, Anna. And I am very happy that you are confiding in me.'

'Thank you. It follows that, no matter what idiocies Freiling may utter, Freddie is not to be interrogated, or even questioned by anyone apart from me until I say so.'

'Well . . . if that is what you wish.'

Anna smiled at him. 'It will not take me more than a couple of days.'

Because after tomorrow it would not matter.

The Führer

I t was three o'clock. Anna left Gestapo Headquarters, had a hot bath, and dressed very carefully. It was cold out but she felt that she had to look as glamorous as possible, so she wore a silk dress over silk underwear and stockings, added her best jewellery, remembering that on their previous meetings Hitler had always appreciated her crucifix: he claimed to be a Roman Catholic himself. She would add her sable and its matching hat. She packed an exact change of clothing, altering the colour of her dress from blue to green for tomorrow, and also decided to take a silk nightdress; she did not normally wear clothes in bed, but she had no idea of Hitler's tastes. Then she carefully packed her shoulder bag. Obviously there could be no weapons on this trip, but the bottle and the lipstick were secured together with several thick rubber bands.

Birgit, popping in and out, was as silently curious as ever, but Anna felt called upon to make some explanation; they had grown steadily closer since the maid had saved the day on the first occasion Essermann had come up to the apartment. 'I shall only be away for one night,' she said. 'But it may be late tomorrow before I return.'

'Yes, Countess.'

Anna smiled at her. 'I am going to visit the Führer.'

Birgit's eyes grew large as saucers. 'Oh, Countess!'

'He has sent for me,' Anna said. 'I suppose he wishes to discuss aspects of my work. But listen. This is a private visit, which he does not wish publicized. Should anyone telephone from Gestapo Headquarters tomorrow morning to find out why I am not at work, tell them that I have a slight temperature and am spending the morning in bed, sedated, and cannot be disturbed. Tell them I will be in tomorrow afternoon.'

Birgit did not look convinced, and the taxi arrived at five fifteen. It was utterly dark, as the driver noted. 'Rangsdorf, Fräulein? Is it not a strange time to be flying?'

'You worry about driving,' Anna suggested, 'and I'll worry about flying.'

He relapsed into discontented silence, and they arrived at the airport at a quarter to six. Rangsdorf, a military airfield, was deserted, save for the security guards, but when they moved forward to check Anna's progress they were immediately joined by a man in a topcoat and slouch hat. 'Countess? Carl Rittner, at your service.' He picked up her valise. 'If you will come with me.'

The guards melted away, and Anna followed her escort through the building and on to the tarmac. A cold breeze was blowing, and she hugged her coat tighter around her shoulders.

'You are carrying no weapons, I hope, Countess,' Rittner remarked as they walked towards the waiting aircraft, which she saw was a twin-engined, long-bodied, Heinkel 111. She had a sudden flutter of butterflies in her stomach: although she had seen airplanes from time to time, as she had told Goebbels, she had never flown; in fact, she had never been close to an aircraft.

'Why should I be carrying a weapon, Herr Rittner?'

'There is no reason. But you understand that you will be searched very thoroughly when you arrive at Rastenburg.'

Ugh, Anna thought, remembering Belinda. 'I understand.'

They reached the plane, where a mechanic waited beside a short flight of steps up to the door; the two pilots were apparently already on the flight deck. The mechanic assisted her up the steps and showed her to her seat, himself fastening the belt round her waist. Then he pulled up the steps and closed the door. 'Shall I take your bags, Fräulein?'

'You may have the valise,' Anna said. 'But I will keep this one. May I ask how long is the flight?'

'Approximately three hours.'

'Three *hours*?'

'It is a long way. You have flown before?'

'No.'

'Ah. There is nothing to be afraid of. It is a clear night with only scattered cloud.' He seated himself behind her.

'Should I not have a parachute?' Anna asked.

'We are not going into combat,' he pointed out.

Anna settled herself, and the engines were started. A moment later they were hurtling down the runway and lifting into the night sky. Her stomach rose rapidly into her chest and then slowly went down again. She was on her way to the Führer.

As the mechanic had promised, the flight was monotonously uneventful apart from the odd bump. Anna found herself nodding off, until the plane suddenly started to descend. She saw a row of lights beneath them marking the runway, and realized that she was going to be landing in a clearing in the middle of a large forest. The airstrip was well protected by watchtowers, although there didn't seem a great deal of room. But a few moments later they were down, and the door was being pushed back. 'That wasn't so bad, was it?' the mechanic asked.

He obviously had no idea who she was, personally, but she had deduced from the matter-of-fact manner in which he had both greeted her and treated the whole flight not only that he had made this journey often but that more often than not he had had a female passenger. 'It was not bad at all,' she agreed, and clambered out, her skirt blowing in the chill breeze. Below her there waited several men, and one of these took her valise. She remained in charge of the shoulder bag, as she was hurried to a waiting car. No one said anything, and a few minutes later she was bouncing along a somewhat uneven roadway through the trees, seated next to an officer who had also not said a word. So she decided not to speak either; she was clearly expected.

The drive took about fifteen minutes, then a fence loomed out of the darkness. A gate was opened for them, and a little further on there was another checkpoint. A further short drive and she saw a group of buildings. These were entirely blacked out, but when the car stopped before the largest of them, outside which there were two armed sentries stamping their feet in the snow, a door was opened for her and she was ushered into a glowing cavern of light, and of warmth as well.

There were about a dozen people, men and women, all in uniform, gazing at her. Behind them were various doors to obvious offices. 'Through there, Countess,' invited the officer who had accompanied her in the car. Anna went through the doorway indicated into an antechamber containing a desk, a long table against the wall and several chairs. The officer followed her and placed her valise on the desk. 'Please wait,' he said, and left, closing the door behind him.

Anna supposed she was being overlooked all the time, so merely strolled around the room, feeling the heat slowly getting through her clothes and into her body. Then the door opened again, and a man in a white coat, another man wearing civilian clothes, and a woman in secretarial uniform entered. 'I am Morell,' the first man announced.

Anna inclined her head; she had deduced that he had to be Hitler's personal doctor, regarded by most of the Party as a dangerous quack but apparently considered indispensable by Hitler himself.

'And these are Hermann, the Führer's valet, and Frau Engert, the Führer's chief secretary.'

Anna had met Frau Engert before, once, when she had attended the Chancellor's office in Berlin, in 1941. She had rather liked her, then. She was not so sure, now. But she wanted to be friendly. 'I suppose you have forgotten me, Frau Engert,' she suggested.

'You are not an easy woman to forget, Countess. Shall I help you with your clothes?'

Anna glanced at the valet, but he obviously had no intention of leaving, was opening her valise. She sighed, took off her shoulder bag and laid it on the desk, then took off her gloves and hat, followed by her sable. Frau Engert stroked the fur as she laid it across a chair, and then carefully folded Anna's dress across the back of the chair. Anna waited, and the secretary said, 'Everything, please, Countess.'

Anna handed her her camiknickers, stepped out of her shoes, and sat down to roll down her stockings.

'What's this?' Morell asked. He was holding the bottle of peroxide.

Anna took a deep breath, but that could have been because he was looking at her and she was naked. 'It is peroxide, Herr Doktor.'

Morell looked at her pubes. 'Are you saying that you are not a natural?'

'I am a natural,' Anna said, 'but I have been finding grey streaks in my hair, and I do not like this.'

Morell looked at Engert, who nodded. 'I am afraid that is a concomitant of the life the Countess has been forced to live.'

'I am told that you are only twenty-three, Countess.'

'I'm afraid that is true, Herr Doktor.'

'Then I am sorry for you. And why is it bound to your lipstick?'

'They rattle so,' she explained.

To her great relief he replaced them without unscrewing the bottle, but then picked up her real lipstick. 'Two lipsticks?'

'I like to vary the shades.'

He made no comment, replaced the tube and closed the bag. But her ordeal was only just beginning. 'Will you lie on the table, please – on your face.' He pulled on a pair of thin rubber gloves.

Anna climbed on to the table and lay on her stomach, her chin resting on her hands. Frau Engert stood by her head. 'Just relax, Countess,' she recommended. 'It will not be so bad.'

Anna felt her buttocks being pulled apart, but at least he seemed to have coated the gloves in some kind of lubricating jelly. 'Does he suppose I carry a gun up there?' she asked.

'This is as much a medical examination as a body search,' Engert explained. 'There can be no risk of any sexually transmittable disease being given to the Führer.'

'How insulting can you get?' Anna remarked, and received a smart slap.

'Roll over,' Morell commanded.

Anna obeyed, and saw with relief that he was donning a fresh pair of gloves.

This examination took longer, probably, she reckoned, because he found it more interesting. 'You have been married, Countess,' he remarked.

'That is correct, Herr Doktor,' Anna agreed, keeping her breathing under control.

'How many children did you have?'

'I have no children.'

'You mean you are sterile.'

'I mean that I have always taken precautions not to become pregnant.'

'Ah, the post-coital douche, no doubt. It is not infallible. And since the dissolution of your marriage . . . When was this?'

'I do not know the exact date. The divorce was heard in England, in my absence. But it was about three years ago.'

'How many lovers have you had since?'

'I will have to think . . .' At least he had taken his fingers away and was stripping off these gloves as well. Clive, Massenbach, Chalyapov, Joe Andrews, Steinberg, Essermann, Laurent . . . and, of course, Heydrich and Goebbels. 'Nine.'

'In three years? You are wanton.'

'It goes with my job, Herr Doktor. I have also been raped.'

He snorted, and touched the blue mark on her right rib cage. 'And this?'

'A bullet wound, Herr Doktor. Being shot also goes with the job.'

'And you are fully recovered?'

'It was four years ago.' As he was no longer touching her, she sat up. 'May I get dressed now?'

'You may put on a nightdress. Frau Engert.'

Engert waited until Anna had dropped the nightdress over her head. Then she said, 'Through here, Countess.'

Anna was aware of more anxiety than she had yet felt throughout the whole traumatic evening, as she followed Engert through another doorway into a somewhat Spartan bedroom, presently unoccupied. Hermann brought in her two bags and placed them on the table, then left. 'Have you eaten?' Engert asked.

'Not since lunch.'

'You must be starving. I will have something sent in to you. I'm afraid it will not be very good: Frau Exner has been dismissed. You have met Frau Exner?'

'I'm afraid I have not had that privilege.'

'Ah. She was the Führer's favourite chef. Such a nice young woman. But then Herr Bormann discovered that she had a Jewish grandmother. You have met Herr Bormann?'

'That is another privilege I have not yet enjoyed.'

Frau Engert glanced at the closed door. 'It is not necessarily a privilege. Just remember that he has the Führer's complete confidence.'

'So what happened to Frau Exner, after she fell out with Herr Bormann? Was she sent to a concentration camp?'

'Oh, no. The Führer does not condemn those he regards as his friends.'

That was reassuring.

'She and her entire family were pensioned off,' Frau Engert said, 'and made honorary Aryans. Not that that will interest you, as you are so clearly an Aryan. Now, you realize that we do not serve meat here. Or wine.'

'Oh.' Anna had been thinking in terms of a steak and a bottle of burgundy. 'Of course. Ah . . .?'

'I cannot say when the Führer will attend you. He invariably works most of the night. He may come in about dawn.'

'May?'

Engert shrugged. 'It depends on what reports are received over the next few hours. If there is a crisis, he may work longer than usual.'

'What happens if he does not come at all?'

'Why, Countess, in that case you wait until he does come. Good night.'

Shit, Anna thought. She had given Birgit no instructions for dealing with a second day's absence. On the other hand, even if Himmler insisted on being told the truth, there was nothing he could do: she had been summoned by his master. But she could not resist a last riposte. 'You mean I am allowed to sleep?'

Engert had gone to the door. She looked over her shoulder. 'Of course, Countess. The only thing you are not permitted to do is leave this room.'

'I cannot go the night without using a bathroom.'

Engert pointed at an inner door. 'The bathroom is through there. You should clean you teeth as well, before retiring. The Führer values cleanliness above all other virtues.'

And yet continues to employ people like Morell, Anna thought. And Bormann.

'I will wish you success,' Engert said, and closed the door behind herself.

There was nothing to do but wait. Certainly Anna could not afford to anticipate. Her supper was served by Hermann and she ate without enthusiasm: it was an unsalted and virtually tasteless plate of vegetables. She cleaned her teeth, made sure she was sweet-smelling all over, debated taking off her nightdress but decided to leave that until his arrival, got into bed and was asleep in minutes – to awake with a start as the door opened.

Hitler stood above the bed, looking down at her. He was almost exactly as she remembered him from their last meeting: the dark hair brushed so that a lock drooped over his eye, the little moustache, the oddly placid features which she knew could become distorted with passion, the black trousers and brown jacket, with the single decoration of the Iron Cross First Class – honestly and gallantly won, as she knew, as a despatch rider in the Great War. Of his health problems there was no immediate sign, save for the lack of colour in his cheeks. She sat up. 'My Führer! I am sorry I was asleep.'

'Why should you be sorry, Anna? What did Queen Isabella of Spain say were the four finest sights in the world?'

Anna got her brain into gear. 'A soldier in the field; a priest at the altar; a beautiful woman in bed; a thief on the gibbet.'

'There! You are a treasure. I should have sent for you long ago. But there have been so many things that needed doing – armies moved from here to there, incompetent generals to be replaced . . . Have you slept with Goebbels?'

Anna remembered from their previous meetings his disconcerting habit of suddenly interjecting a question into the conversation.

'There is no need to be embarrassed,' Hitler said. 'The good Doctor has slept with just about every worthwhile woman in Germany. Besides, he told me about it. Was he as good as he thinks he is?'

'He is very large,' Anna conceded, cautiously.

'And that is important to you.' He turned away and began to undress.

'The size of a man is immaterial, my Führer. It is what he does with what he has, before, during and after, that is important.'

He turned back to face her, naked. 'And if he cannot do . . . anything he might wish to?'

He was certainly somewhat small and not revealing any great enthusiasm. Anna swung her legs out of bed, got up, and took off her nightdress. 'There can still be pleasure in it.'

She made to take him in her arms, and he held her away. 'My Führer?' She was genuinely alarmed.

'I wish to look at you.' And now at last there was a twitch. 'So much beauty. So much perfection.' He touched her, lightly, his forefinger circling her left nipple before sliding on to her stomach. 'You make me think of Eurynome.'

'Sir?'

'You have not heard of Eurynome? There, you see: you are not infallible. Eurynome was the Pelasgian goddess of Creation. She emerged from Chaos, naked, long-limbed, long-haired and utterly beautiful, and danced her way across the Heavens. But her passage through space and time created the North Wind, Boreas, who took the form of a gigantic serpent, Iphion, who – I quote the myth – became lustful for the beautiful goddess, and wrapped himself around her thighs. From their union there came earth and water, and all living things. You'll note the resemblance to Adam and Eve, and their serpent, although I must confess I find the Pelasgian myth slightly more stimulating.'

And I must blow this man to pieces, she thought, who *is* a monster however pitiable. But not for a few hours yet. 'I am here to please you, my Führer. You have but to say what you wish.'

'What I wish,' he muttered, and sat on the bed. He did not appear to have noticed the wound. Or perhaps he had read her file.

But the problem remained. She sat beside him. 'When one is exhausted, it can take time.' She took him in her arms, and he turned to her. They fell across the bed together. But half an hour later nothing had been accomplished, although they were both dripping sweat. Then he pushed her away. 'Do you know the real reason I have not sent for you before now? It is because I feared that not even you would succeed. And I knew that the man who could not make it with you naked in his arms has no right to call himself a man.'

'Oh, my Führer,' she protested. 'Of course that isn't so.' But he was definitely agitated. 'Will you settle for half a cake?'

'What do you mean?'

She slipped off the bed and knelt between his legs.

'How can you hope to make me ejaculate if I cannot erect?' he asked.

'Erection is not a necessity,' she assured him, and only a few moments later proved her point.

Hitler lay back across the bed, panting. 'You are a treasure,' he said again, 'an absolute treasure. Now tell me, how much do you know about these conspiracies?'

'Sir?' She was taken completely by surprise, by the question itself, and at such a time as she had supposed him exhausted.

'You're not going to tell me you don't know what is going on? You work for the SD.'

Think, God damn it. Did it matter what she told him, if within a few hours he was going to be dead? But what he might do in those few hours . . . 'Yes, sir. I know there is something going on. Herr Himmler is investigating it. In fact, he has given me some names to work on myself, when I get back to Berlin.'

'He knows you are here?'

'No, sir. It is just that the job was given me. For tomorrow.'

'Is General Oster on your list?'

'General Oster, sir? I understand he has been retired.'

'He was sacked by Admiral Canaris, from the Abwehr. Officially for incompetence. But my private information suggests otherwise. I wouldn't be surprised if Canaris was involved as well. In fact . . . I am going to disband the entire Abwehr. They have proved utterly useless. I am going to merge them with the SD. Does this please you?'

'Well, sir . . .' Anna had no love for the Abwehr, who, unaware that she was SD, had once arrested her. 'If you think it is best.'

'Yes. It will be best. But I would prefer it if you did not confide that to Himmler for the time being. And I would like you to keep me informed of the progress of your investigation, Anna. I want names. I will send for you again soon, and you will bring me a list. Now leave me. I need to sleep.'

'You would not like me to be here when you wake up?' Anna was not entirely sure what she wanted the answer to be.

'If you were here, I would attend to no more business, and we could well lose the war. A car will take you to the airstrip, and the plane is waiting for you.' He squeezed her hand. 'You have made me very happy.'

Anna kissed him, dressed herself, and went into the bathroom. Now she had to be her ice-cold working self, and give not a thought to the unhappy man lying on the bed. At least she had made him happy, however temporarily. She renewed her make-up and brushed her hair, then made sure that the false lipstick was still securely fastened to the peroxide, and carefully punctured the top. Instantly liquid oozed out and on to the glass. She fastened the bag, and returned with it to the bedroom. Hitler was already asleep, snoring faintly. Anna stood by the bed for a moment, looking down at him. But now her emotions were entirely under control.

She placed the bag on a chair beside the bed and left the room, carrying her valise. Hermann was seated in the antechamber, and rose at her entry. 'The Führer . . .?'

'Is asleep and does not wish to be disturbed. He said there would be a car waiting for me.'

'Of course, Countess.'

She gathered this was a regular routine. As she reached the car, she was joined by Engert. 'Is he happy?'

'I think so,' Anna said, and seated herself.

'Then I will not again wish you good fortune,' Engert said, closing the door, 'because yours is already made.'

She stepped back, and the car moved away. Anna looked at her watch. It was only five minutes since she had punctured the bottle. Fifteen minutes to the airstrip, another five to be airborne. Then she would be beyond anyone's reach, and as she had no doubt there would be complete confusion following the explosion, she would be in Berlin well before anyone got around to wondering just what had caused the explosion . . . and how.

Then . . . She had not been in a position to alert Steinberg as to what she was going to do. But she had established that she would be interrogating him the moment she returned. He would then have to contact Beck and set the coup in motion. Until then, again, there should be no thinking, even about what Hitler had said – no brooding, no anticipation.

The airstrip was in sight, with the waiting Heinkel. But . . . 'What is that noise?' she asked the driver.

He looked in his mirror. 'It is a motorcycle, Fräulein.'

'Following us?'

'I believe so, Fräulein. Shall I stop?'

'No. Go on. It cannot be important.'

But of course the motorcyclist would catch them up before she could gain the plane. Her throat was dry, her stomach light. She could not imagine what had happened. There was another ten minutes before the bomb was due to explode. Had Hitler woken up and looked into the bag? The thought of being dragged back to face him after what had happened between them . . . But had she an alternative? She had no weapon, and for this trip she had carefully not packed her capsule; it would certainly have been found when she was searched and would have aroused suspicion – would any woman, summoned to share the Führer's bed, travel with a suicide pill?

Now . . . The car stopped, and the door was opened for her. 'Fräulein!'

Anna had to make a mental effort to move her legs. She got out, and the motorcycle pulled to a halt beside her.

'What is the matter?' the officer demanded.

The rider saluted. 'I have something for the Countess von Widerstand.'

The officer looked at Anna.

'I am the Countess von Widerstand,' she said. If she was about to die, no doubt horribly, she was determined to do so with dignity.

The rider reached into the side pocket of his machine and produced her shoulder bag. 'You left this behind, Countess.'

Anna took the bag, slung it on her shoulder, and climbed into the plane. The temptation to throw it away was enormous. But that would have been an admission of guilt, and to die quickly in a sudden vast explosion was infinitely preferable to what would seem a lifetime in a Gestapo torture chamber followed by a slow hoisting from the floor, her naked body wriggling and kicking – just as she had described to poor Bartoli, she remembered. Talk about being hoist with one's own petard. So, think of the bomb against her shoulder as the capsule she did not have; death would certainly be instantaneous.

But what would happen then? Would anyone ever know exactly what had happened to the aircraft, which was now taxiing to the end of the runway? She doubted there would be many pieces left to be picked up. In fact, would anyone outside the inner Nazi circle ever know that anything had happened at all? Clive and Joe certainly would be left entirely in the dark: their prize agent, and possession, would simply have disappeared without trace. Goebbels and Himmler might shed a crocodile tear; perhaps even Hitler would mourn her, briefly. Essermann she felt might genuinely regret her demise. Laurent would consider her as a ship that had passed in the night, pausing only just long enough to give him an unforgettable experience. And all of the beauty she possessed, all of her mental ability, her physical skills, would be gone to perdition.

As for the fate of her family, that did not bear consideration. The plane was now airborne, winging its way into the bright morning sky, following the path of the still rising sun. She looked at her watch: she had left the bedroom twenty-five minutes ago. Five minutes left. She gazed at the back of the mechanic's head: this morning he was sitting in front of her. He seemed utterly relaxed, utterly confident. But why should he not be, as he was only doing what he had done so many times before?

But . . . Why not shout in his ear that if he wanted to live he should allow her to throw something out? But that would be tantamount to signing her own death warrant; she could not hope to take over the plane: she had no idea how it worked.

She realized that she was holding her breath, let it go in a rush, and again looked at her watch. Too late! Thirty-one minutes! But she was still alive! Well, she supposed it was impossible to achieve spot-on accuracy with a device like this. But . . . She found herself staring at the second hand, proceeding slowly on its way, round and round . . . The temptation to look inside the bag was enormous. But she dared not, at this moment. Besides, what did she want to find?

Another five minutes passed, and she realized that the device had failed. How, she had no idea. But she was going to live! An enormous glow spread through her body. On the other hand, Hitler was also going to live. Suddenly her euphoria was tempered by anger. As with the assassination of Heydrich, London's elaborate plans had come to nothing, because of the inadequacy of their weapons, and she had been exposed not only to terminal risk but also to a sexual experience she could have done without. Now . . . Hitler knew something was going on. And, like Himmler, he expected her to do something about it. Because she was his most trusted aide. And she had no means of contacting London! As for Freddie – should she warn him to call the whole thing off, or solidify her position with the Führer by arresting him and forcing him to confess and name names? To secure her future and that of her family . . . and to damn herself through all eternity.

The aircraft was descending, and she caught her breath. However aware she, and every other Berliner, had been of the immense blows the RAF had rained on the city almost every night for the past six weeks, their concept of what was happening had been limited by what they had been able to see or hear from the ground. This was a bird's-eye view, and wherever she looked there was nothing but devastation. From the smoke still rising on the still winter air, she knew there must have been another raid last night, while she had been in the relative safety of Rastenburg.

There were craters on the runways at Rangsdorf, but the pilot brought the machine down safely, and a car was waiting on the tarmac. As before, her escort did not speak, merely held the door for her. She sank on to the cushions, gazed at the shattered buildings and rubbled streets as she was driven to . . . 'Is my apartment building damaged?' she asked.

'I'm afraid it is, Countess.'

Shit! she thought. Talk about disasters. She saw what he meant when they rounded the last corner, and she looked at a fresh pile of rubble. The building itself still stood, but part of the roof had collapsed into the street, and workmen were boarding up the shattered windows of the lower apartments. She picked up her valise and went into the lobby. 'Countess!' the concierge said. 'It is good to see you back.'

'Tell me that it is good to be back,' Anna said. 'Is my apartment still there?'

'Oh, it is still there,' he assured her. 'But all the apartments have been damaged.'

'Fräulein Birgit?'

'I do not think she is hurt.'

Anna went to the elevator. 'That is not working,' the concierge said. 'I am sorry, Countess, but there is no electricity.'

Anna made a face and began to climb the stairs. Fit as she

was, she was exhausted, more emotionally than physically, she knew. She reached the sixth floor, opened the door, and Birgit came running from the kitchen to throw herself into her arms. 'Countess! Oh, Countess!'

Anna hugged her. 'Are you all right?'

'Oh, it was terrifying! I thought I was going to die.'

Anna released her. 'But you didn't, did you? Always look on the bright side.' She went into the lounge, gazed at the shattered windows over which a workman was busy nailing some boards, at the sideboard which was a litter of broken glass, filling the room with the odour of alcohol, and then up at the crack in the ceiling; there were four more apartments above hers.

'A man was here from the Gestapo,' Birgit said. 'He said that the building is not safe, and we should move out. But I refused, until you returned.'

'You told him I was away?'

'Well . . .' Birgit licked her lips, anxiously.

'Of course you had to,' Anna agreed. 'He could see I wasn't here.' She went into her bedroom. Here too the window had been shattered, but the wardrobe, and thus her clothes, seemed undamaged. And the bathroom was untouched. But there was no water. 'Damnation,' she said. She desperately wanted a bath. 'All right,' she said. 'It looks as if we will have to move out. Pack my things up, and yours, and wait here. I will make arrangements and come back for you.'

'Oh, Countess, do you think we could leave the city?'

'I doubt that will be practical, right now. But I will see if I can find somewhere safer for us to live. Now leave me.'

Birgit closed the door. Anna opened her shoulder bag, inhaled the strong smell of the acid. The lipstick had certainly been punctured, and the acid, as predicated, had spread everywhere, ruining her toiletries. But it had only scarred the glass bottle. What a fuck-up!

She emptied the remaining acid down the toilet, bundled the shoulder bag and its contents up in the sheet, which was covered in plaster from the ceiling in any event, and stuffed them into the dirty-clothes hamper; she did not suppose Birgit would waste her time delving into that while packing in a hurry. Then she repacked the valise with her office uniform, her Luger and her spare jewellery. 'I will be back for you, hopefully, in a couple of hours,' she said. 'Please be ready.'

She went down the stairs and to the gymnasium, picking her way through the rubbled streets. It was just coming up to ten, and Stefan was surprised to see her at that late hour. But he was also delighted, and hastily dismissed the three other young women he had been working out. 'Countess!' He peered at her. 'Are you all right?'

Anna undressed. 'Do I not look all right?'

'You look . . . agitated.'

'I have every reason to be agitated. I have been bombed out of my home.'

'My God! But you are unharmed. And a good workout is the best answer to jangled nerves.'

'My nerves are not the least bit jangled,' Anna snapped, both irritably and untruthfully. 'And I have no desire to work out. I wish to use your shower, and then I must get to my office.'

As usual, he followed her into the shower stalls. 'Where is it going to end?'

'I don't think it is something you wish to think about,' Anna recommended, and turned her face up to the flowing water.

'Anna!' Himmler as usual looked about to embrace her, but as usual thought better of it at the last moment. 'I did not expect you in today. I have been so worried. They told me your building had been hit, but the man I sent along to see if you were all right could not find you.'

'The water main burst,' Anna explained, fudging the time issue, 'so I went along to the gymnasium to work out and use their shower.'

'Good heavens! What dedication!'

'What I now need,' Anna pointed out, 'is somewhere for me and my maid to live.'

'Ah! Yes. Quite. I had been planning on moving you anyway, in view of these continuing raids. I want you to be safe, Anna.'

'I would like that too, Herr Reichsführer.' She was in a thoroughly abrasive mood.

'So I have had an apartment prepared for you, downstairs. You will be absolutely safe down there. Nothing can possibly get to you, and even if the building were to collapse, there is a solid concrete floor – or roof, I suppose.'

Anna nearly exploded herself. 'Did you say *downstairs?* You mean, under this building?'

'It is the safest place.'

'How do I breathe?'

'Oh, there is constant air conditioning. Several of our leading people have moved down there already.'

You are turning me into a troglodyte, Anna thought. She had always valued fresh air more than most other things. And how would the air conditioning work if the building did collapse on top of it? 'How long will I have to live there, sir?'

'Until – well, things have been sorted out. In that regard, I wish you to take another little trip for me.'

Oh, shit, she thought. She needed time to think, and hope-fully plan what came next. Right that moment she had no idea. Only that London, and New York, were going to wake up one day very soon to the realization that the year had ended and Hitler was still alive. It was never going to occur to them that it was their incompetence that was at fault.

On the other hand, to see Laurent again would be a treat – especially after last night's ordeal – and . . . She wondered if he could be turned; if she dared take the risk of attempting it?

'Sit down,' Himmler invited, and she sank on to the chair before his desk. 'I wish you to go to Stockholm.'

Anna could not believe her ears. Could he really be giving her an out? – a means of contacting London? But she had to ask, 'Has Herr Laurent let you down?'

'No, no. This is nothing to do with transferring funds. I merely wish you to carry a letter to an acquaintance of mine. Now, I must warn you that this man moves around a lot and although I shall inform him that you are coming to see him, he may not be immediately available. So it may be necessary to remain there for a day or two before you are able to contact him.'

Again Anna could not believe her ears; he might as well have been working for MI6.

'Of course,' Himmler went on, 'I know that this is the worst possible time of year to be visiting Stockholm, but you survived a Russian winter three years ago, did you not?'

'Yes, I did,' Anna said bravely. 'When do I leave?'

'Not for a week or so.'

Damn, she thought. But she merely said, 'Oh!'

'There is the matter of this conspiracy to be sorted out first.'

Suddenly even the winter sunshine disappeared. 'Sir?'

'I understand that you intend personally to interview Freddie von Steinberg.'

'Well, yes, sir. I told Colonel Essermann that I felt, as Count von Steinberg and I are acquainted, that I could get more out of him with a friendly conversation than with threats.'

'You mean you told Hellmuth.'

'Sir?'

'Oh, come now, Anna. You and Essermann are lovers, are you not?'

There could be no point in denying what he obviously knew. 'You told me I should cultivate him, sir.'

'So I did. I entirely approve. But, ah . . . you do not confide in him as to the secrets you and I share?'

'Of course I do not, sir. Whatever my . . . carnal desires, my allegiance is only to you.'

'I was sure of it. You are a treasure. However, this conspiracy thing . . .'

'I find it difficult to take it seriously, sir. This man Freiling is clearly demented, and now that he has been found out he is throwing out accusations left and right.'

'Ah, but Anna, you have overlooked something. Even Homer can nod, eh?'

'Sir?'

'Freiling was not found out. He went to the Gestapo of his own free will.'

'He could still be suffering from dementia,' Anna insisted.

'For all your brains and your beauty, I fear that you are, still, just a woman – reluctant to give up a point of view, even in the face of overwhelming evidence.'

Anna refused to be offended; she could not afford to be. 'I still do not see where this overwhelming evidence is, Herr Reichsführer. One man's denunciation?'

'Straws in the wind, Anna. Straws in the wind. Such as a reported conversation between Colonel Ballon and another person.'

'Colonel Ballon?'

'Colonel Ballon is aide-de-camp to Field Marshal von Beck. Did you not know that?' He seemed surprised that Anna did not know everything.

Oh, my God! Anna thought. What had Steinberg started? If this got back to Hitler, on top of his suspicions . . . and he wanted her to report direct to him! But she kept her voice even. 'General von Beck retired some time ago, sir. When I was a junior operative.'

'He was sacked by the Führer,' Himmler said severely. 'That breeds resentment.'

'And this Colonel Ballon was heard saying what, and to whom?'

'The conversation was indistinct to our listener, and he cannot say to whom it was addressed. What he did hear was the name of General Stieff, who is, I quote, "definitely one of us". I assume you know General Stieff?'

'He commands the Berlin Garrison,' Anna said slowly.

'Correct. That is to say, he commands a large body of troops on our very doorstep. But that is not all. The other person went on to say, "Stieff may be important, but the man we want is Rommel. With Rommel on our side we cannot fail."'

'We still do not know about what they were speaking,' Anna said desperately.

'Oh, come now, Anna. Beck is our senior soldier, even if he is in retirement. Stieff commands a force which could dominate Berlin. He is not at this time engaged with any enemy. Rommel has just been appointed commander of our Atlantic defences. What possible project can they be sharing, either for aggressive action against our enemies or for the defence of the Reich? There is a plot afoot, Anna. It is our business to discover just what this plot is, against whom it is directed and, above all, who is involved.'

Was there a ray of hope? Like all the Nazi leaders, with the possible exception of Goebbels, this idiot was so obsessed with maintaining his own position, with the fear of being somehow undermined, that he could not see the obvious.

'Of course, sir,' she agreed. 'But can any of this be connected with Freiling? Or with Freddie von Steinberg? Surely that is just a coincidence.'

'I do not believe in coincidences, Anna. When you see a dog chasing a bitch on heat, and immediately after see another dog running in the same direction, is that a coincidence? Or an obvious indication that they are both after the same thing?'

Anna allowed herself to look a little shocked at the crudity of his imagery, and he hurried on.

'Forgive me. These scum make my blood boil. I wish you either to bring me proof that Freddie von Steinberg is involved, or that he is innocent.'

Anna inhaled. 'Yes, sir. Is this to be before or after I go to Sweden?'

'It is to be done now. Immediately. Steinberg is not a strong character. It should not take you more than a day or two to break him down.'

'Yes, sir.' Anna stood up. 'If it is necessary to hurt him . . .'

'Then do so. You have my full authority.'

'Thank you, sir. Heil Hitler.'

Anna felt quite breathless. There were so many things to be done – with no certainty that she could do any of them, successfully. She began by returning to the apartment block and collecting Birgit. Birgit had never been inside Gestapo Headquarters, and gazed around herself in a mixture of awe and terror as they were escorted down the stairs, two agents following with their bags.

They passed the punishment level and plunged still deeper into the ground. Even Anna had never been down here; as she had told Himmler, to this minute she had not known such a subterranean world existed. There were glowing electric bulbs, and soft air conditioning, but nothing could subdue the stench of dampness.

'Are we in prison, Countess?' Birgit asked.

'We are here for our own protection,' Anna told her.

'But there are no windows!'

'There is nothing to look at anyway. But you are free to go out whenever you wish, either for a walk or shopping. And this is not too bad.'

She gazed around the apartment. Of course it could not compare with her previous accommodation, being smaller and utilitarian rather than luxurious. But there were two small bedrooms, if with a single bathroom between them, a well-equipped kitchenette – there was also a mess hall at the end of the corridor – and carpets on the floors; and even if it was December it was warm enough.

'But how long will we have to live here?' Birgit wailed.

'Until the bombing stops.'

'I will get ill.'

'Don't tell me you suffer from claustrophobia?'

Birgit hugged herself. 'I feel that I am in my grave.'

'Well, look at it this way: when you *are* in your grave it won't feel so strange. Now, you can spend the rest of the day unpacking and making us comfortable.' She gave her a purse of money. 'Go and buy some flowers and something nice for dinner. And lay in some drinks. And smile.'

'Yes, Countess. But you will not be here?'

'I will be here for dinner, goose. I don't know about lunch. Now, I have work to do.'

She went up to her office and called Essermann to join her. 'Anna,' he cried. 'I heard that your building had been hit!'

'I have the impression that the experts feel it is about to fall down.'

'But how can you go on living there?'

'It appears that I cannot go on living there. I am now situated about five floors beneath where we are sitting.'

'But you are all right. That is because you were not there when the bombs hit.'

Anna raised her eyebrows.

'I telephoned you, last night, about nine o'clock. Just before the raid started. I thought we might have supper together. But your woman said that you were away for the night.' He paused, staring at her.

This attack had to be met head on. 'I was away for the night, yes. But you knew I was. You were there when I received my instructions.'

'I did not know you were going for the whole night. Who were you with?'

'I think that is my business.'

'I thought we had an understanding.'

'We do have an understanding, Hellmuth. The understanding is that when we are both free from duty we can enjoy each other's company. Last night I was working. As you know, I do not discuss my work with anyone apart from the Reichsführer. Now I am working again. I understand that you have made some progress.'

'Yes. One of my people tapped the telephone line of Colonel

Ballon and recorded a conversation of his. A very incriminating conversation.'

'The Reichsführer told me of it. But you do not know who he was speaking to.'

'Unfortunately, no.'

'I should like to hear the recording. But you are quite sure it was not Count von Steinberg.'

'Not unless he is very good at disguising his voice.'

'So you have nothing incriminating on him apart from Major Freiling's wild accusation.'

'That is true.'

'And is Freiling under arrest?'

'No. He was questioned and released. To this moment he has committed no crime. He is under surveillance, just in case he makes contact with anyone else who may be of interest to us.'

'You mean any of the names you have obtained from your phone-tapping.'

'Well, yes.'

'Which is all that you have to go on. Why were you tapping Colonel Ballon's phone in the first place?'

'Simply that he is Field Marshal von Beck's aide-de-camp.'

'And what made you suspicious of Beck?'

'After Freiling's accusation, we placed Count von Steinberg also under surveillance.'

This was getting worse and worse. 'And what did you discover?'

'Amongst other things, that he has been paying regular visits to Beck's house.'

'I believe the Field Marshal is a friend of his family.'

'That is true. It is still not usual for a young man to pay regular visits to a friend of his father's – unless they happen to be in same profession, and he is attempting to learn from his senior's experiences. Beck has been a soldier all his life. He knows nothing else. Steinberg has never been a soldier. What does he have to learn from a veteran?'

'As usual, you're revealing great powers of analysis, Hellmuth. I congratulate you. Not that I consider anything you have so far turned up links Freddie to any plot save in Freiling's ramblings.'

'You say that because you do not wish to find anything against him. Because he was, or is, your lover.'

'Are you keeping me under surveillance as well?'

'Well, no. But . . . you went with him to the opera.'

'And you assume that every time I accompany a man to the opera, I sleep with him afterwards? Is that because, when *you* take me to the opera I sleep with you?'

'Well . . .' He flushed.

She reached across the table to squeeze his hand. 'It is fortunate that I am so fond of you. Now listen. I will admit that I do not believe that Freddie is guilty of anything save perhaps picking his friends unwisely. On the other hand, your reports have succeeded in agitating the Reichsführer, and unfortunately I have to go away for a few days.'

'Again. Go where?' He was again instantly jealous.

'I am not in a position to tell you that. It is on the Reichsführer's private business.'

'You mean you are going to Switzerland. Again.'

'You are entitled to your own opinion.'

'What do you do there?'

Anna could not suppress her Irish sense of humour. 'Why, Hellmuth, I go to see my lover.'

'You . . .'

She smiled. 'You are a sweetie. I go on the Reichsführer's business. What that business is, I have no idea. I am only a messenger girl. It is not something I wish to discuss. Before I go, I am going to have a word with Freddie. In view of what you have told me, it should be a simple matter to trip him up if he is guilty. But our meeting will have to be tête-à-tête. I am telling you this because I do not wish you to get any wrong ideas.'

'Hm. I do not like it.'

'I do not propose to fuck him.'

'But if you see him privately, without a witness, and he *is* guilty, and things get sticky, don't you realize that if he were to be arrested, he may well attempt to involve you?'

Which was what she had been waiting patiently for him to suggest. 'That is why I am telling you now, Hellmuth. You will be my insurance. I work for the Reichsführer, and nobody else. You know that. And I love you, and nobody else. I hope you know that too.'

'Oh, Anna! Anna! I adore you. When . . .?'

Anna appeared to consider. 'As I may be away for a few

days, I think you should come and have supper with me tonight.' She giggled. 'In my dungeon.'

'Now listen very carefully,' Anna said, gazing across her desk at Steinberg. This was actually the safest place for them to meet, as it was one of the few places that was not bugged. But she had to choose her words very cautiously: she suspected that were this idiot to learn that Hitler was aware there was something going on, he would lose his head completely. 'I think I have managed to throw enough doubts in everyone's mind so that they will not proceed in any direction without a lot more proof than they now have. But they are busily trying to obtain that proof. I don't think they still suspect you, save for the fact that you have been seeing too much of Beck. But they definitely suspect Beck.'

'But how? He has done nothing save talk to me in private.'

'Freddie, you naivety terrifies me. Beck is a famous man, used to authority and to making decisions. You are, if you will excuse my frankness, a nonentity who is a political dreamer. You planted the idea in his head. But it is in his nature to take control. You deal in ideas. But as I have said, he deals in action. You propose to eliminate Hitler. He may be willing to leave that to you. But he understands what will need to be done immediately the assassination is successfully carried out. He has thus contacted General Stieff, who, as I am sure you know, commands the Berlin garrison. He is also, as he is a general, used to dealing with business through subordinates, and has confided the plan to his aide-de-camp, who seems to have been given the task of contacting as many generals and other commanders who may be sympathetic as they can think of. To put it in a nutshell, it would seem that half the senior Wehrmacht officers in Germany know what is going on.'

Steinberg had turned quite white.. 'But . . .' Then he frowned. 'How can you know this?'

Anna related her conversation with Himmler, while Steinberg's face seemed to disintegrate. 'Then we are finished.'

'That is not inevitable.'

'But if Himmler knows . . .'

'He does not intend to do anything about it at this moment.'

'I don't understand.'

'Frankly, neither do I. It is difficult to know what goes on in his mind.' In every direction, she thought. 'It could be that he means to join you, at the right moment. Or it could be that he intends to cast his net as wide as possible before pouncing.'

'My God! What are we to do?'

'Sit tight.'

'I must warn Beck.'

'To be more discreet – nothing else.'

'But . . . we are just about ready to go.'

'What?'

'I think I have found the right man, at last.'

'You have found someone to commit suicide?'

'Well, obviously we hope it will not come to that. We have still to work out the details.'

'Who is this would-be martyr?'

'Well . . .' Steinberg twisted his fingers together. 'Claus von Stauffenberg.'

Anna raised her eyebrows. 'Stauffenberg? I remember him, from before the war. Oh, yes, he would be the ideal man.' She recalled that tall, handsome, dashing young officer, a great-grandson of the immortal Gneisenau. 'But he is, or was, a fervent Nazi.'

'He was. Perhaps he still is, at heart. But he is a German before that. Like you, he can see that Hitler is leading us – leading the German people – to destruction. And since the end of the North African campaign, he has been on the staff of General Fromm, you know, the commander of the home army. As such he is regularly required to report to the Führer. He is never searched.'

'I find that hard to believe.' Anna remembered her own experience.

'Well, you see, he is above suspicion.'

She would not have thought that anyone was more above suspicion than herself. 'What makes him so special?'

More finger-twisting. 'Well, you see, in the North African campaign, he was seriously injured. His car drove over a mine.'

'Oh, good God. When you say seriously injured . . .'

'Well . . . The mine blew off his left arm.'

Anna stared at him.

'And two fingers and the thumb of his right hand.'

Anna leaned back in her chair.

'And he is virtually blind in his left eye.'

Incident in Stockholm

Anna all but fell forward as she sat up. 'Have you completely lost your senses?'

'He has the courage, and the determination. He has virtually taken over the entire project.'

'To do what? Can he fire a pistol? Can he *hold* a pistol?'

'Well, no. But we were thinking in terms of a bomb. It would be in his briefcase. With a timer, of course. It's a special thing, developed by the British. Johannsson gave it to us. He seems to have some contacts over there. It's very complicated, so I won't attempt to explain it to you. But it will give him ample time to get away before it goes off, and it is virtually undetectable.'

Anna realized that her mouth was open. They had written her off, but were sticking with that original and faulty contraption – because they didn't know hers hadn't worked! They must think she had lost her nerve. Now she simply had to get in touch from Stockholm.

Steinberg was misinterpreting her expression. 'Believe me, Anna, it is going to happen. I – we, have every confidence in Stauffenberg. Would you like to meet him?'

'Under no circumstances. I hope he does not know of me?'

'I gave you my word, Anna. No one knows of you.'

'Not even Beck?'

'No one. I swear it. All that they know is that someone close to the Reichsführer and well regarded by him is favourable to our cause. Actually, they think it is Nebe.'

Anna frowned; Arthur Nebe was Himmler's head of Internal Security – as such he was, effectively, Essermann's boss. 'What makes them think that?'

'He has been in conversation with one of our people.'

'For God's sake,' Anna said. 'Is there anyone in Berlin who does not know of this plot?'

'We are attracting more and more sympathizers, yes. Although I did not know that Beck was openly canvassing for support. But we are relying upon you to convince Himmler that it is his duty to co-operate with whoever takes over the government when Hitler dies.'

'How masterful you have become,' Anna remarked. 'Now, I am going away for a week or so.'

'Going away? Where?'

'I am not in a position to tell you that. But when I come back, I may have important and constructive news for you, regarding Himmler's attitude. I would certainly recommend that you do nothing until I return. And for God's sake be careful as to who else you attempt to recruit.'

'Well?' Himmler inquired. 'I will not wish you a happy New Year because it may not be one. What have you learned from Steinberg?'

'As far as I can ascertain, sir,' Anna said, 'Freddie is a completely harmless young man who lives in a dream world. He may never have been a soldier himself, but for that reason he fantasizes of military glory. I think he knows that even were he to be given the opportunity to fight he would not know how to go about it. But Field Marshal von Beck is apparently willing and eager to talk about the past, and Freddie loves to listen.'

'And Beck has never mentioned any subversive ideas to him?'

'Not that he is aware of. He is not very bright, you know, sir. As for the rest, I have studied all the various reports assembled by Essermann, and I cannot find anything incriminating in what was said. I will, of course, continue my investigation, if that is what you wish . . .'

She held her breath, but he merely waved his hand. 'I hope you are right. Anyway, there are more important matters. Have you heard the latest news?'

What now? Anna wondered. 'No, sir.'

'It is not being released for publication at this time. *Scharnhorst* is gone.'

'Gone where, sir?'

'To the bottom of the sea, you silly girl. How Bey ever got to be an admiral I do not know. The idiot allowed himself to be lured into a trap laid by the Royal Navy, and attacked a convoy to Russia, unaware that they were supported by a task force led by the *Duke of York.* Can you imagine? A battle cruiser attempting to take on the latest battleship in the British navy. Nine eleven-inch guns trying to match ten fourteen-inch. What absurdity. But there it is. With *Tirpitz* out of action, our very last capital ship has gone.'

'Is the Führer upset?'

'Upset? My God! Right this minute he is berserk. But we have our own canoe to paddle. This makes your mission to Stockholm even more important.' From his desk drawer he took a heavily sealed envelope. 'This is to be delivered, by you personally, to Count Folke Bernadotte of the Swedish Red Cross. Have you ever met Count Bernadotte?'

'Yes,' Anna said. 'I have met him at a reception here in Berlin.'

'Then I have no doubt that he will remember you. But this must be given to him personally. No one else. I wish you to be very clear about this.'

'Yes, sir.'

'But as I told you before, although I have written him to expect a courier, I understand that the Count may not be immediately available, and so you may have to spend a few days in Stockholm. Are you prepared to do this?'

'If you require it, sir,' Anna said bravely, while her heart was singing.

'Well, then, you leave tomorrow. You are booked in at the Falcon Hotel. I am told it is very comfortable.'

'Very good, sir. And my identity?'

'As Count Bernadotte knows who you are, it would be pointless to use a false name. You are the Countess von Widerstand, and you are on a diplomatic mission for the Reich.'

'As you say, Herr Reichsführer.'

'Just remember that no one, but no one, is to know the contents of this letter other than Count Bernadotte. In this regard, you must be prepared to take any steps necessary to protect it. And yourself, of course.'

'You wish me to be armed, sir?'

'I think that would be appropriate.' He held out a little booklet. 'This is your diplomatic passport, which will see you through any Customs post, and you have your carte blanche.'

He took off his glasses to gaze into her eyes. 'Both our futures are at stake, Anna.'

'I understand that, sir. But . . . am I to await the Count's answer?'

'Yes. It may just be a preliminary answer. But a great deal will depend on it. Our lives are in your hands, Anna.'

'I shall remember that, sir. And I shall return as soon as is practical.' Anna stood up. 'Auf Wiedersehen.'

Birgit, of course, was aghast. 'You are going away for a week, Countess? And I am not to come with you?'

'It is simply not practical,' Anna explained, 'and it will only be for a few days, really.'

'And I am left here in this . . . this dungeon.'

'By the time I return, I expect you to have turned this dungeon into the sort of home we have both come to appreciate. I give you carte blanche to spend whatever you think necessary. If anyone questions what you are doing, refer them to Herr Himmler.'

Essermann was equally perturbed. 'You say you do not know how long you will be away?' he asked as he sat beside her on the drive to Lübeck. ' Is that not very irregular?'

Anna shrugged. 'I am on the Reich's business, which, as I am sure you appreciate, must come before any other consideration.'

'Of course. But ah, you are not travelling to – well . . .'

Anna squeezed his hand. 'As far I am aware, Hellmuth, I am not being required to kill anybody.' Unless I have to protect the contents of the letter, she thought.

His fingers were tight on hers. 'Oh, Anna, the thought of anything happening to you . . .'

She kissed him.

Needless to say, Werter was on the dock. 'Why, Herr Werter,' she said. 'How nice to see you again.'

He looked decidedly apprehensive, and the more so at the sight of Essermann, wearing his black uniform, into whose arms Anna allowed herself to be swept for a farewell kiss. But he determined to get in a point of view. 'I assume you are coming back, Countess?'

Anna smiled at him. 'You will have to wait and see.' She squeezed Hellmuth's hand and boarded the ferry.

Then at last she could allow herself to think. The sealed envelope was, of course, burning holes in her new shoulder bag far more quickly than London's acid had done. But the temptation to open it, at least at this stage, had to be resisted. As it obviously did not contain money, it had to be some kind of proposal – from the Reich, with the full authority of the Führer? or from Himmler personally? It had to be the latter. If Hitler wanted to communicate with the Swedish government, which could only be with a view to ending the war – an impossible thought in any event – he would do so through their ambassador in Berlin. But if Himmler was seeking a personal salvation . . .? Would that turn the conspirators' plans on their heads, or did that mean that she had been wrong in her assumption that he would never risk seeking power as the next Führer? She did not think so. If he was aware, as now seemed certain, that there was an incipient plot against the Führer in existence, and intended to take advantage of it, then the only reason to involve the Swedish government was to find out, through them, if the Allies would be prepared to deal with him. She was absolutely sure they would not, but this might still be a vital piece of information for MI6 . . . and the OSS. She would have to wait and see what, if anything, Count Bernadotte might let slip.

But all of that, possibly earth-shaking as it was, ranked below the fact that she was being given the opportunity to contact Clive. She should be very angry. And in fact that was still simmering – that she had been exposed to such an experience, and to such a risk, with defective material. Would they want her to try again? She honestly did not think she could handle another night like that. And if Stauffenberg was willing to take on the burden . . . But if he was going to have to do it with the same duff material as she had been given . . . That also needed sorting out.

By Clive! She was aware of a slowly growing excitement as she caught the train from Malmö to Stockholm, having sailed through Swedish Customs by presenting her diplomatic passport. The journey took several hours, through country entirely blanketed by snow, through which the red roofs of the houses poked picturesquely. Stockholm was equally shrouded in snow, the lakes frozen. The train had been full, and it was necessary to wait half an hour for a taxi, stamping her feet on the frozen ground. But at last she was at the Falcon Hotel, being shown to a very comfortable room, where she could stand for fifteen minutes beneath a hot shower while she thawed out. Then she had a room-service supper and went to bed, enjoying – as she was sure she would have done in Geneva but for the unwelcome interruption, and had done in Lucerne – the utter peace of an air-raid-free city, which was made more peaceful yet by the sound-deadening effect of the snow.

Next morning she had to control her impatience until nine o'clock, breakfasting in her room. But at nine sharp she telephoned the Swedish Red Cross Headquarters. 'I need to speak with someone who understands German,' she said, in that language. As she had told Himmler, Swedish was not amongst her many accomplishments.

'I speak German, Fräulein,' the woman said.

'Then I would like to speak with Count Bernadotte, please.'

'May I have your name?' the woman asked.

'I am the Countess von Widerstand. Count Bernadotte is expecting me.'

'Count Bernadotte is not in yet. If you will leave your telephone number I will inform his secretary that you called, Countess, and no doubt he will contact you.' Her tone suggested, *supposing he has either the time or the inclination to wish to speak with some itinerant German.*

'Thank you,' Anna said, and gave the hotel number as well as that of her room, reflecting that with any luck Bernadotte would be out of town and be unable to see her for a few days, which would give her a legitimate excuse to remain in Stockholm for a while.

As it would still be only ten past eight in London, again she had to wait, so she had a bath and dressed. She was in the middle of her make-up when the phone rang. 'Countess von Widerstand?' A man's voice.

Damnation, she thought. 'I am she. Count Bernadotte?'

'I am Count Bernadotte's secretary, Countess. Count Bernadotte would like you to have lunch with him today, if that is convenient.'

'Today?' Shit! 'Of course. That would be entirely convenient.'

'Do you know Stockholm, Countess?'

'This is my first visit.'

'Ah! In that case, a car will pick you up at twelve thirty.'

'Twelve thirty,' Anna agreed, and hung up.

That was bad luck, but at least it was now ten o'clock, or nine in London. 'I would like to make a long-distance call,' she told the girl on the hotel switchboard.

'Certainly, Fräulein. The number?'

Anna gave her the long-memorized unlisted number of MI6 headquarters and waited through a succession of thumps and clicks. Then the number was repeated by an English voice. 'Good morning,' Anna said. 'I would like to speak with Mr Bartley, please.'

'Who is calling, please?'

'Belinda.'

'Belinda. And where are you calling from, please?'

'Stockholm.'

'Stockholm!' There was a moment's silence, then the woman said, 'I will connect you with Mr Bartley's office.'

More clicks. Anna had no doubt that the call was now being monitored. But a few moments later another woman said, 'Did you say, Belinda?'

'That is correct. Who is this?'

'I am Mr Bartley's secretary.'

'Well, kindly connect me with your boss. It is very urgent.'

'Ah . . . I'm sorry, Count— Belinda, but Mr Bartley is not in the office.'

'Oh, shit!'

'Countess?'

'Forget it. Listen, when do you expect him?'

'In about four days' time.'

'*What?*'

'He is presently out of the country.'

'For God's sake! Then who is in the country?'

'Would you like to speak with Mr Baxter?'

Anna considered. She had only met Billy Baxter once, on the occasion in 1940 when she had agreed to work for MI6 and Clive had considered it necessary for her to become acquainted with her ultimate boss. As she remembered the occasion, she had not liked him, and she suspected that he had not liked her, either – although Clive had told her it was just that Billy was apprehensive of forceful women. But it was absolutely essential that she talk to someone with some clout, and thanks to Bernadotte's prompt response she only had a couple of days to play with. At least Baxter should be completely au fait with what she was doing. 'All right,' she agreed.

'Can you hold, for five minutes?'

'Five minutes.'

Amy dashed up the stairs and arrived panting before Baxter's desk. 'Mr Baxter . . .'

Billy looked up. 'Don't tell me something's happened to Clive?'

'No, sir. I don't know, sir. But . . . she's on the line.'

'Take a deep breath, Barstow,' Billy recommended. 'You are yammering.'

Amy took several deep breaths. 'The Countess von Widerstand is on my line. She says it is very urgent.'

'You mean she's alive? And telephoning from Germany? Holy shit!'

'Sir?' Amy was pained. As a well-brought-up young woman she was unused to the indiscriminate use of obscenity. And now she had been presented with the S-word twice in ten minutes.

Billy ignored her, ran down the stairs to pick up the phone. 'Countess?'

'At last,' Anna commented, somewhat acidly; she had been wondering how she was going to explain what was clearly going to be a staggering phone bill on her expenses.

'Where are you?' Billy demanded.

'I am in Stockholm, Sweden. I will be here only for about two days. It is of the utmost importance that I meet one of your people in that time. But I understand that Clive is not available.'

'That is correct. Can you not discuss your problem now?'

'Over the phone? I don't think that would be a very good idea, sir.'

'I see. Well, leave it with me. I'll get someone across to you.'

'Within twenty-four hours,' Anna reminded him.

'Ah, yes. Yes. Within twenty-four hours.'

'It would be of great assistance for me to know who my contact is going to be.' Perhaps, she thought, he could send the real Belinda. That would be rather fun.

'Whoever it is,' Billy said, 'will use the Belinda code, and will be known to you. Give me your address.'

'The Falcon Hotel, Stockholm.'

'Very good. You will be contacted.' He replaced the phone and looked at Amy, who was looking at him.

'Shall I contact Miss Hoskin, sir?'

'No. I do not think that would be appropriate.'

'There is no one else in the office known to the Countess.' She snapped her fingers. 'We could use the Americans. I believe the Countess has met that chap Andrews, and I know he is still in England.'

'I don't like that idea either,' Billy said. 'They are trying too hard to muscle in as it is.' Anna Fehrbach, he thought. Quite the most exciting woman he had ever met. So she was a mass murderess, or, as she would call it, a mass executioner. But she was actually his possession, as long as he kept her out of the hands of the Americans.

'Then who will you send, sir?' Amy asked. 'You promised her it would be someone she knew.'

'Yes,' Billy said. 'I did, didn't I?'

Anna remembered, correctly, that Folke Bernadotte was a tall, intensely handsome man, a descendant of the Napoleonic marshal who had been elected King of Sweden and founded the present dynasty. She was also aware of his work with the Swedish Red Cross that had alleviated the fate of many thousand concentration-camp victims. What Himmler, the man responsible for creating such camps, could expect of him . . .

To her surprise, the Count wore uniform, but he bowed over her hand most gallantly when she was escorted through the crowded restaurant to his table. 'Countess von Widerstand! This is an enormous pleasure. I suppose you do not remember me.' He spoke flawless German.

'I remember you very well, sir. But I am surprised that you remember me.' Anna allowed herself to be helped out of her sable by the maître d', and she also gave him her fur hat. She was wearing a pale-green woollen dress and her best jewellery; her hair was loose save for its usual retaining band on the nape of her neck.

'Yours is not a face one easily forgets. Do sit down. Will you accept a champagne cocktail?'

'I will, thank you.' Anna seated herself opposite him, and the drinks were brought.

'The communication that I received,' Bernadotte said, 'from the German embassy, was that you wished to see me on an urgent personal matter, and that you had the blessing of Reichsführer Himmler in doing so.'

'Whereas, I am sure you have deduced that the personal matter is not my own.'

'I had no doubt that you would enlighten me. Shall we order?' Anna accepted his recommendations, and a bottle of wine was served. Then he asked, 'Would you prefer to discuss business now, or later?'

'I actually have no business to discuss, Count Bernadotte.' He raised his eyebrows and she smiled at him. 'I am merely a delivery girl.' She opened her bag and handed him the envelope. 'From Herr Himmler.'

He regarded both her and the envelope for some seconds, then laid it beside his plate as the hors d'oeuvre was served. 'I assume you know the contents?'

'No, sir. I do not.'

'But, as I understand it, you are Herr Himmler's Personal Assistant.'

'That is correct, sir.' Anna ate her salted-fish pieces, carefully.

'But he does not confide in you.'

'He confides in me what he wishes me to know.'

Bernadotte considered this while their main course was served, then drank some wine. 'May I ask you a terribly personal, and impertinent, question, Countess? If you are offended, you are welcome to slap my face, or throw your wine over me.'

Anna drank in turn. 'I am not easily offended, sir.'

'Well, then . . . as you occupy so important a place in the German Secret Service, may I assume you are a Nazi?'

'You may *assume* that, sir.'

He raised his eyes to meet hers as the emphasis registered. 'Well, at any rate, you must necessarily support the actions of your government, and of Herr Himmler in particular.'

Anna chose her words carefully. 'I am not required either to approve, or to disapprove, the actions of my government, sir. I am only required to carry out my orders, as and when

I receive them. My current orders are to deliver that letter to you, personally, and to receive from you a reply, personally.'

He continued to gaze at her for some seconds, but was too much of a gentleman to continue his interrogation after so pointed a snub. 'As you say,' he agreed, and used his clean butter knife to slit the envelope and take out the two sheets of handwritten paper. 'Do you mind if I read this now?'

'I would like you to.'

He scanned the sheets, his expression never changing. When he was finished, he looked up. 'You say you have no idea what this says?'

'No, sir, I do not.'

'I think you are probably fortunate. Try to keep it that way.'

'And your reply?'

'Now, Countess, if I were to give you a verbal reply, you would have to know what I am talking about and, as I have said, it would be far better, and safer, for you not to become involved. Besides, it is not something to which I can reply, off the cuff, as it were. I shall have to consider the matter.'

'Herr Himmler will be impatient to hear from you.'

'I am sure he will. But I am sure he will understand the situation. Lunch with me here the day after tomorrow. My car will pick you up at your hotel. At that time I will give you my reply, in writing, and sealed. Will that satisfy you?'

'It will have to, sir,' Anna said, and drank her coffee.

She knew she should be desperately curious as to the contents of the letter, and what Bernadotte would have to say in reply. If, in view of what was going on in Berlin, she had a pretty good idea of the subject matter, she could not determine why Himmler would wish to involve a neutral who, although well known internationally, was not actually a statesman, and was certainly not a Nazi sympathizer. But she could not stop herself from considering the coming twenty-four hours as far more important – as they were, however great her disappointment that it would not be Clive knocking on her door. It would be delightful to see Belinda again, but Baxter had obviously not made up his mind who to send, and besides, if Clive was away, was it not possible that Belinda was with him? Grrr. So it would probably be Johannsson, a man who was setting up to be a nuisance, if only because he did absolutely nothing for her, sensually. But if it was to be

him, she would at least be able to tear a strip off him for the
failed bomb.

Meanwhile, as in Lucerne, she was stuck, as she dared not
risk being out when her contact arrived. Not that she had any
great desire to go out. She had read that Stockholm, known
as the Venice of the North, was one of the most beautiful
cities in Europe, and her brief glimpses of the architecture
seemed to support that claim, but that afternoon it began to
snow quite heavily, and by the time she went down to dinner
it was blowing a blizzard. She had no idea how her contact
was going to reach her – although if it was to be Johannsson
he would surely already be here – but if he, or she, was flying,
there might be a problem.

There was an all-male dinner party going on, with a great
deal of loud toasting. They were all naturally interested in the
glamorous young woman dining alone, but she only glanced
at them, and after the meal went straight to bed, where, having
the mental control to empty her mind of all stressful thoughts,
she was asleep in seconds – to awake to a winter wonderland,
with the ploughs moving slowly along the streets to clear
paths through the waist-high snow.

She got dressed, had breakfast, and settled down to wait.
There was no point in putting off the maid, and as the girl
obviously did not speak German, she merely gestured towards
the bed and nodded. By the time she went down to lunch she
was beginning to feel agitated. In another twenty-four hours
she would be seeing Bernadotte again, and after that there
would be no excuse for remaining in Stockholm a moment
longer. 'I am expecting a caller, perhaps this afternoon,' she
told Reception when she left the dining room. 'I shall be in
my room.'

'Of course, Countess. The name of the . . . ah . . .?'

'The caller will give *my* name,' Anna said, and went upstairs.

She settled down with a pack of cards and was playing her
fourth game of solitaire when her phone rang.

'Countess? There is a gentleman here to see you. I'm afraid
he refuses to give me his name, but he says you are expecting
him.'

'Yes, I am, as I told you. Please ask him to come up.'

She put away the cards, took her Luger from her shoulder
bag, unlocked her door, and waited. A few minutes later there

came a tap. Anna stood against the wall beside the door. 'It's open.'

A brief hesitation, and the door swung in. 'Why, Mr Baxter,' Anna said. '*What* a pleasant surprise.'

Slowly Billy turned towards her, then looked at the pistol. 'Do you always answer the door like that?'

'I'm alive,' Anna pointed out, and stepped behind him to close and lock the door.

He advanced into the room. 'What on earth made you choose to rendezvous in a climate like this? We may as well be at the North Pole.'

'I'm told it is very beautiful in the summer,' Anna said. 'Actually, it is very beautiful now, if you can overlook the temperature. And I am sure you know, Mr Baxter, that I do not choose places for a rendezvous. I am sent to places, and I try to arrange the rendezvous around that fact. Do sit down.'

Baxter sat in the one armchair. 'Would you mind putting away that thing.'

Anna laid the gun on the table, sat in the chair beside it. Baxter felt in his pocket and produced his pipe. 'Do you mind?'

'Yes, I do,' Anna said.

He hesitated, then put the pipe away again.

'But I can offer you a drink.'

He looked at his watch.

'Of course,' she agreed. 'It is not the correct hour. I know! A cup of tea. Would you like a cup of tea?'

'Thank you.' He remained watching her as she picked up the phone and dialled room service. 'Is this merely a rendezvous, or are you carrying out a mission for your employers ?'

'Both.'

'And perhaps you can offer an explanation for the failure of the mission you were supposed to be carrying out for us? It was to be completed by the end of the year. That was a week ago.'

'I did complete my mission,' Anna said.

'There has been no report of it?'

'That is because the bomb failed to go off.'

'Oh, shit!'

Anna raised her eyebrows. 'You don't sound very surprised.'

He grimaced. 'There have been some failures.'

Anna pocketed the pistol, answered the knock on the door, waited while the waiter placed the tray on the table, and locked the door again. 'So you sent me on what was virtually a suicide mission with duff equipment,' she remarked, pouring. 'Not for the first time. Shall I put the arsenic in now, or would you like some sugar?'

'Two lumps. I am most terribly sorry.'

Anna handed him his tea and sat down. 'Words I shall remember when they put the rope around my neck.'

'We actually thought you had been caught and executed.'

'Clive thought that?'

'He refused to accept it. Neither would that fellow Andrews. They were both very upset. '

'Even while refusing to accept that I might be dead. Well, you must give them my love and the bad news that I am still around. No thanks to them.'

'Look, you have every right to be upset. But you're here, aren't you? Looking, if I may so, more beautiful than ever.'

'You say the sweetest things.'

He flushed. 'And the bomb has been remade. It now includes a wire connection, between the acid and the explosive. The acid eats into the wire, and is conducted to the explosive. The new version has been tested several times and has never failed to work. So—'

'Count me out.'

'What?'

'I don't know how much you understand about the situation, Mr Baxter, but let me put you in the picture. In order to gain access to Hitler, he has to want to receive you. Now, he does receive, fairly regularly, staff officers and the like with important information. But I am not a staff officer. I have nothing to tell the Führer that he does not already know. Therefore there is only one reason for him to wish to receive me in his private quarters. *Comprende?*'

Baxter slowly put down his tea cup. 'You mean you . . . my God! You actually . . .'

'Carried out my orders to get close enough to him to place the bomb. That meant I had to be close enough for him to do whatever he wished to do to me. Are you all right?'

He had gone very red in the face.

'I think you should loosen your tie,' Anna suggested. 'In fact, take off your coat and jacket. I really do not wish you to have a heart attack. I have so much trouble explaining dead bodies in my room to the authorities, especially outside Germany.'

'It is quite warm in here.' Baxter got up and removed his coat and jacket, then loosened his tie.

'I am sure you can appreciate that it is not an experience I wish to repeat. However, we are not quite bereft.' She outlined the progress of the conspiracy, omitting certain details, such as Stauffenberg's disabilities and the fact that both Hitler and Himmler were obviously aware that there was some kind of plot going on but had so far decided not to do anything about it. That was something she wanted to probe for herself.

'Hm,' Billy commented. 'You say that your friends already have a bomb. Given them by Johannsson?'

'Associates, Mr Baxter. Associates. Didn't you authorize Johannsson to give them a bomb?'

'No, I did not. Those damned Yanks are acting on their own. Not for the first time. What exactly is your role in this?'

'I do not have a role.'

His eyebrows went up.

'I cannot be involved with the conspiracy as such. As far as anyone in Germany is aware, I am a faithful servant of Herr Himmler, and I must remain so, or my position would become untenable.'

'But you're dealing with these people.'

'I am dealing with one of them, who only knows me as Himmler's PA. He believes that I can persuade Himmler to take over the government should Hitler be removed.'

'Hm. I'm not sure that we would wish that.'

'I'm not sure that he could be persuaded. He has his own agenda.'

'Which you possess?'

'Not entirely. As far as I can work it out, he is preparing to do a bunk if the going gets too rough. I reported this to Clive back in August.'

Baxter nodded. 'I remember. He is salting money away in Switzerland . . . and here in Sweden?'

'I don't think so. He believes his money is safest in Switzerland, but I think his idea is to seek political asylum in Sweden.'

'And you are prepared to help him do this.'

'I am prepared to carry out his orders, Mr Baxter. Because I have no choice if I, and my family, are going to survive.'

'Message understood. Have you anything else for me?'

'Yes. Everyone expects the Allies to invade this summer. Is that correct?'

'Now, you know I can't tell you that, Anna.'

'You just have,' she pointed out.

'You are too quick for your own good. I asked if *you* had any information for me.'

'Only that you do need to invade, as rapidly as possible. Do you know anything about the secret weapons Germany is developing?'

'We hear rumours.'

'They happen to be fact. The Luftwaffe has developed a huge rocket, an unmanned flying bomb, if you like, which will fly at over four hundred miles an hour and deliver a payload of a thousand pounds on any designated target at a range of several hundred miles. It is in its final stage of preparation now, and will be operational, probably by June. The objective is to deliver heavier attacks on your cities than you did on Hamburg or are currently doing on Berlin.'

'Hm. Just let me write those figures down.' He took a notebook from his pocket. 'Frankly, I think this is pie in the sky.'

'They do have them,' Anna insisted.

'I'm sure they do. And your information will be invaluable to the RAF. But I would say that we have the planes to cope with them. Well, this has been a most informative meeting and, as usual, a very valuable one.' He stood up, put on his jacket.

Anna looked at her watch. 'It is five o'clock. Won't you stay and have a drink with me? It is very close to drinking time even by English reckoning.'

'I can think of nothing I would like more, Anna. But my plane is waiting to take me straight back.'

'You mean you're not staying even for one night?'

'I'm afraid not. Anyway, I don't think you would find my company as congenial as Clive's.'

'Don't you think I might regard that as a challenge.' She smiled at him. 'Just joking. But I would like to think we are now friends.'

'We have always been friends, Anna, even if I have from time to time found your methods – well, a little hair-raising. Do you expect to survive this war?'

'I'm working on it.'

'Well, then, I sincerely hope to see you when that day arrives.'

'Oh, I am counting on that. Until then . . .' She took him in her arms and kissed him on the mouth.

He responded, but then moved away. 'Shall I give Clive your love?'

'I asked you to, didn't I?' She opened the door for him, then closed and locked it. She wondered if, like Himmler, he was afraid of her?

'My reply.' Count Bernadotte slid the envelope across the table.

Anna looked at it. 'The envelope is not sealed.'

'It is sealed, Countess. But not with *a* seal. Will you open it?'

'It is not my business to do so.' Anna opened her shoulder bag and placed the envelope next to the Luger that lay in the bottom.

'You conceive of your business as the requirement to serve Herr Himmler, and therefore the Reich, faithfully and to the best of your ability.'

They had had a long, slow, enjoyable lunch, and he had waited until they were drinking their coffee before producing the envelope. Anna had not pressed him. She had enjoyed the ambience, as she was enjoying the ambience of all Stockholm, the tranquillity in such total contrast to the freneticism of Berlin. But now a certain tension had crept into the conversation. 'Do you criticize me for that, Count?'

'On the contrary. I consider loyalty to one's position and one's superiors to be the greatest of virtues. But it is, of course, possible for loyalty to be misplaced.'

'I do not understand what you are saying,' Anna lied.

'I was wondering if you are aware that Germany cannot win this war – in fact, that she is almost certain to lose it.'

'Would such an awareness justify disloyalty?'

'Is not the greatest of all loyalties to oneself? – to one's ideals, to one's family, to one's personal sense of honour, certainly. But eventually it must come down to one's desire to survive.'

How wonderful it would be if she could bare her soul to this kind, gentle and honourable man. But as that was not possible . . . 'No, sir. One's desire to survive must be subordinate to one's sense of personal honour, which is involved with one's awareness of duty. Whether one rates one's principal duty to lie in serving one's employers, or one's country, or' – she drew a long breath – 'one's family, has got to be a personal decision. But once made, it cannot be altered.' She dared go no further than that.

He studied her for several seconds. Then he said, 'I am glad you hold that point of view, Anna von Widerstand. But it distresses me to consider that when the edifice of Nazidom comes tumbling down, as it must do, you may be buried in the rubble. You are too . . .' He reflected for a moment, choosing his words. '. . . unique a personality to be lost to the world, at least for a long time.'

'Thank you, sir,' she said. 'There are quite a few people who would disagree with you.' Twenty-five at the last count, she thought.

'Should that time come, it may be that only my opinion will matter.'

They gazed at each other for several seconds. 'I shall remember that, Herr Count. And now . . .' She looked at her watch.

'Of course. My car will take you back to your hotel.'

'I would prefer to walk, if you do not mind.'

He raised his eyebrows. 'It is virtually dark outside, and below freezing.'

'I have my coat. As this is my last afternoon in Stockholm, I would like to *feel* the place.' She smiled. 'It is so very different from Berlin. Can you understand that?'

'Yes. You say this is your last afternoon here? You're leaving tomorrow?'

'On the early train. Herr Himmler will be waiting for your letter.'

'I imagine he will.' He stood up, bent over her hand. 'These two meetings have been a very great pleasure. Remember our conversation.'

Anna went to the lobby, put on her sable, tucked her hair

out of sight beneath her fur hat, watched with interest by the doorman, and pulled on her gloves. It was indeed dark outside, and her breath misted in front of her nostrils. But it was so deliciously clean.

The streets were all but deserted; judging from the glow of lights in the buildings around her it was obviously still office hours, and would be for another hour. She turned towards the lake side, walked about fifty yards, and a man appeared beside her; he must have been following her for some time, his footfalls deadened by the snow.

'Will you come with me, please, Countess?' he asked, in German.

Anna looked at him, but in the gloom it was difficult to identify any prominent features in his face; on the other hand, he wore a slouch hat, which was suggestive. 'I might, if you will tell me why I should?'

'We need to ask you some questions.'

'Are you a policeman?'

'I am Gestapo, Countess.'

'Ah.' Now here is a conundrum, she thought. How did he know who she was, and if he did know who she was, how did he know she was in Stockholm? 'Have you authority here?'

'We have authority over every German citizen anywhere in the world, Countess.'

But it did not appear as if he knew who she actually was, or, certainly, that she was SD. The situation was worth investigating. And at that moment a car arrived beside them. 'If you would be so kind, Countess. It is far too cold to walk.'

The door was opened, and Anna got in and sank on to the cushions. The man got in beside her; the only other occupant was the driver. 'I did not know the Gestapo had offices in foreign capitals,' she remarked, conversationally, although of course she did; Feutlanger had contacted the Geneva office to have her tailed from the railway station.

'We have offices everywhere,' he said proudly.

'And the Swedish government permits this?'

'Not officially. They know we are here, of course. But we represent ourselves as an import-and-export firm, and as long as we keep a low profile they do not trouble us.'

'That is very interesting,' Anna said. 'How many people man this import-and-export office?'

'There are three agents and a secretary.'

'Fascinating,' Anna said. 'And what exactly do you wish to speak to me about?'

'Herr Bochner will explain.'

'Herr Bochner being the boss man. Yes. Tell me, Herr . . . ah . . .?'

'Tobler.'

'Herr Tobler, what would you have done if I had simply refused to accompany you?'

'I am afraid I would have had to use force, Countess.'

'Do you regard that as keeping a low profile?'

'Well, no one would have known. The street was dark, and deserted, and it would have been very quick. I am an expert,' he added, more proudly yet.

'I am sure you are. Thank you for being so frank.'

'Well, you are not likely to be repeating anything I have said to anyone else, are you?'

'I would say that is unlikely,' Anna agreed.

'There, you see. We do endeavour to keep things civilized. We have arrived.'

The car had entered a small courtyard, surrounded by buildings, in which almost every window was illuminated. But this made the courtyard totally dark. The doors were opened, and Anna was ushered into a small hallway and up a staircase, the two men immediately behind her. Then she went along a narrow corridor, to arrive at a doorway. 'It is unlocked,' Tobler said.

Anna opened the door and entered a sparsely furnished office; another open door led to what might have been a waiting room. Behind her, the chauffeur closed the outer door, this time locking it.

'The Countess von Widerstand, Herr Bochner,' Tobler said.

Bochner, who had been seated behind the desk, stood up. He was a tall, heavy man, who vaguely reminded her of the Russian commissar Ewfim Chalyapov. That was a sufficient cause for her to dislike him, even if she had not been conditioned to dislike all Gestapo personnel on sight.

'Countess,' he said. 'Please sit down.'

Anna sat in the straight chair before the desk, her shoulder bag dangling against her right side. Bochner returned behind the desk, Tobler stood beside him, and the chauffeur stood against the door; she could have been back in Geneva. 'Your goon suggested that you would tell me what this is all about.'

'My goon. Ah, ha ha. That is an Americanism, is it not? I do not think the lady likes you, Tobler.'

'But I like her, Herr Bochner.'

'Well, you will have to be patient. There are three of us.'

So that's how you would like it to be, Anna thought. It did not encourage her to feel any sympathy for him. 'You still have not told me why I am here,' she pointed out.

'You are a very arrogant woman.'

'Well, of course I am. I am the Countess von Widerstand. Have you never heard of me?'

'I have heard the name.'

'When last did you work in Germany?'

'Three years ago.'

'Ah. But someone told you I was coming to Sweden.'

'We were informed by Herr Werter of the Lübeck office.'

'Ah,' Anna said again.

'I believe that you have met Herr Werter?'

'Indeed I have. And he told you of me.'

'He said you are employed by the SD, but in what capacity he is not quite sure. He felt that your activities were suspicious, and suggested that we keep an eye on you while you are in Stockholm.'

'So you have been following me,' Anna said, pleasantly. 'And I was unaware of it. I congratulate you. So what have you found out?'

'You had lunch with Count Bernadotte the day before yesterday, and again today.'

'And this is of interest to you?'

'On your first meeting with Count Bernadotte you handed him a sealed envelope. Today he gave you an envelope back. I think we need to see what is in that envelope.'

'What makes you think that it is of the least interest to anyone except me?'

'Well, Countess, would you not say that coming all the way to Stockholm to exchange letters with Count Bernadotte, in preference to merely using the post office, is suspicious? And when it is taken in conjunction with your meeting with a man who apparently flew in from England just to see you and then flew out again – well . . .'

'It is very unfortunate that you found all of this out,' Anna said. 'But again I congratulate you on your diligence. However, I'm afraid I must refuse either to show you the contents of Count Bernadotte's letter, or to answer any more questions.' She stood up. 'So if you will excuse me . . .'

'You are not going anywhere, Countess, until you have satisfied us' – he grinned – 'in every possible way. It is not often that we have the privilege of entertaining such a handsome woman.'

Anna glanced at the door.

'You cannot get out. Nor is there any use screaming; these offices are sound-proofed. And there is no one in all Stockholm has any idea that you are here. Except Count Bernadotte. But as you have a seat booked on tomorrow morning's train to Malmö, he will not expect to hear from you again. If anyone else is interested, you will simply have disappeared on your walk back to your hotel.'

'Suppose I had elected to be driven back?'

'Then we would have had to force an entry to your hotel room. But this way is much more convenient for us.'

'Of course it is. You must consider this your lucky day. May I ask one more question before you start enjoying yourself?'

'What is it?'

'Is your secretary going to have a go at me too? I do not see her.'

'My secretary only comes in for a couple of hours every morning. By that time, you will no longer be here.'

'You have been so co-operative,' Anna said, 'in telling me everything I need to know. Well, in all the circumstances, I suppose I had better give you the letter.' She opened her shoulder bag and put her hand inside.

'That is a very sensible decision,' Bochner agreed. 'But you do realize that, after everything that has been said, we are not going to let you go without interrogating you.'

'I was sure of it,' Anna said, bringing up the Luger and shooting him in the chest, then turning the gun on the other two men before either could react. Tobler died instantly, shot in the heart. The chauffeur, hit in the stomach, and clearly in great pain, still managed to reach for his gun, but Anna shot him through the head before he could use it.

Bochner, hit on the right side of the chest and spewing blood, was grasping for the desk drawer. Anna stood above him. 'I don't know anything about Gestapo training methods,' she said, 'but in the SD one of the first essentials we have to learn is: always search a suspect the moment he, or she, is arrested. But it's too late for that, for you.'

She shot him again in the chest, sending him back to the floor, then went to the chauffeur, took the pistol from his hand and shot the dying Bochner in the forehead. Then she wiped the pistol clean of her prints, and placed it back in the chauffeur's hand, making sure the fingers were tight enough to leave their prints. Next she did the same for her own gun, wiping it clean before placing it in Bochner's hand. She looked around the room, but there was no trace of her presence to be seen. She let herself out, closing the door behind her, went down the stairs, and walked back to the hotel.

In her room, she ordered supper and a bottle of wine all to herself, then sat and gazed at Bernadotte's letter for some moments. But steaming it open would be highly risky. She had no doubt that whatever was in it would come out, eventually. Twenty-eight, she thought. And had a hot shower.

Crisis

'H m,' Himmler commented, studying Bernadotte's letter. 'Hm.'

'Not bad news, I hope, sir,' Anna said.

It was late at night and she had just regained Berlin, after an all-day journey from Stockholm, highlighted by the expression on Werter's face when she had stepped off the Malmö ferry and given him her brightest smile. But he was someone to be dealt with later. More immediately, her late arrival had meant getting Himmler out of bed, and he was even less prepossessing than usual, in his striped pyjamas and tousled hair – such as there was of it.

He raised his head. 'Did Count Bernadotte discuss my letter with you?'

'No, sir, he did not. He merely said that he would provide a written reply. But it took him two days to do so.'

'Yes. These Swedes are damnable people, so dour, so pessimistic. Still, they are the best we have.'

'The best for what, sir?' Anna asked innocently.

'For whatever we need them for.' He went to the sideboard and poured two balloons of cognac, gave her one. 'You had no trouble?'

'No, sir.'

'Hm.' He sat down and threw one leg across the other. 'I received a quite startling report from our Stockholm embassy this afternoon.'

'Sir?' As she knew what was coming, she was prepared for it.

'Did you know that we maintain a Gestapo office in that city? In fact we do in most neutral cities. It is illegal, of course, and so they operate under a variety of disguises. These are generally known to the local police, but as long as our people do not break the law they are tolerated.'

'And the Stockholm office has broken the law?' Anna allowed herself to look anxious.

'It is difficult to say. The Stockholm office no longer exists.'

Anna sipped her brandy. 'I do not understand, sir.'

'There was a three-man staff, with a Swedish secretary. Apparently, when the secretary went in this morning, she found our three agents all dead.'

'Good Lord! But how?'

'It would appear that they shot each other.'

'Sir?'

'Two of them were holding guns. The police have recovered the bullets and they are undergoing ballistic tests now, but there can be no doubt that they all came from the guns held by two of the dead men.'

'What a terrible thing,' Anna commented. 'Have the police a theory on what might have happened?'

'No. As I said, although our people were operating as trading agents, the Swedes knew who they were, which is why they immediately reported the incident to the embassy, presumably in the hope of obtaining some relevant information; but they could offer no explanation.'

'Perhaps they quarrelled over a woman,' Anna suggested.

'What, all three of them?'

'Well, two may have quarrelled, and the third attempted to interfere.'

'My God, what is this country coming to? These people are supposed to be the best we have. Still, as long as you were not in any way involved . . .' He peered at her.

'I did not go near any of our people in Stockholm, Herr Reichsführer' – which was no lie: they had come near her. 'You gave me the impression that my mission had to be secret.'

'Well, of course. And you have, as always, carried it out without a hitch. You are a treasure. I only wish Bernadotte had found it possible to be more positive. Still . . . Now you go downstairs to bed. I wish to see you first thing tomorrow morning on a very important matter.'

'Yes, sir.' Anna drained her glass and stood up. 'Heil Hitler.'

As no one had known how long she would be in Sweden, there had been no car waiting for her, and she had caught the train, which was why it had taken her so long to regain Berlin. So at least she did not have Essermann hanging round her neck. But she suspected that relief was only going to be temporary. If she seemed to have unloaded her responsibility for the murder of Hitler, and thus any risk of involvement, she had accumulated a new problem: Werter. As he had been the one who had alerted the Stockholm office to her visit, when the news reached him that that entire staff had been wiped out, he would have to be very thick indeed not to wonder if there wasn't a connection. Perhaps she should have told Himmler the truth. She had only been carrying out his orders that no one should learn the contents of those so-mysterious letters, and he could have no idea of the more important point: that no one could be allowed to know of Baxter's visit. And to further muddy the water, he was obviously about to send her off on another jaunt. Well, she thought, a couple of days in the company, and hopefully the arms, of Henri, would be a very pleasant relief.

Birgit was in bed, but scrambled up to greet her mistress, wearing striped pyjamas reminiscent of Himmler's though far more attractive. 'Oh, Countess, I am so glad you are home.'

As she was always greeted like this, Anna did not regard the maid's enthusiasm as exceptional. But she asked, 'Have you got us settled in?' The little apartment certainly looked comfortable enough.

'I have done my best. Your sister was here, yesterday.'

'What?'

'She apparently found out that we are living in this building, and wanted to see you.'

'What about?'

'She did not say.' Birgit peered at her. 'She is your sister?'

'Yes,' Anna agreed. 'Well, no doubt she'll come back if she has something on her mind. I am very tired and so I am going to bed.'

Was this another looming problem? she wondered, as she slid beneath the sheet. But it could keep. Himmler's problem, whatever it was, came first.

'Good morning, Anna. Sit down.'

Anna lowered herself into the chair before the desk.

'Now, this conspiracy business . . .'

Oh God, she thought. She had assumed that was buried.

'You are aware that there can be no doubt that the Allies are poised to carry out an invasion of France.'

'I know they have been building up forces, sir. But surely they cannot yet be ready for such an undertaking.'

'My information is that that they are entirely ready. The whole south of England has been turned into one vast armed camp. It seems certain that they are waiting only for the end of the winter with the promise of good weather in the Channel. So it may happen as soon as Easter. Certainly our army commanders expect it before the end of May. I do not understand about these things, but it seems that it will depend on the moon and the time of dawn and the correct tide. Obviously, we intend to smash them when they come, but we must do everything to make sure of this.'

Smash them when they come, Anna thought. Is that why you are negotiating so anxiously, and at the moment unsuccessfully, with Bernadotte? and why you are frantically moving as much money as possible out of Germany?

Baxter had given no indication that an invasion was close. But he would not, even to her; whatever his kind words, she knew he had never fully trusted her. But that was irrelevant, if they were actually coming, if the end of this nightmare in which she lived, and which had been going on now for six years, was actually in sight.

Himmler had been studying her. 'I know that it is an immense concept, Anna,' he said, 'which is why we must take all possible steps to make sure it ends in a victory for the Reich. If we can meet this invasion, and smash it, it will throw their plans back at least a year, and by the end of this year all our secret weapons will be operational.'

'Yes, sir.' She had heard so much about these secret weapons, but all she had been able to discover for certain was that they involved the new kind of bomb she had described to Baxter. In any event, her ability to remit information to London had ended with the demise of Bartoli, and since then her English masters had been more interested in the plot against Hitler than in any information about possible secret weapons she might have been able to obtain.

'That is why it is necessary for us to consider the possibility of there being a conspiracy amongst the high military command in a serious manner.'

'I thought we had dismissed it as fantasy.'

'No, no, Anna. You convinced me that Freddie von Steinberg could have had nothing to do with it. But I have been keeping track of things. That is my job, eh? – gathering straws in the wind; and some of these straws have been remarkably solid. There can be no doubt that Beck is up to something.'

Oh, my God! She thought. 'But . . .'

'Why haven't I arrested him? I will tell you why, Anna. It is because the information I have received convinces me that there are quite a few serving generals involved. What do you think the Führer would say if I placed half of the Wehrmacht's commanding officers under arrest? What would the Wehrmacht say? Would they fight to the last drop of their blood to defeat the Allies if they felt their generals were not wholeheartedly with them?'

'What a terrible situation,' Anna muttered. She was not thinking only of the Wehrmacht, or its officers. He did not seem to realize that Hitler was thinking along the same lines.

'Exactly.'

'May I ask, Herr Reichsführer, how many people know of your suspicions?'

'Well, of course, quite a few people know that I am keeping Beck, and certain other people, under surveillance. But no one knows exactly why.'

'But you have told the Führer?' She held her breath.

'No, I have not. He has more than enough on his plate without being worried by talk of a conspiracy, whether real or imagined. Besides, if there is a conspiracy, how do I know which of *my* people is involved. I have confided only in you, Anna, because I know that you are absolutely trustworthy.'

'Thank you, sir,' Anna said, remembering that Shakespeare had had his character Puck, in *A Midsummer Night's Dream*, reflect: *What fools these mortals be.*

'But I realize that you cannot carry out an investigation of this magnitude entirely on your own. However, your assistants must be absolutely as trustworthy as yourself. I assume you have total confidence in Essermann?'

'Ah . . .' But if she was going to have an assistant, Hellmuth was certainly the best prospect. 'Yes, sir. I do.'

'Then I will appoint him to be your aide. But you will also need a secretarial assistant who must be equally trustworthy.'

'I will find one, sir.' Even if she had no idea who it could be.

'Do not worry. I have the very person. Your sister.'

'*What?*'

Himmler raised his eyebrows. 'Don't you trust your sister? Wouldn't you like to have her working with you?'

'Of course I would like that, sir. But in a project of this magnitude . . . She has no experience.'

'She will learn from you. There could be no better teacher. I must tell you, Anna, that she has, so far, proved something of a disappointment.'

'Sir?'

'She seems to have a streak of – what shall I say? – squeamishness that you entirely lack. You remember your first big assignment? – that fellow Bordman?'

'Yes, sir.'

'You were told to seduce him, and you did it so successfully that he married you.'

'Yes, sir.'

'Tell me, what did he do to you, that first night? Or, ha ha, what did you do to him?'

'I did nothing to him, sir, except to make it plain that I would neither slap his face nor scream for help if he made advances. I was a virgin.'

'So, what did he do to you?'

'He fucked me, sir.'

'How?'

It was Anna's turn to raise her eyebrows.

Himmler flushed. 'I mean, was it strictly – well, the missionary position?'

'The first time, sir.'

'He did it more than once on your first night?'

'He was very enthusiastic, sir.'

'My God! But the second time . . .?'

'Was a rear entry, sir.'

Himmler produced a patterned handkerchief to pat his fore-head; he obviously had a vivid imagination. 'You did not object to this?'

'Well, actually, sir, I preferred it to the first way. I didn't have to look at his face.'

'Ha ha. You are a treasure. But tell me, suppose he had tried – well . . .'

'To sodomize me, sir?'

'Ah . . . yes. Would you have accepted that?'

'General Heydrich's orders were that I should refuse him nothing.'

'Did he ever, ah . . .?'

'No, sir.'

'Because he was an English gentleman, eh?'

Anna reflected that he obviously knew very little about too many English gentlemen. 'No, sir. It was because he could never sustain a hard enough erection long enough for such a difficult entry.'

The handkerchief was back at work. 'Perhaps you were fortunate. But if he had managed it, you would have accepted it, because it was your duty to do so. You would not have hit him with a . . . ah . . . chamber pot and run screaming from the room with nothing on.'

Oh, my God! Anna thought. 'Is that what happened?'

'He was a Turkish gentleman.'

'I see. So . . .?'

'She should have been dismissed from the service, sent to an SS brothel. You are not allowed to run screaming from your room in one of those situations. As for using a chamber pot as a weapon . . . This man was a very important member of the Turkish government, and he was quite put out.'

'I can imagine. And Katherine?'

'She has been suspended. As I said, she should have been immediately downgraded, but I intervened. After all, she is your sister, eh?'

'Thank you, sir. I am most enormously grateful.'

'I am giving her another chance, in your care. Not that there will be any sexual problems in this case, eh? Very well, Anna. I am relying on you.'

'Yes, sir. May I ask, is there a time scale involved?'

'Well, obviously, the sooner we can wrap this up the better. However, there must be no flaws in the evidence we present to the Führer. Be thorough, but exact.'

'Yes, sir. You understand that I will probably have to speak to some of these people, to get at the truth.'

Himmler frowned. 'You mean, put them under interrogation?'

'No, sir. I think that would be counterproductive at this stage. If I may say so, the secret of such successes as I have had lies in my ability to make people feel that I am on their side, that I understand their points of view, perhaps even that I am prepared to go along with them in whatever they are planning. This enables me to gain their confidence, as a result of which they are inclined to be indiscreet.'

'Ha ha. Yes. That is brilliant.'

'It is also open to misinterpretation by possibly hostile outsiders, especially as I will not be able to explain my actions to anyone except you.'

'Good point. What do you require?'

'A blanket carte blanche, sir – to cover any action I may be forced to take. There should be two, exact copies – one for me to carry with me in case I am arrested by any overzealous Gestapo agent; the other for me to keep in a safe place in case I am robbed of the first.'

Himmler stroked his chin. 'You realize that you are asking for unprecedented power.'

'I regard this is an unprecedented situation, sir. I hope you understand that my only desire is to serve you. As you have reminded me often enough, the facts of my career mean that my future is irretrievably bound to yours. And, of course, you will always have the power to revoke the carte blanche should I let you down.'

'Do you know, Anna, your powers of perception, your clarity of thought, make you unlike any woman I have ever met, or even heard of. I am not sure I would like to meet another. You will have your carte blanche. I just want to make one point: whatever you find out, you are to take no executive action without referring to me first.'

'Of course, sir,' Anna said. 'I am your servant.'

Had everything fallen into her lap? How she wanted to believe that. If the plot were successful, and Beck became head of state, Himmler would obviously lose much of his power. There remained pitfalls, but she had survived sufficient pitfalls in the past. And now she had to hurry.

'Oh, Anna,' Katherine sobbed. 'I have had such a terrible time.'

'I know,' Anna said.

Katherine frowned through her tears. 'You know about—'

'Your Turkish friend, yes. You know what should have happened to you?'

Katherine licked her lips. 'I could not stand that.'

'Well, you may not have to. As of this moment you are working for me.'

'For you? Oh Anna!' Katherine threw her arms round her sister's neck.

Anna allowed her a hug and then disengaged herself. 'It may not all be beer and skittles. Come with me.' She led her upstairs and into her office, where Essermann waited. 'This is my sister, Hellmuth.'

'I would have known that,' he said. 'But actually, we have met.'

Katherine simpered, and Anna wondered. But Hellmuth's sexual habits were strictly orthodox.

'Well,' she said. 'Now you are going to work together, with me, on a top-secret project.' She repeated the relevant parts of her conversation with Himmler.

Katherine listened with open-mouthed wonder. Hellmuth scratched his ear. 'I thought that business was finished,' he remarked.

'Apparently it isn't. But we have to proceed very cautiously, because there is no saying, at present, just how deep and widespread this conspiracy is, who, perhaps very highly placed, may be involved. Therefore not a word of what we say or record must ever be uttered outside this room.' She glanced at their faces. 'That will count as treason. Now, our first task is the collection and correlation of all the existing evidence, obtained as part of our surveillance operations over the past few months. That is your task, Hellmuth. I want you to accumulate all of this material from every available source – Gestapo, Abwehr and SS. If anyone objects, you are operating under the direct orders of Reichsführer Himmler and they can refer to his office. But none of the evidence must be shown to anyone except me. That is an order from the Reichsführer. He is relying on me to keep him fully up to date, and he will make the decision as to when we move, on anyone.'

Hellmuth looked as if he might have toothache at the idea of her having all the power in their relationship, but he nodded.

'Now, Katherine, you will tabulate and cross-reference all of that material, as Hellmuth brings it in. That may not sound very exciting, but remember that you are working for the Reich at the very highest level.'

Katherine also nodded, looking suitably determined.

'And what will you be doing?' Hellmuth asked.

Anna smiled at him. 'I am going to see if I can infiltrate this conspiracy.'

'What?' Hellmuth and Katherine spoke together.

'It is the Reichsführer's idea,' Anna explained.

'Are you sure?' Steinberg asked. 'I mean, the risk . . .'

'The time has come when we have to take risks,' Anna said. 'Himmler is launching a top-level investigation into all people who can possibly be involved. This is mainly the fault of your various associates who have been acting quite irresponsibly, making absurdly open telephone calls without apparently suspecting that their lines might be being tapped.'

'My God! Then we are finished!'

'Not at the moment. I have been placed in charge of the investigation.'

'You? But—'

'I will have to deliver, and fairly soon. But if you can carry out the assassination before I do, then we will all be in the clear.'

He sighed. 'There is a complication.'

Oh, shit! she thought; another one? 'Stauffenberg has changed his mind?'

'No, no. He is as keen as ever. But Beck . . .'

'Don't tell me he has got cold feet?'

'I don't think so. But he has been corresponding with other senior officers who are prepared to join us . . . But I suppose you know that.'

'Yes,' Anna said grimly. 'So does Himmler.'

'Well, they are of the opinion that killing Hitler will not be enough.'

'What do they want you to do – blow up the Chancellery? In any event, he is hardly ever there, nowadays.'

'We know. He spends much of his time in Berchtesgaden or in Rastenburg. But he is visited, regularly at both addresses, is he not, by his senior officers?'

'Of course. He depends on his staff officers for reports on which he bases his decisions. That is how Stauffenberg will get in.'

'And Himmler and Göring are often present, are they not?'

Anna leaned back in her chair. 'Just what are you trying to say?'

Steinberg licked his lips. 'I know he is your boss, and you work very closely with him, but you cannot like the man. I mean, he is a vicious monster.' He flushed as he gazed at her expression. 'Isn't he?'

'You have not answered my question.'

'Well . . .' Another nervous lick of the lips. 'It is the opinion of the generals, with which Beck concurs, that merely getting rid of Hitler is not sufficient, that if Göring and Himmler were left to take over the government, we would be no further ahead.'

'I see. Göring *and* Himmler. Why not go the whole hog and include Goebbels?'

'They do not think he is important. Göring has the Luftwaffe at his command. Himmler has the entire police force. Goebbels has the Ministry of Propaganda. That is meaningless. The question is, can you accept this?'

Anna continued to study him for some moments. In her opinion, Goebbels was the most dangerous man in Germany. But she knew she might be prejudiced. And there was a good deal of sense in the generals' point of view. Himmler might not himself be a man of action, but he was certainly capable of *re*acting. And if he were to go up with Hitler, she would be the only person who would know of the nearly two million dollars he had salted away. Apart from Laurent, of course. But she had no doubts of Laurent's loyalty – to her – now. While again, if Himmler were to go up with Hitler, she would surely, if she acted quickly enough, retain sufficient clout to get her parents out of their Polish prison before anyone else could react.

Steinberg was encouraged by her silence. 'You could help us by providing a list of Himmler's schedules . . .'

'And I suppose you have someone at the Air Ministry to keep you informed about Göring's movements.'

'Yes, we do.'

'You may be creating an unnecessary additional problem. Every day you delay increases the risk of detection.'

'But you are in charge of the investigation. You have said you could stall it.'

'I can for a while, but only a while.'

'It will happen at the first opportunity. You have my word. Anna . . . when can I see you again?'

'Business before pleasure,' Anna reminded him. 'In any event, you cannot see me again, outside this office, until after it is over: I am now living in the basement of this building. So . . . I will wait to hear from you.'

'A directive from the Führer,' Himmler announced. 'He handed it to me personally when I saw him at the Berghof, yesterday. You won't believe this, Anna.'

Anna hardly believed he was standing in front of her desk. Every time he went to the Berghof for a conference she was not sure he would come back. But perhaps Göring had not also been there, or Stauffenberg's presence had not been required. She was completely in the dark as to what the conspirators were doing. But that was at her request, and it was how it had to be, if she was to have any hope of surviving. So she said, 'Yes, Herr Reichsführer?'

'The Abwehr is to be amalgamated with the SD, under my orders.'

'Good heavens!' She had almost forgotten that was going to happen.

'You understand what this means?'

'I would say that OKW is dissatisfied with their perform-ance,' Anna suggested.

'Well, they have every right to be. But it is more serious than that. The Führer is convinced that they are the centre of the conspiracy.'

Anna registered disbelief in her face. 'But . . . Admiral Canaris . . .'

'You have nothing on him?'

'No, sir, I have not.'

'Well, maybe I will give him to you to interrogate, one of these days. Would I be right in supposing that you do not like him?'

'I have only met Admial Canaris once, sir.'

'But it was one of his people who tried to rape you, while pretending to arrest you, two years ago. As I recall, you broke his neck.'

'I was defending myself, sir,' Anna said modestly. 'I do not believe that Admiral Canaris had anything to do with that.'

'Well, we shall have to see what you can find on him, when you come back.'

'Am I going away, sir?' Again, she thought.

'I have a delivery for Herr Laurent.'

'A million plus,' Henri said, 'to add to the million plus he already has. How does he get all this stuff?'

'By arresting everyone he can and confiscating every penny they possess,' Anna said.

'Well . . . it's all here, whenever you want it. I would say you've enough now to get out and live a very good life.'

They were in his Lucerne apartment, to which she had gone immediately on arriving. The sense of well-being, the ability to relax in Switzerland itself, much more in his company, was overwhelming. She had hoped to achieve a similar period of

R & R in Stockholm, and it hadn't happened. Now it was suddenly threatening not to happen here either. She turned to face him, seated beside her on the settee. 'I can't touch that money, Henri.'

'Say again?'

'It isn't mine.'

'Didn't Himmler say he'd share it?'

'Yes, he did. But it's not his to share, either. It belongs to a whole lot of innocent people, whom he has either murdered or locked up just to get his hands on their wealth.'

Laurent's hand had been resting on her breast. Now he moved it to scratch his head. 'I don't understand.'

'Henri, I have been forced to do a lot of very nasty things in my life, but I am not a thief.'

'Yet you bring this stuff to me.'

'While I am required to work for the Reichsführer, I must obey his orders, without question.'

'I am getting more befogged by the moment. You say you are required to work for him. Whose orders are you obeying? – Hitler's?'

'Please don't ask me that, Henri. And please don't be angry with me. You are more precious to me than almost anyone else.'

'I could never be angry with you, my dearest girl. But supposing – well, that Himmler never gets around to claiming the money? What do you propose to do with it?'

'With your help, give it back.'

'To whom? You say most of these people are dead, or are very likely to be by the time it's ours to give.'

'Then we'll think of some worthwhile charity.'

'You really are unique. Knowing you has been the greatest experience of my life.' He took her in his arms.

Anna was no stranger to tension: she had lived surrounded by it for five years. But the next few months were the tensest of her life. She provided Steinberg with a list of Himmler's projected movements over the coming weeks, and then could do nothing more than wait, a business complicated by the number of times he returned from Rastenburg; had Göring given up going?

There was also the matter of stalling – both Himmler and

her staff. Essermann accumulated a mountain of information, which was duly handed to Katherine, who meticulously categorized it and filed it. Both were aware that they had more than sufficient evidence to make a whole raft of arrests. Anna put them off by telling them that Himmler had not yet made up his mind to take action, and they accepted this. Indeed, they became quite a jolly little team and celebrated her twenty-fourth birthday in her office with a couple of bottles of champagne. To Himmler she kept insisting that they lacked various vital pieces of evidence but that they were on the verge of making the final breakthrough. This he in turn accepted, as he had become accustomed to accepting everything she told him. But time was running out.

For everyone. He appeared in her office on the morning of 6 June. 'Well,' he announced. 'It's happened!'

'Sir?' For a moment she supposed he was referring to Hitler's death. But then she realized he couldn't be, as he himself was still alive.

'The Allies have landed. In Normandy.'

'But . . . Normandy?'

'I have been on the phone to the Führer. He says it has to be a feint; the only sensible place for them to cross the Channel is at its narrowest point, the Pas de Calais. But apparently there are an awful lot of them.'

'But they have got ashore?'

'Yes. As I say, in considerable numbers. Oh, we are holding them, but the situation is complicated by the fact that we have to maintain our strength in the Calais area, to handle the real invasion when it comes. What is worrying is that they seem to have many more men and ships available than have been reported by our spies, if they can launch a feint on this scale and still have their main force poised to attack in the north. That is another failure of Abwehr.'

'Perhaps it isn't a feint,' Anna murmured.

'My dear girl, you know nothing of military matters. It is sixty miles of open water between England and Normandy. No modern army can be sustained across such a distance. Think of the logistics involved, the vehicles, the fuel required. No, no, it has to be a feint. It is just a matter of how soon they give up trying and get back into their ships. It will not be long, because I have something else to tell you. Our V-bombs are ready. We are going to rain such a devastating series of blows on London that all war production will cease. We are now approaching the climactic battle of the war. Victory or death, eh? Are you afraid, Anna?'

'Not so long as you are in control, Herr Reichsführer.'

She was not lying. As long as overconfident and totally misguided idiots were in control of German strategy, defeat was staring them in the face, even if they seemed unable to see it. She remembered Baxter's calm certainty that the RAF could deal with the V-bombs. He had never been wrong in his judgements before, however unlikely some of them had appeared in the early days of the war.

After a month even the High Command started to realize that the Normandy landings had not been a feint, as the Allies poured more and more men and materiel across the Channel. The Wehrmacht fought desperately, and at this stage were retreating only step by step, but they were retreating, and everyone knew that once the open country beyond the bridgehead was reached, the Allies' superiority in planes and tanks would explode.

Could it really be the end? Anna wondered. It was a scenario that she had never expected – that the Allies might get into and across Germany and reach Berlin from the west before the Russians got there from the east. In that case, she and hers would be saved. So was it worthwhile continuing the plot against Hitler? Or was it more important than ever, because as long as he remained in control Germany would fight to the last man, and in the process be utterly destroyed?

As she had heard nothing from the conspirators, and Himmler still paid regular visits to either Rastenburg or Berchtesgaden – as, presumably, did Göring – and always returned unharmed, she had to wonder if the conspirators had been drawing the same conclusions as herself. But then, at the end of the first week of July, with the resistance in the west at last beginning to crumble, Himmler paid one of his visits to her office, carefully closing the door behind himself.

'Herr Reichsführer!' Anna rose from behind her desk.

'Herr Reichsführer!' Katherine rose from behind her desk.

'At ease.' Himmler frowned at Katherine, as if he could not remember who she was.

'My sister, sir,' Anna explained. 'You placed her on my team.'

'Oh, yes. I remember. Leave us.'

Katherine glanced at Anna, and received a quick nod. She hurried from the room.

'Is she proving a success?' Himmler inquired.

'Yes, indeed. She is a very hard worker.'

'Well, the time for work is over. Now we must have action.'

'Sir?'

'Things are not going well. You know that.'

'Yes, sir.'

'The Führer has come to the conclusion that there is a severe lack of enthusiasm in our commanders on the Western Front. He smells treachery.'

'Sir? But . . . Field Marshal von Rundstedt? Field Marshal Rommel?'

'Even them. What have you got on them?'

'On Rundstedt, nothing. On Rommel . . . His name has been mentioned in some of our monitored telephone calls, but I have no proof that he is actually involved, only that his involvement is desired by the conspirators.'

'Well, as I said, we must act, now. The Führer has summoned me to the Berghof on Sunday, and I know he is going to inquire about the state of our investigation of the conspiracy. I must have something for him. If he were to find out that we have been accumulating all this information for months and made no arrests – well . . . it might be difficult to explain. I wish a list of names to give him.'

My God! Anna thought; I have finally run out of time. 'Including the two field marshals?'

'Well, Rommel, certainly. And anyone on whom you have any information at all. Bring Nebe into your team if you think that will help.'

Think, think, think. 'I have to advise you, Herr Reichsführer, that we do not actually have sufficient proof against any of them to stand up in court.'

'You are thinking of an ordinary court in ordinary times. But these are not ordinary times. If the Führer gives the go-ahead, we will put them before one of Freisler's people's courts. He'll find them guilty, with or without sufficient evidence. Once he does that, and we get them into our interrogation chambers, we'll soon get all the proof we need. Don't forget, Anna. I want that list by Saturday afternoon to take with me.'

Catastrophe

H e left the room, and Katherine hurried in. 'He seems very upset.'

'He is very upset.' So was she. She dared not create any further delays. Steinberg had told her that Nebe was in the conspiracy, but as he did not know that *she* was in it, it would be sticking her neck out unacceptably far to approach him except in strict accordance with Himmler's instructions. On the other hand, the conspirators had to be warned, and immediately, that they would be liable to arrest by the beginning of the next week. Once again she had to risk everything. She picked up her telephone. 'Put me through to the Foreign Ministry.'

Clicks and bumps. 'Foreign Office. Who is it speaking, please?'

One of Ribbentrop's arrogant innovations, which never ceased to annoy her. 'This is the Countess von Widerstand. I wish to speak with Count von Steinberg.'

'I will just see if he is in his office, Countess.'

More clicks and bumps. 'Anna?'

'I wish to see you, Count,' Anna said in her coldest tone. 'Immediately.'

'Ah . . .' He was obviously taken aback. 'You mean now?'

'That is what immediately means, Count. Would you like me to send a car for you?'

'Are you placing me under arrest?'

'That depends on what you have to say to me, Count. I will expect you in fifteen minutes.'

She hung up, and looked at Katherine, who had never seen her sister in full flow before.

'I think I had better see him alone,' Anna said.

'*Are* you going to arrest him? I thought he was your friend.'

'No one is my friend, Katherine, if they turn out to be an enemy of the Reich. Now off you go.'

Katherine gulped, and left the room, and Steinberg arrived a few minutes later, looking anxiously left and right as he came in, as if expecting SD agents to be waiting for him.

'Come in, Freddie,' Anna said. 'Sit down.'

He obeyed. 'What is the matter?'

'I am hoping you are going to tell me that. You haven't been in touch for two months.'

'There has been nothing to report. Stauffenberg has twice been to Berchtesgaden with the bomb in his briefcase, but on neither occasion has either Göring or Himmler been present.'

'I warned you that such a stupid reservation would cause trouble.'

'Our time will come.'

'No, it will not. Your time is just about up. Listen.' She outlined her meeting with Himmler, watched his face pale, and then, to her surprise, glow again.

'Then as you say, we can wait no longer. Well, Stauffenberg is also summoned to the Berghof on Sunday. Göring is going to be there, and now you say Himmler as well? He'll do it then.'

'You realize that will be too late to stop me giving Himmler that list.'

'That is not relevant, if both he and Hitler are dead before they can act on it.'

Anna regarded him for several seconds. 'It could just work,' she agreed. 'What exactly will be your plan?'

'Stauffenberg will attend the meeting and place his briefcase as near as possible to where Hitler is standing. This meeting always assembles at eleven. I am to telephone and ask to speak with him at ten past. He will leave the room to take the call but not do so. Instead he will get into his car and wait. The moment the bomb explodes, and he sees the entire conference room go up, he will call me back and we will set everything in motion here. Stieff has his men ready, and will take over the city the moment I call him. Stauffenberg will return here as rapidly as possible, but by then the coup will have been completed.'

'And if something goes wrong?'

'If he answers the call I will know he has been unable to plant the bomb. In which case I will abort all troop movements.'

It is too elaborate, Anna thought. 'What about the people left here?'

'What people?'

'Well, Goebbels, for starters.'

'That little cripple?' Steinberg said contemptuously. 'He is Hitler's creature. Without Hitler, he is nothing.'

I hope you're right, Anna thought.

'I suppose Essermann might be a nuisance,' Steinberg mused. 'But you can handle Essermann, can't you, Anna?'

'I can handle Essermann,' Anna said, thoughtfully.

'Thank God for that,' Essermann said. 'I thought he was never going to make up his mind.'

'He hasn't made up his mind,' Anna pointed out. 'He wants the Führer to do that. The list of names we have, if acted on, would just about tear the heart out of the Wehrmacht.'

'But if they are in any event traitors . . .'

'It's not our business to make judgements, Hellmuth. Our business is simply to supply facts. Let me see your list.'

He handed it to her, and she scanned it. 'General Stieff?' she inquired. She had deliberately kept him out of the investigation. 'What is his name doing here?'

'Well . . .' Essermann looked embarrassed. 'He commands the Berlin garrison.'

'And that makes him a conspirator? I would have said the fact that he has been given such a responsible position must mean that he is the most trustworthy officer available.'

'But don't you see, Anna, that holding such a command, *were* he to be a member of the conspiracy, he would be in a position to take over the city, take over the government, in a matter of hours.'

Anna leaned back in her chair. 'Really, Hellmuth, your paranoia is beginning to disturb me.'

'But—'

'Tell me, who at this moment, and in the absence of the Führer, is the most powerful man, militarily, in Berlin?'

'Well . . . I would say the Reichsführer.'

'I agree with you. Then why is his name not on this list?'

'What?'

'You say that Stieff's name is here simply because he is in a position to subvert the government, not that you have any proof that he intends to do so. But you have just agreed that the man who is in the best of all positions to subvert the government is the Reischsführer. Ergo, his name has to be on your list.' She held it out. 'Write it down.'

Essermann gulped. 'I could not possibly do that.'

'Why not?'

'Well . . . it could not be true.'

'You are too selective in choosing your truths. But you are correct. The only truths that matter here, where we are dealing with life and death, are those supported by positive proof. You have no evidence that General Stieff is engaged in any subversive activity, and there have been no inexplicable telephone calls from his office. Therefore . . .' She placed the sheet of paper on her desk, picked up her pen, and struck out Stieff's name. 'Now, all these others – you are sure that you have sufficient proof for each one?'

'I have recorded telephone conversations that are highly suspicious.'

'Hm.' She could see no way out of virtually condemning all of them.

'May I see your list?' Essermann asked.

'I have told you that it ties in with yours, in most aspects.'

'Is Steinberg on it?'

'I do not see him on yours.'

'I have not been allowed to investigate him. *You* have not allowed me to investigate him.'

'Because he is not worth investigating. I have told you this.'

'You are protecting him.'

'Oh, really, Hellmuth, why should I do that? I do not even particularly like the man.'

'Is he not one of your lovers?'

'That is absurd, and insulting. Now kindly leave me. I have work to do.'

She waited until he had stamped from the office before allowing herself to find her handkerchief and dab sweat from her neck.

How slowly the week passed. Anna deliberately hung on to the list for as long as possible. She could not say why. Perhaps she was hoping for a miracle, although hourly she expected her phone to ring and Himmler to summon her to his presence to demand it. But he never did, and when they met in the corridors he gave her his invariable benevolent smile.

But as he had certainly told her he wanted the list ready by Saturday afternoon, she felt she had to deliver. If he was going all the way to Berchtesgaden, he might well be leaving tonight. Besides, she was curious as to the reason for his sudden lack of interest after such a direct order. She went to his office, found him seated at his desk reading a report. He looked up. 'Ah, Anna. Are you off?'

'I have that list you asked for, Herr Reichsführer.'

'The list? Of course. Keep it for the time being, will you? I'll look at it next week.'

'Sir? Aren't you due at the Berghof tomorrow?'

'Oh, that's been cancelled. Something must have come up.'

Almost Anna sat down without being invited: her knees felt weak.

'Instead I am to join him at Rastenburg on Thursday. You'll never guess why?'

He was absolutely right; Anna's brain was still overwhelmed by this sudden reprieve. But was it a reprieve? It meant that the assassination would have to be postponed yet again, and every postponement increased the risk of betrayal or discovery. 'No, sir,' she said. 'I cannot.'

'The Führer is to be joined by Il Duce, to discuss the formation and operation of this new Fascist republic. He wants all of us military departmental heads to be present. What a bore. You know my opinion of this new idea – of Italians in general.'

'And the list, Herr Reichsführer? You will present it then?'

'I will take it with me, and see if I have an opportunity to present it. But I am sure you appreciate that it is something that is going to need a good deal of discussion.'

'Of course, sir.' Anna could feel the relaxation slowly seeping through her system – although there remained a lot to be done. But that would be Freddie's business; all she had to do was contact him.

She returned to her office, sat at her desk, and telephoned the Foreign Ministry. 'I am sorry, Countess,' the girl said, 'Count von Steinberg has already left the office.'

Shit! Anna thought. 'Then kindly tell me his home telephone

number.' This was undoubtedly tapped, which was why she had never used it before; but all she had to do was summon him to her office.

'I do not think that the Count has gone home, Countess. I understand that he was leaving Berlin for the weekend.'

Shit, shit, shit! Anna thought. But what was she getting so upset about? So Stauffenberg would go to Berchtesgaden tonight or tomorrow – supposing his visit had not also been cancelled – find that neither Göring nor Himmler was there, and answer Freddie's call. So he would then do his duty as a staff officer, and come home again. She just wished it hadn't all been so elaborate.

She had an early dinner, went to bed and slept soundly. As it was a Sunday, she was not required in the office; and as she couldn't get hold of Freddie, there was nothing she could do about the conspiracy either. So she remained in bed after breakfast, reading a novel to occupy her mind. When she got up, she had a bath, dressed, and was disturbed by the sound of tramping boots in the street above her head. 'What is going on, Birgit?' she asked.

'I do not know, Countess. There are soldiers marching about the place.'

My God! She thought. Can he have gone ahead and done it? Remaining hidden away was out of the question. She went upstairs. There was only a skeleton staff on duty, and these were mostly gathered at the windows, looking out. 'What is happening?' she asked.

'I do not know, Countess,' said one of the female secretaries. 'They seem to be expecting trouble. Look, over there?'

On the street corner, overlooking the headquarters, a machine-gun post had been set up, a mini-fortress of sand-bags. Anna felt quite cold. This could only be happening by Stieff's orders, therefore . . . But Himmler was at home in his apartment. She had no idea where Göring was, but in view of what Himmler had told her, it was very unlikely that he was at the Berghof either. But if Stauffenberg had gone ahead anyway . . .

She realized that she could be in considerable danger. Freddie had sworn that no one knew of her part in the conspiracy other than himself – and Johannsson, of course.

But Johannsson was undoubtedly safely in Stockholm, and to the average German, certainly everyone in this building, she was the most fervent upholder of the regime in the country. Her execution would be at the top of every hit list, at least until Freddie himself turned up.

She returned downstairs to her apartment, to find that Birgit had gone out – obviously to find out what was happening. Well, the woman would have to fend for herself; she had no intention of tamely presenting her neck to an executioner's sword: her business was to stay alive until Freddie came for her. She locked the door, checked that her new Luger was loaded and placed her two spare magazines on the table before seating herself behind it, facing the door.

She sat there for two hours, never moving, her brain totally concentrated on what might lie immediately ahead. Then there was a rasp of a key in the lock, but as Anna had left her key in place, whoever was out there was unable to make an entry. On the other hand, the only other person who possessed a key to this apartment was Birgit.

Not that Anna intended to take any risk. She got up and stood beside the door, gun resting against her shoulder. 'Who is it?'

'Countess? It is me, Birgit.'

Anna turned the key. 'It is open.'

She wrapped her left hand round the butt of the pistol on top of her right, and levelled the weapon. Birgit opened the door, stepped inside, and closed it behind her, only then turning to look at Anna. 'Countess!' she cried.

'Just being cautious,' Anna assured her, lowering the gun. 'What is happening up there?'

'It is all so strange, Countess. There were all those soldiers, soldiers everywhere.'

'I saw them,' Anna said. 'What were they doing?'

'That is the funny thing. They were there for a few hours, and then they went away, back to their barracks.'

'Do you know,' Anna said, 'I feel like opening a bottle of champagne. Will you join me in a glass?'

'What exactly happened here yesterday, Anna?' Himmler asked on Monday morning.

'I don't know, sir. It was very odd.'

'I am told that it was an exercise. But now Stieff is unavailable for comment. Yet it was carried out on his orders. Here in Berlin! What enemy is he expecting to take over the city, this far from any fighting front? Unless . . . Have you got him on your list to be investigated?'

'No, sir.'

'Why not?'

'Well, there is no suggestion that he is, or could be, associated with any of the conspirators.'

'He may be smarter than you think – even you, Anna. Get me everything you can on him, before Thursday.'

It was Wednesday morning before Essermann again came to her office, and then only because she sent for him. In that time she had heard nothing from Steinberg. But she could work out what must have happened. Freddie must have made the telephone call, had no reply, and passed the word for Stieff to move – without waiting for confirmation. It must have been only after that that Stauffenberg had discovered that neither Himmler nor Göring were attending the Berghof that day, and been able to contact Freddie and abort the action. As she had felt from the start, it had just been too complicated. They had been enormously lucky that no one had actually been arrested, that no attempt had been made actually to take over any government departments – though that was itself redolent of looming disaster, in that Stieff's failure to take immediate, decisive action pointed to a great deal of uncertainty on his part.

But now she had no choice other than to wash her hands of the whole thing, and obey Himmler's directive. 'Where have you been?' she inquired.

'Working,' Essermann replied.

'Without referring to me?'

'I had gained the impression that you were no longer interested in my opinion.'

'Really, Hellmuth, you are behaving like a teenager. So we had a difference of opinion. Do you expect us to agree on everything all of the time?'

He looked suitably abashed.

'Well,' she said, 'The list is complete, and will go to the Führer tomorrow. So . . .' The phone rang. For a moment she hesitated before picking up.

'Are you alone?'

Shit, she thought. Shit, shit, shit. He was the last person on earth she wished to hear from at this moment. 'No.'

'Well then, just listen. Did you know that Rommel has been blown up?'

'My God! He's not . . .?'

'He's not dead. His car was strafed by one of those RAF things – a Tornado. But he is very badly hurt and will be out of action for some time. One more blow, eh? The Führer is very upset. He wishes to see you.'

'Me?' Anna could not prevent her voice rising.

'Yes, you, you silly girl. Who else would he want to see?'

'But . . . when?'

'Be at Rangsdorf at six this evening. It will be the same procedure. You will return tomorrow.'

Anna stared at the phone. She could not believe this was happening.

'Did you hear me, Anna?'

'Yes, Herr – sir.'

'Then is something the matter?'

'No, sir. I was surprised. I had not expected to be called again.'

'You are too modest. He adores you. He feels that you can relieve the tension. Six o'clock. I look forward to hearing from you when you return.'

The phone went dead. Anna slowly replaced the receiver.

'That sounded like bad news,' Hellmuth suggested.

'What makes you think that?'

'You look quite concerned.'

'It is *very* bad news. Field Marshal Rommel has been badly wounded. His car was strafed by the RAF.'

'His name is on our list.'

'I know that. But as he is going to be out of action for some time, I think we can leave him off for the time being. But you will deliver the other names to the Reichsführer tomorrow morning.'

'You do not wish to do this yourself?'

'I will not be here. I am going out of town tonight.'

'Where are you going?'

'That is my business, Hellmuth. But I can tell you that it is state business.'

He snapped his fingers. 'That telephone call! Who was it from?'

'That also is state business. Now, I am going down to my apartment to change my clothes. I shall be leaving in a couple of hours. I will see you tomorrow.' She got up and went to the door. 'Believe me, Hellmuth,' she said. 'There are some things it is better for you not to know.'

She went down to the basement, found an embarrassed Birgit just going out.

'Countess? I was going to the shops. The queues are terrible. It took me two hours this morning to get a loaf of bread, and the butcher's was closed by the time I got there. But the sign said they would be opening again at five.'

Anna looked at her watch. It was a quarter to four.

'I thought I'd get there early,' the maid explained.

'That seems sensible. But I will not be in for dinner.'

'Oh. But . . .'

'Buy something for yourself. Do not expect me in tonight. I will be back tomorrow.'

'Yes, Countess.' She hurried off.

Anna went into her bedroom, stripped off her clothes and ran a bath. She had not yet allowed herself to think. Now she had to. But what was there to think about? she wondered as she sank into the suds. She had no idea if the conspirators would try again tomorrow, when it appeared everything they required would be in place, or if their morale had been too shattered by Sunday's debacle. She personally would not be involved; she would surely be there and back long before the conference convened. The embarrassment of possibly encountering Himmler could be overcome by referring him to Hitler, and in any event would be irrelevant if he were about to be blown up. The ordeal of having to spend another night with Hitler, or at least part of one, might be a personal catastrophe, compounded by the knowledge that she was having sex with a dead man. Going on what had happened the last time, it was going to be a very long twenty-four hours. But she had endured very long twenty-four-hour – even forty-eight-hour – periods more than once in the past. This one was just compounded by the possible enormity of the occasion. But she could do nothing more than practise what she had always done so successfully. She knew what had to be done, and in what order. It was simply a matter of concentrating, and taking it one step at a time.

It was all so dreadfully familiar. Even the mechanic was the same; he greeted her as an old friend. But the flight was completed in daylight and, as before, she was driven directly to Hitler's bunker.

Frau Engert also greeted her as an old friend. 'Dr Morell is waiting for you.'

'Don't tell me I have to be searched again?'

'It is the rule, I'm afraid. And he does enjoy it so.'

The Doctor was as sharp as ever. 'Aha,' he remarked. 'I see you have a new shoulder bag.'

'Why, yes, Herr Doktor. My maid spilled something on the other one, and stained it.'

He was examining the contents. 'And you have given up using that peroxide.'

'It didn't seem to be doing much good.'

'Such accessories are a waste of time.' He gestured towards the table.

'You know the form,' Frau Engert said when the ordeal was completed. 'Your dinner will be sent in to you.'

'Do you have any idea when the Führer will be in?'

'None at all. He is very busy, as you can imagine, what with everything that is going on. However, I know there is a staff conference scheduled for tomorrow, and also that Il Duce is arriving tomorrow afternoon. I imagine the Führer will wish a good night's sleep.' She peered at her. 'Does he sleep, when he is with you?'

'Of course.'

'Before, or after?'

'It was after, the last time.'

'But only briefly. Do you not remember? He woke up only minutes after you had left, and found that you had forgotten your bag. And immediately sent it after you. He is genuinely fond of you. If you do not do or say anything stupid, you may have a brilliant future.'

My future, or certainly, the future of which you speak, is not in my hands, Anna thought, had her supper, and prepared herself for bed. She knew the drill now, fell asleep, and awoke at Hitler's entrance.

He seemed more ebullient than the last time, and certainly pleased to see her. 'Anna!' He embraced her, holding her very tightly. 'You are, as always, a breath of Heaven.'

That was a remarkable compliment, coming from the ruler of Hell. 'As you are, my Führer,' she assured him, 'I am so happy to see you looking so well.'

'Why should I not be looking well? We are on the verge of great things. And you know, I feel that *I* will accomplish great things, with you, tonight.'

Oh Lord! Anna thought. But she could not resist asking, 'And the war is going well?'

'As well as we could wish. Oh, the Allies are making some progress in France, and poor Rommel has managed to get in the way of a bomb, but they must know that they are lost.'

'Ah . . .'

He began to undress. 'My V-bombs, Anna. My V-bombs!'

'They are being successful?'

'Oh, indeed. The V-1s have not been quite as deadly as I had hoped. They are not fast enough, and these new RAF planes, the Mosquitoes, can catch them. But our new model, the V-2, flies at a thousand miles an hour, and is unstoppable. They will have to negotiate a peace long before they can exploit any victories they may be gaining in France. Anyway, it is in their interests to do so. Even that madman Churchill, for all his rhetoric, must realize that Soviet Russia, were she to succeed in defeating us, would be the greatest threat to world peace since Genghis Khan. Did someone not once say, "If Germany did not exist, it would be necessary to invent her"? – just to keep out the Asiatic hordes. Oh, yes, we shall be fighting shoulder to shoulder with the British and the Americans before the year is out. Now, no more politics.' Naked, he took her in his arms.

It was no less exhausting than the last time, but at least he managed to enter her and ejaculate in her, which apparently pleased him enormously. When she made to move afterwards, he said, 'Stay. I want to sleep with you in my arms.'

She could only hope that he did not mean to try again, but actually fell asleep, to awake when Hermann brought breakfast in. She looked at Hitler, who was also awake.

'Hermann,' he said. 'What time is it?'

'Eight o'clock, my Führer. You said you wished to be called at eight o'clock.'

'Yes. Thank you, Hermann.'

The valet cast another hasty glance at Anna, who realized that she possessed only a fraction of the sheet; but it would have been juvenile to react. Anyway, this man had been present on both occasions when she had been searched.

Hitler got out of bed, put on a dressing gown, and sat at the table to pour coffee. 'For you?'

'Thank you.' Anna also got out of bed, and reached for her own dressing gown.

'No,' he said. 'I prefer to look at you as you are. I think that you, naked and tousled, are the sight any man would wish to carry with him through all eternity. You are Eurynome come to life.'

My God, she thought. Can he be prescient? She sat opposite him, sipped orange juice. 'You are my Führer. Should I not be preparing to leave?'

'Your aircraft will wait until you are ready. I have a tiring day ahead of me. This morning there is a conference, at which everyone will present his own gloomy point of view. They are incapable of seeing the greater picture. They lack vision. And then I must entertain Il Duce. Oh, he is a great man. I have never doubted that for a moment. But even he has become a pessimist. I do not blame him, after the way he was stabbed in the back by the very men he led to greatness. But he is a difficult conversationalist. You were to report to me on the progress of your investigation into this conspiracy.'

Accustomed as she had become to his habit of interjecting questions into apparently innocent conversations, Anna was still taken by surprise. But her wits were quick enough to respond. 'You were going to send for me, my Führer.'

'So I was. I have been busy. *Is* there a conspiracy?'

As Himmler was in possession of her findings, she could take no chances on being caught out, even if they were about to be blown to perdition. If they were not, if the conspirators missed this chance as well, they would have to fend for themselves; she did not see them getting another and, in fact, they would not deserve one. 'I'm afraid there is, my Führer.'

He had been munching a piece of toast, which he lowered
to the plate. 'And you have done nothing about it?'

'I have reported my findings to the Reichsführer. He was
to present them to you on Sunday, but the meeting was
cancelled. I understand he is bringing them with him today.'

Hitler resumed eating his toast, while staring at her. Then
he asked, 'Are your findings conclusive?'

'That is for you to determine, my Führer. My evidence
consists of reported meetings, telephone conversations . . . As
to whether these are sinister or merely grumblings . . . As you
have just said, there seems to be a tendency to pessimism at
the moment . . .'

'Do you share in that?'

'Of course I do not, sir.'

'Why not?'

'I have absolute confidence in you, my Führer.'

Again he stared at her for several seconds, and she wondered
if she might have laid it on a little too thick. Then he said,
'You almost make me wish to put you in command of my
armies. As for these swine . . .' Suddenly his voice became
shrill and his eyes blazed. 'I shall destroy them all. I shall
make them rue the day they were born. I shall . . .' Again,
with unexpected suddenness the passion ended; he wiped a
fleck of foam away from the corner of his mouth. 'Oh, look
at the time. Half past eight. They'll all be turning up over the
next couple of hours; the conference is scheduled for eleven.
I'm afraid, Anna, that our little idyll must end. For today.'

'Of course, sir. May I bathe?'

'Certainly. May I watch you?'

He watched her dress as well. He had said he wanted to carry
her image through eternity. She wished him joy of it. When
he was ready, he held her in his arms for a final kiss. 'You
have served me very well, Anna. I shall send for you again.
Soon.'

Then she was in the car, and able to relax, just a little. That
brief glimpse into the molten torment that was his mind had
been as frightening as it had been startling. What might happen
if he lived to study her report did not bear thinking about.
But it was out of her hands, now.

She arrived at the airstrip just after ten. Her aircraft was, as promised, waiting for her, and another plane was just landing. She got out of the car, watched the several passengers disembarking, her heartbeat quickening as she saw the unmistakable figure of Stauffenberg. They came towards her, and several gave her an uncertain smile or nod of the head; they knew who she was even if they could not immediately decide what she might be doing there. To her relief, Himmler was not amongst them; as this conference had definitely not been cancelled, she had to presume that he was either there already or was coming on a later plane.

Stauffenberg walked past her without a greeting, although he certainly also knew who she was. But to him, as to all the others, she was Himmler's creature.

They got into the waiting cars and were driven off, and she boarded. Her mechanic soon got the message that she was not in the mood for conversation, and they flew in silence, landing just after one. A car was waiting for her, and she reached Gestapo Headquarters in fifteen minutes, to her invariable enthusiastic greeting from Birgit.

'Oh, Countess, I am just preparing lunch.'

'I don't think I will have any lunch, thank you, Birgit.'

'Countess? Are you all right?'

'Yes, I am all right. I just do not feel like eating. I will have a good dinner.'

Her stomach in fact felt tied up in knots. What she really wanted to do was have a stiff drink and go to bed. But she had to act as normally as possible and also be available to go into action the moment things started to happen. She changed into her secretarial uniform, went up to her office, found Katherine typing away.

'Anna! I did not know if you were coming in today.'

'Well, I am here now.' She sat behind her desk. 'Is there anything important?'

'I don't think so. I don't know what I am supposed to do, now that we have completed our investigation.'

'I am sure Herr Himmler will think of something.' She looked at her watch. A quarter to two. Whatever was going to happen must have happened. It seemed incredible that she should be sitting here, in the peace of her office, while the whole German world might already have fallen apart. Hitler, dead. Göring, dead. Himmler, dead. She almost told Katherine, but she didn't know her sister well enough, after so long a separation. Telling her would have to wait until things started to happen here. She gave her some filing to do, which sent her into the next room, pretended to read some files herself.

She was no stranger to waiting for a crisis to develop, but that was the longest afternoon of her life. It was past three when her door was thrown open and Steinberg almost fell in. 'Freddie? What . . .' A look at his face told her the crisis had become a catastrophe.

'Anna!' He was shaking, held on to her desk to stay upright, 'It's happened!'

'Freddie . . .'

'He's dead!' Steinberg cried. 'Don't you understand? Stauffenberg telephoned before leaving Rastenburg. The bomb went off. Everyone in the conference room must have been killed. He's on his way here now.'

'Then . . .'

'He told us to act immediately. But that idiot Stieff won't move. He says he must have proof that Hitler is dead. Proof! What more proof does he want?'

Presumably, Anna thought, his nerves are still shattered from Sunday's fiasco. But Katherine might be listening. 'Why have you come to me?' she asked, coldly.

'Tell me what we must do – how we can make him move.'

The door opened again, before she could think of a reply. 'Anna!' Hellmuth stared at Steinberg. 'You? Here?'

Steinberg reached for his pocket, and Essermann drew his pistol and shot him in the chest. Steinberg fell without a sound.

Katherine appeared in the inner doorway. 'Oh, my God!' she shrieked.

Essermann ignored her. 'Anna?' he said again, and her phone rang.

She picked up the receiver. 'Yes?'

'Anna?'

'Yes, Herr Doktor.' She kept watching Essermann, who was staring at her while he tried to figure things out, but he had holstered his gun. She was holding the receiver in her left hand; with apparent absent-mindedness she opened the shoulder bag that lay on her desk. 'Can you tell me what is going on?'

'There has been an attempt on the life of the Führer.'

'An attempt?'

'Someone planted a bomb in the conference room.'

'You mean the Führer . . .'

'He is badly shaken, but he is not dead.'

Another dud, Anna thought. An utterly catastrophoic dud. 'That is a miracle,' she said.

'It is, you know. It has to be. The blast wrecked the room. It was contained in a briefcase, planted next to where the Führer was standing by some traitor on the staff. Purely by chance, or, as you say, by some miracle, an officer talking to the Führer found his feet blocked by the case and moved it to the other side of a solid upright, seconds before the bomb went off. The upright absorbed the force of the explosion.'

'A miracle,' Anna said again.

'As the Führer said, it was a divine intervention. But listen, almost his first words on leaving the conference chamber were of you.'

'Me?' Her squeak was genuine.

'He said, "Anna knows who these scum are. She told me so, last night. Tell her to have them all arrested, now. Shoot any who resist. Give her carte blanche." That is what I am giving you now. Get the SD moving, and then report to me, with your list. If anyone refuses to obey you, refer him to me.'

'Yes, Herr Doktor,' Anna said slowly.

'Then carry on. I expect to hear from you within the hour.'

The phone went dead. She and Essermann remained looking at each other, and Katherine still stood in the doorway. Goebbels had a penetrating voice, and both of the others had heard every word he had said.

Now Essermann spoke, almost in a dream. 'You! You knew what was going to happen. You planned it. You have obstructed the investigation from the start.'

'Don't be ridiculous.' Anna slipped her hand into her bag. Essermann might know something of her reputation, but he had never seen her in action.

'Then why did Steinberg come running to you? Why did he attempt to shoot me the moment he realized I would find out?'

'I think you will find that he was unarmed,' Anna said, 'and you have committed murder.'

'And now you have carte blanche to make sure the conspiracy continues.'

'Hellmuth, I think you want to be very careful what you say.'

'You! The arch-traitor!'

He reached for his holster, but Anna's fingers were already curled round her pistol. In one lightning-fast movement she drew, aimed and fired, hitting him in the centre of the forehead.

Feet drummed in the corridor, and several men and women burst into the room. 'Countess! Those shots . . .?'

'These men were plotting against the Führer,' Anna said. 'Remove the bodies, and then report to me here. We have a lot to do.'

The bodies were lifted and carried away.

'Anna,' Katherine said. 'Those men . . . weren't they your friends? Your lovers?'

'Sleeping with a man does not necessarily make him a lover. Or even a friend. They were traitors.'

'Yes. But just to shoot Colonel Essermann! I don't understand.'

'You must have heard what Dr Goebbels said. The conspiracy must be stamped out, and he has given me full authority to do this. Do you want to go on working with me?'

'Well, yes, of course. But—'

'Then you do not have to understand.' Anna got up, went to her sister, and embraced her. 'Just obey me, without question.'

Epilogue

'As you say,' I suggested, 'a total catastrophe.'

Anna gave a little shiver. 'Do you know the truth of it?'

'I know there were quite a few . . .'

'Five thousand, men and women, died. Once a few were arrested, as I had warned Freddie from the start, everyone *implicated everyone else. One or two escaped the worst. Rommel, for instance, was allowed to commit suicide and given a state funeral. But the majority were quite horribly executed – senior officers like Beck, strung up on piano wire with no belts to their pants so that they slipped down to their ankles as they wriggled while the cameras rolled . . . ugh!'*

'Do you regret any of it?'

Anna sighed. 'I have reminded myself, often, that they were all Nazis, enemies of the free world, that they were happy to see the Jews driven into the gas chambers, that they were interested only in saving their own skins. But then I think, If only my bomb had gone off, or the conspirators had been less elaborate and used the first opportunity they had instead of wanting anything to be just so . . .'

'What about Steinberg?'

She made a moue. 'He was a boy trying to operate in a man's world. I was fortunate that Essermann shot him, or I would have had to do it myself, or risk betrayal.'

'And Essermann? He had been – well . . .'

'My lover? Yes. But I had always known I would have to kill him one day. Oh, the whole thing was such a mess.'

'But you were triumphant, as always. The heroine of the hour.'

'It was not my proudest achievement.'

'Yet you were there, to see the end of it all – of them *all: Goebbels and Göring, Himmler and Hitler – and to rise, phoenix-like, from the ashes, with three knights in shining armour waiting to set you free. Will you tell me who won the prize?'*

Anna Fehrbach smiled.

Withdrawn